Praise for  bestselling author

"Fast-paced and intense... most heartfelt installme... fans will love it."
—*Publishers Weekly* on *Cowboy to the Core*
(starred review)

"Multidimensional and genuine characters are the highlight of this alluring novel, and sensual love scenes complete it. Yates's fans...will savor this delectable story."
—*Publishers Weekly* on *Unbroken Cowboy*
(starred review)

"Grant and McKenna's steamy and refreshingly honest progress toward a romantic relationship is intertwined with stories of the other Gold Valley residents from past and future books, adding extra satisfaction for series fans."
—*Publishers Weekly*
on *A Tall, Dark Cowboy Christmas*

"The banter between the Dodge siblings is loads of fun, and adding Dallas (Bennett's surprise son) to the mix raises that humor up a notch or two."
—*RT Book Reviews* on *Untamed Cowboy* (Top Pick)

"Yates' new Gold Valley series begins with a sassy, romantic and sexy story about two characters whose chemistry is off the charts."
—*RT Book Reviews* on *Smooth-Talking Cowboy*
(Top Pick)

"This fast-paced, sensual novel will leave readers believing in the healing power of love."
—*Publishers Weekly* on *Down Home Cowboy*

"[A] surefire winner not to be missed."
—*Publishers Weekly* on *Slow Burn Cowboy*
(starred review)

MAISEY YATES

Cowboy
Christmas
Redemption

Recycling programs
for this product may
not exist in your area.

HQN™

ISBN-13: 978-1-335-00990-6

Cowboy Christmas Redemption

For anyone who needs some extra hope this season.
Romans 15:13

Cowboy Christmas Redemption

CHAPTER ONE

ELLIE BELL COULD sometimes imagine that she lived an entirely different life. Not because she didn't love so much about what she had, but because it was nice, even for a little while, to set down the various burdens that she carried around with her and just focus on the moment.

Getting chickens had been an interesting endeavor, one that had proved to be quite a bit more sanity-preserving than she had anticipated.

Sometimes when she was out collecting eggs, she felt like she'd fallen through a time warp. Where she was younger than twenty-eight. Not a woman with a heavy burden of responsibility, or the crushing weight of loss deep inside her.

But somebody liked. Somebody carefree. Whose only responsibility was to collect eggs and look out at the beautiful view that stretched out before her.

Her little farmhouse was modest, and it was old, with a porch that had white peeling paint that she hadn't been able to rally herself to fix. But she'd hung baskets of flowers from the rafters, and she supposed that was something.

At least it was something she was much more up for than painting.

Maybe someday she would get it together and do all the renovation that the place needed.

She took a deep breath, and she focused her gaze on the horizon. On the long stretch of emerald field that faded into the evergreen-covered mountains, currently bathed in a rose-gold glow from the setting sun. The days were getting shorter, heading into the Christmas season, and honestly, that was something else that just made her tired.

She had to do things.

For Amelia's sake.

Well, handily, Tammy Dalton was always around to do something. The Daltons had been her late husband's surrogate family, and after Clint's death, had become hers and Amelia's, as well.

Tammy always made a wonderful Christmas dinner, and the gathering that they had was spectacular. And it gave Ellie an excuse not to make a big fuss about Christmas at her house, which always felt vaguely sad to her.

She didn't want to drag out the ornaments that she had gotten with Clint. And she didn't want to get rid of them and get new ones, either. They'd had cozy Christmases in their apartment back by the high school in town. Their own ornaments. First Christmas, with a bride and groom. The Bells, on a big silver bell…

She'd loved him so much. Right from the beginning. He was just a nice man. In spite of the fact he'd had a rough upbringing. He'd been open, and he'd laughed easily. He'd taught *her* to laugh a little easier.

He'd taught her to love in a way that was so different from the way she'd known love as a child.

She'd spent her growing-up years craving her mom's attention, while her mom craved only the attention of whatever man had her heart at the time.

She'd hated it. And she'd sworn off love herself.

But then she'd met Clint.

He'd been tall, with dark hair and a slight build. Rangy and athletic. He was the kind of guy who had to climb up the side of a rock face on a hike if there was one; the kind who had to jump over obstacles just as easily stepped over.

He'd been the one thing to distract her even slightly from her laser-focused vision. She'd wanted to go to college, be a teacher. Because it was teachers who'd given her the support, the help, that her own mother didn't.

She'd made Clint wait to get married until she was finished with school. She'd been strong that way. She'd been determined to forgo boyfriends, especially while she was studying. But she hadn't been able to stay away from him. He was so magnetic and happy, and she'd wanted that.

As soon as she'd graduated, they'd gotten married.

They'd lived in little apartments near the high school, and Ellie had gotten jobs substitute-teaching in the area, and then spent a year as a teacher's assistant at the school right near their house.

They'd been young when Clint wanted to try for a baby, but he'd been so excited about it. So they'd started trying, and not just for a baby but also to find a house.

They'd found the farmhouse. She'd found out she was pregnant.

He'd been the proudest, happiest man alive that day.

And four weeks later he'd died.

Before they'd moved into their home. Before he'd ever even gotten to hear his child's heartbeat.

She'd never had a Christmas in the farmhouse. Her and Amelia's Christmas traditions were built around the Dalton family, and that was okay with Ellie.

Her egg-collecting was feeling terribly sad at the moment. But she blamed the upcoming Christmas season for that.

It was inescapably bittersweet.

Always, she thought about that first Christmas without him. When she had been eight months pregnant and so miserable. So alone.

Alone, except for Caleb Dalton.

The entire Dalton family had been good to her in the years following the loss of Clint, but no one had been quite as good as Caleb.

Caleb had been Clint's best friend in the world. A man who was like a brother to him, so he'd said often. He'd talked about Caleb all the time, from the beginning of their relationship. She could still remember going to her first Dalton family barbecue with Clint. He'd been nervous, because it had been like meeting his parents, he'd said.

All three Dalton brothers had presence. A perfect combination of their father Hank's charm and charisma, and their mother Tammy's beauty and quick wit.

Caleb had been unlike any man she'd ever met. A daredevil with an easy smile, and he was so big. Larger than life, both in height and in presence.

He could fix anything. If her car needed a tune-up or an oil change, Caleb could just do it. Why call the landlord when their apartment had an issue? Caleb could always handle it. She'd been in awe of that. The way his hands worked to puzzle together anything that might have been broken.

She could see why Clint loved the family the way he did, and Caleb in particular. She'd bonded with him easily, quickly.

And now…

Caleb had become her best friend in the entire world. She'd always liked him. But he became something more during these long, lonely years.

He'd become her rock. Her salvation.

He was always on hand in an emergency. If she needed cold medicine in the middle of the night for Amelia, yet didn't want to drag her little girl to the store, she could call Caleb. And he would go get the cold medicine. He would bring it to her. If she wasn't well, he would be the first person to come by with soup, and to make sure that Amelia was taken care of while she convalesced.

He had built her chicken coop. Had been the one to help her figure out what you were supposed to do with chickens in the first place.

And when she had partnered with his brother Gabe to help start the school that she now taught at on the Dalton family ranch, Caleb had immediately partnered with her, too.

He had helped make her dream a reality, the moment that she was able to have dreams again.

She felt much happier, thinking about Caleb.

He was definitely a lot more of a safe space than Christmas could ever be.

As if thinking of him conjured him up, she heard the sound of truck tires on gravel, mixed with the sound of an old engine from a Ford F-150.

It was Caleb, coming home with Amelia. Amelia had spent the day with Tammy. The school that Ellie had been part of founding, and that she worked at full-time, specifically geared toward troubled boys, was on the Dalton family ranch, and Hank and Tammy Dalton lived there in a large house. Tammy had graciously offered to watch Amelia after preschool on the days when Ellie worked.

It just so happened that today, by the time Ellie had finished up, Amelia and Tammy were in the middle of a baking project.

Usually, Ellie would have hung out, but today she had been eager for escape. For a moment in silence. Out of time.

And she wasn't even sorry it was over. Because Caleb was here. And so was Amelia. No matter how difficult or chaotic life could seem, she loved the people in it.

She stepped out of the coop, her basket clutched in her hands, and she made her way across the field, toward her driveway. Her floral dress caught the breeze and fluttered around her legs, strands of blond hair whipping across her face. She pushed them away and smiled as Caleb got out of the truck.

"Was she good for you?" Ellie asked.

"We've been singing the theme song to a show I've never heard of for twenty minutes," he said, opening up the driver-side door wider so he could put the front seat down.

And there was Amelia, strapped into her car seat and looking extremely pleased with herself. "It was *Shimmer and Shine*, Caleb," she informed him.

"Shimmer and Shine," Caleb amended, directing that toward Ellie. "I think I like *Peppa Pig* better."

"You and me both," Ellie said.

She took a step toward the truck and Caleb grinned. "I've got her."

He pushed his black cowboy hat back on his head, his blue eyes catching the light. He had a dusting of light stubble on his jaw, not unusual for him at this hour of the day, and his muscular arms were still streaked with dirt, she noticed, as he began to unfasten Amelia's seat belt.

He had battered workman's hands. He worked the ranch that his family owned, and he was a firefighter by trade. He'd ridden rodeo for a while before that, though not for very long. But still, everything he did had a certain amount of labor involved, and no small amount of danger.

She'd always liked curling up on the couch with a book, safe indoors, over doing anything outside. She knew that for his own reasons, that would be torture for Caleb. He was a man who needed movement, who needed open spaces. A man who preferred hands-on learning over book learning.

It unnerved her that he continued to fight wildfires, even after what had happened to Clint. But she knew that it was unreasonable to ask him to quit his job.

Didn't mean she didn't want him to.

He set Amelia down gently on the ground, and her little girl launched herself at Ellie. She swung her up for a hug before depositing her back in the driveway. "Did you have a fun day with Grandma Tammy?" she asked.

Tammy Dalton was the closest thing Amelia had to a grandmother.

Both Clint and Ellie hadn't had involved families at all. In fact, it was one of the things that had bonded them together when they'd met.

Ellie had been cautious. She'd never dated. Not after watching the way her own single mother had burned through men, the quality of which had been incredibly variable.

Of course, she had ended up a single mother anyway.

Which seemed fully unfair, given how very much she had tried not to perpetuate the cycle she'd been born into. She'd gotten into school. She'd finished. She'd started a teaching career. Gotten married.

But she'd been widowed.

If there was one thing she'd learned, it was that you couldn't plan everything, no matter how much you might want to.

"It was good," Amelia said. "We made chocolate chip cookies and peanut butter cookies."

"And where are the cookies?" Ellie asked.

"We ate them all," Caleb said.

"Did you really?"

She hunted around behind him, trying to see if she could find a plate of cookies in the truck.

"Of course not," he said. "I have some for you."

"Can I take the eggs in the house?" Amelia asked.

"Sure," Ellie said, handing her daughter the basket.

She raced up the stairs as quickly as her little legs could carry her, her pink cowgirl boots glittering with each movement. A gift from the Daltons. So of course, they were Amelia's favorite.

"Thank you," Ellie said. "It was nice to have a few minutes to myself this evening."

"No problem. You're on my way home."

"I am. It's handy."

It really was. More than handy. A lifeline. The man was like one of the mountains that surrounded her home. Stalwart and steady, never changing, even as the seasons around them did.

Evergreen.

He reached into the truck and pulled out a plate of cookies, handing it to her. She didn't wait. She dived in, taking a peanut butter one from the top and helping herself to a large bite. "Your mom is a genius," she said. "I try, based on everything she's taught me, but they still never turn out this good."

"I don't even try," he said, shrugging. "I just eat them."

As if to demonstrate his point, he grabbed one of the chocolate chip ones from the top and put the whole thing in his mouth.

"That's mean," she said. "You could have taken some more from your mother's house."

"I did," he said.

"Then you have no call taking my cookies."

"It's a delivery fee."

"For my child or for the snacks?"

"Thanks for reminding me," he said, this time taking a peanut butter one.

She expected him to go then, because it had been a long day, and it wasn't like she hadn't seen him at work earlier. But he didn't. Instead, he stood for a moment, his expression uncharacteristically thoughtful. "I might not be able to drop Amelia off at home as often in the future."

"Oh?"

It was abrupt and weird. Especially considering she'd just been thinking about what a stalwart Caleb was.

"Yeah," he said. He braced himself on the truck, and her eyes were drawn to his biceps, to the way the muscle shifted beneath his tanned, scarred skin.

She wondered what the scar on the inside of his arm was from. Barbed wire? An angry bull? Maybe just from a youthful misdeed. It was very hard to say with a man like Caleb.

It really was a wonderful arm. It had to be said. Objectively speaking, Caleb was a perfect masculine specimen.

He wasn't pretty. No, he was too raw to be anything like pretty. Even with those blue eyes, which were the kind of blue that women had difficulty letting pass by without remarking on. But he was scarred, and he was weathered from working outdoors, and, as she had previously been thinking, his hands were rough.

Though, they could be gentle when they needed to be.

If she had a single friend, she would definitely set her up with Caleb.

"I... Why?"

"I'm buying a new piece of property."

"Really?" Caleb hadn't given any indication that he was thinking of moving away from the acre lot that he lived on.

"Yeah," he responded, maddeningly opaque.

"Details, Caleb." Having a man for a best friend could be annoying, because they didn't tell you things, like the fact that they were considering moving. And then, when they finally did tell you, they didn't tell you anything about it.

"I bought Jehoshaphat Brown's place."

"You didn't," she said.

Jehoshaphat Brown was an eccentric who lived a few miles up out of town, and had the largest Christmas tree farm in the area. "I did," he said. "I mostly don't believe it because I don't believe he would move. But he is. He's moving to Hawaii."

"Now, I really don't believe that," she said.

"Hey," he responded, "believe whatever you want, but he is. He's moving to Hawaii, taking a job as a bartender at a resort. Oceanside. He bought a condo with the money I paid him."

"But you are… You're going to run a Christmas tree farm?"

"At least temporarily. Everything's ready to go now, which means finishing out the year, or the next few years, is guaranteed money in the bank to begin other ventures. There's contracts already made with outfits around the country, truckers on hand to drive the things to their destinations. And he owns that small lot down on the main street of town. So, I'm all set not only to sell this year's crop around the country, but also sell it here."

"But you don't… You don't actually want to…be a Christmas tree farmer?"

"My ultimate goal is cattle," he said.

She'd had no idea. None at all. Not that he wanted his own ranch, not that he'd been unhappy at the school. Was he unhappy at the school? Was he leaving?

"What does this mean for your position at the school?"

"I will be leaving. Which I will be talking to Gabe about later tonight."

"But…"

"With West Caldwell coming into town, there's no need for me to hang around. He's going to be working on the ranch."

"Your half brother that you've never met. That's putting a lot of stock in a man you don't even know."

"Gabe figures we owe him. And, since Gabe is awash in guilt over the whole half-sibling thing, I figure that works in my favor."

As much as Ellie loved Hank Dalton, the patriarch of the Dalton clan, it was becoming more and more clear that he was problematic. A couple of years ago it had been discovered that he had a daughter that none of them had known about. McKenna Tate. She'd come into town after discovering the identity of her family, and after some adjusting, the Dalton family had welcomed her into the fold. But on the heels of that revelation had come another one.

There were three more children. All adults now.

Hank had never known about them. But Tammy had. It had changed the relationship, that reveal.

But Hank was awash enough in the guilt from the actions in his past, that the two of them were trying to work through it, to an extent. And Ellie really hoped that they did. For some selfish reasons, if she was honest. Because she loved them, and they were the closest thing to a family for her, and she didn't want to lose them.

"But… Don't you want to wait and see if it's going to work out?"

"No," Caleb said. "I don't want to work at the school forever. This is what I want."

That made her…angry, and she couldn't figure out exactly why. He deserved to have dreams; of course he did. But she'd just…assumed he was happy with the way things were. She'd somehow meshed his dreams together with hers.

Had decided that what she was doing with his family ranch, with the school, was what he wanted, too.

But if she didn't feel great about him fighting fires anymore, maybe he didn't, either. And she'd never asked. She'd only thought about it in terms of her own comfort. That wasn't right at all.

Still, the idea of him having his own endeavors, his own life farther away from her and not right all around her while they worked…

She *needed* him. She really had. She still did.

She didn't like this…this change. But she should be

happy for him, and it made her feel… She felt bad. And she didn't like feeling bad about something that was good for her friend.

"I'd… Well, congratulations," she said. Even though she didn't feel like congratulating him at all. She felt like having a tantrum.

She really didn't know why.

"Thank you," he said, his mouth quirking up into a half smile that made it very clear he was well aware she wasn't having the best reaction to his news.

"I'll miss seeing you." The words more plaintive than she'd intended.

"I'm not moving away," he said.

"Yeah, but I see you *all the time*," she protested.

"You will still see me *all the time*."

"But you won't be dropping Amelia off when I want you to."

"Probably not."

Her stomach twisted, but that wasn't what was upsetting her. She knew it wasn't.

And then it hit her, as strongly as that melancholy had when she'd realized it was nearly the Christmas season.

This phase of life was over.

The one where he was here to carry her. Where she had a crutch to get her through what life looked like without Clint. Being a single mother.

It was changing.

It had begun to change months ago, when the idea for the school had come about. She had gone back to work.

But she'd been a fledgling, and he'd been there to help her.

In the years since Amelia was born, she had lived off the insurance settlement she'd gotten after Clint's death.

And settlement money from the helicopter company, which had been found negligent. It was overloaded, and they knew it, knew that it didn't have the capacity to carry the number of people that had been on it.

Every man who'd been on the helicopter had died.

Money didn't bring back people you lost.

It in fact seemed like a laughable pursuit when you were grieving a husband. But once she'd had it she'd realized why it mattered. Because she hadn't been able to do anything beyond the bare minimum to keep herself alive. And she was having a baby.

It was how she'd bought this house.

And all the furniture in it. Everything that had made the place a home that she and Amelia could inhabit. And even when it had been difficult to care about such a thing, part of her had known that she had to.

And it had been Caleb, of course, who had assembled it all. Who had helped with everything.

And now she was being a jerk about something that he'd achieved. After all he'd done for her.

Well, the little scolding session she gave herself was nice, but she still felt unhappy. But that didn't mean she had to act unhappy. She had ample experience with pretending to be more okay than she was. She should be able to do it now.

"I'm happy for you," she said. "Really. I'm sorry. We can go get furniture that's difficult to assemble, and I'll help you put it together."

"Meaning?"

"I'll…offer you a drink while you put it together?"

"Right." He nodded. "Sounds about right. Hey, don't worry about it, Ellie. Things are going to be fine."

There was so much she wanted to say to him, but

she didn't know how to articulate it. Mostly because she couldn't quite explain the discomfort happening in her own chest. So instead, she just watched him get into his truck, and didn't even scold him when he stole another cookie.

She tried to figure out exactly what the feeling was as she watched his truck disappear down her driveway. Then she turned and walked to her porch, sitting down on the bottom step.

"What is wrong with me?"

And suddenly, it hit her.

He was moving on, and she hadn't.

It was different, because of course, he had been Clint's best friend. She'd been Clint's wife. So Caleb moving on from the whole situation was easier. More expected.

But she wished... Well, she wished for a whole lot of things.

Things that were coming up more and more often. Her best female friend at the moment was Vanessa Logan. Vanessa was pregnant, getting ready to have a baby with her husband, Jacob, a man who loved her so much that just looking at the two of them together made Ellie's whole body hurt.

She didn't want that. She didn't want to fall in love. She didn't want a relationship. But she wanted...

It would be nice to be kissed under the mistletoe, maybe. To have something to wear a dress to. To go dancing in that dress.

And suddenly, those thoughts she had in the chicken coop, about those moments that felt out of her life, that felt like an escape, crystallized.

That was what she wanted. Just some moments. To

feel like something other than a tired single mother, or a sad, grieving widow.

A moment to feel like a woman.

Maybe she needed to make some changes, too.

Maybe, instead of dreading Christmas, she needed to get started on her wish list.

CHAPTER TWO

CALEB DALTON HADN'T had much to smile about for a long time. It had been a bear of a few years, since his best friend's death, and while time might ease a wound, it wouldn't ever bring Clint back.

But that permanence made space for movement, around the grief, around the pain. And finally toward a future he'd been planning for a long time.

Clint had been, honest to God, one of the best men on earth. The hole he'd left behind had been huge, and Caleb had dedicated himself to caring for his friend's widow and child in his absence.

That had been his life, his whole life, for nearly five years. And it was fair, because it had been Ellie's life, too.

He cared for Ellie. A hell of a lot. He'd met her because of Clint, but she'd been in his life now for more than ten years.

His feelings for Ellie were complicated. Had been from the beginning. But she'd been with Clint. And there was no doubt Clint was the better man. More than that, Clint was his brother. Maybe not in blood, but in every way that counted.

Caleb had never claimed to be a perfect friend. Clint was one of those people who'd drawn everyone right to him. He was easy to like. Caleb's own parents had been bowled over by Clint from the time they were kids.

And Caleb's jealousy had gotten the better of him once when they'd been younger. Something that made him burn with shame even now.

He hadn't let it happen when they'd been adults. No matter how tempting it had been. No matter how much he'd…

A muscle in his jaw ticked.

He gave thanks that there was a space in front of the Gold Valley Saloon, and he whipped his truck there up against the curb, ignoring the honk that came from behind him.

He turned around and saw Trevor Sanderson in his Chevy, giving Caleb the death glare.

"Hold your damn horses, Trevor," he muttered as he put his truck in Park.

He should have been quicker.

Hell, that was life in a nutshell. Sometimes, you were just too late. For parking spots, and for women.

He'd tried to get that image out of his head. More times than he could count over the past decade. Had tried to erase that first time he'd seen Ellie.

It was at his parents' barbecue. Late one summer afternoon.

He'd been talking and laughing with his brothers, and he'd lifted a beer to his lips and looked out away from the party. Then he'd frozen.

It was like the world had slowed down, all of it centering on the beautiful blonde walking toward him. The golden light from the sun illuminated her hair like a halo, and her smile seemed to light him up from the inside out.

As she'd gotten closer, he'd taken in every last detail. The way the left side of her cheek dimpled with that grin; her eyes, a mix of green and blue and a punch in the gut. Her lips were glossy pink, and he wondered if it was that stuff that women wore that smelled and tasted like cherries. He couldn't decide if he hoped that it was or not.

Twenty years old, more experienced with women than he probably should be, and ready right then and there to drop down to his knees and propose marriage to the one walking in his direction.

It took him a full minute to realize that the beautiful blonde was holding hands with someone.

And that that someone was Caleb's best friend on earth.

It was a surreal moment. It had been a sea change in his soul. When his feelings for Ellie had tipped over from nothing to everything.

A revelation he hadn't been looking for, and one he sure as hell hadn't enjoyed.

It was like the whole world had turned, then bucked, like a particularly nasty-ass bull, and left him sprawled out on the ground.

It had been the beginning of a thorny, painful set of years. As he'd gotten to know Ellie, as his feelings for her had become knit deep into his heart, into his soul. She'd become more than his friend's woman, and more than a woman he'd desired. She'd become a friend to him.

In many ways he was thankful for the depth of the feeling, because it was the reason he'd been able to put aside the lust. The idea that he'd fallen in love with her at first sight.

When Clint had first started dating her, she'd been in school, so she hadn't been around all the time. But during the summers, and on breaks, she came around with Clint.

Went to the lake with them. Went fishing. Came to Christmas and Thanksgiving.

The summers at the lake, though, that had been a particular kind of torture. All of them swimming out in the water, her and her swimsuit. A tiny bikini that had left little to the imagination.

And he had been so very interested in imagining all the things that it did conceal.

And he'd felt like the biggest, most perverse asshole.

Then there had been the time that Clint had asked him to take her out riding.

Just the two of them.

Because Clint trusted him. Of course he did. Why wouldn't he trust his best friend? So he'd done it.

Had taken her out on the trails that wound behind the Dalton family property, up to the top of a mountain. And he looked over at the view with her, watched the sunset. And everything in him had wanted to lean over and kiss her on the mouth. To act on the feelings that were rioting through his chest.

For just a breath she'd looked back at him, met his eyes. And he'd thought maybe she'd wanted it, too.

Yeah, it would have exploded his relationship with Clint, but for a minute it seemed like it might be worth it.

Then she'd looked away. And then he'd come back to himself.

Clint was his brother. In every way but blood.

And he couldn't betray his friend like that.

Anyway, Ellie loved Clint.

She didn't love Caleb.

And no matter how much he might not want to, he had to respect that.

So he hadn't kissed her. They had ridden back down

that mountain, and nothing happened between them. But late at night, Caleb had taken himself in hand and fantasized that it had.

Two days later Clint and Ellie had been engaged.

Caleb had agreed to be the best man.

She'd married Clint. And while his feelings for her had remained, they'd shifted. As they'd had to.

He wasn't perfect. He'd never touched Ellie. Not like a man touched a woman, though that hadn't stopped him from going over the accidental brush of fingertips, of their elbows touching, over and over in his mind if it had happened on accident.

It hadn't stopped him from keeping and cherishing secrets with her, even when he knew he shouldn't. Hadn't stopped him from pushing some boundaries that not even Ellie had realized he'd been pushing at.

Ellie was the one who'd realized, for the first time, that he was dyslexic. And he'd sworn her to secrecy. And in that secrecy had come secret reading lessons.

And he'd…well, he'd lost control of his own feelings again. And once he'd recognized that, he'd cut them off. Cut her off.

But then Clint had died, just a month later. And everything changed again.

Since then, his relationship with Ellie was about their coming together to try to fill the gap Clint had left behind. His helping where she needed it.

Helping with the house, with her grief, with Amelia. That was all.

He got out of his truck on a groan and pushed the door open to the Gold Valley Saloon. It wasn't too busy, being early on a weeknight, but the locals were definitely out, drinking and playing darts. Sitting around eating fried food and complaining about their bosses and day jobs—which around here often meant livestock.

A rancher was beholden to his animals, and Caleb did know that.

He wasn't under any illusion that a life raising cattle would be an easy one. But it was the one he wanted.

His dad had wanted better for his sons. He'd said that, in his own words.

Hank Dalton had been poor trash from the trailer park made good. He'd earned himself a whole lot of money on endorsement deals and championship purses in the rodeo, and he'd expected that it would make his sons want to be scholars. Just because they had the opportunity to go to college.

Sadly for Hank, none of them had a very deep abiding interest in higher education.

After Gabe had gone to the rodeo, followed by Caleb and Jacob, he'd seemed to accept that more or less.

But Caleb knew that Hank had been hard on his oldest son.

Sometimes, Caleb wondered if it was because he had the foresight to not want them to be like him.

He hadn't seemed to possess that level of concern with Caleb.

He'd wanted Gabe to go to college. He'd wanted it for Jacob, too.

He hadn't even thought for a moment that Caleb would go.

But then…he'd been right. Caleb would have rather had metal rods shoved under his fingernails than continue on in school a minute longer than he had to.

Though whatever Hank did, it might have had a lot more to do with being worried his boys would follow in his footsteps. His bad behavior had caused a lot of turmoil during their growing-up years, but it was recently that the full extent of the consequences became clear.

First with the appearance of McKenna, and then with the revelation that followed about West Caldwell, and about the other as yet to be named half siblings.

All Hank's infidelity, wandering out there in the world. Mistakes that were more than thirty years old.

Caleb frowned. He supposed that wasn't fair. To think about other people as mistakes.

For his part, he hadn't thought much at all about his half siblings. Gabe seemed to feel driven to make it right, and given the fact that his brother was the only person who knew that those half siblings existed back years ago, he could understand why Gabe felt some guilt about it.

Caleb had too much guilt and responsibility as it was, and he couldn't take any more on.

He saw his brother sitting at a table over in the corner and he made his way over there, crossing the scarred wooden floor and scanning the room as he did.

There were two women who made eye contact with him. Offered him a smile.

And he waited.

For something.

For a lick of interest.

Something to make him feel hot. To make him feel that tug low inside of him. That anticipation of a potential hookup. A conversation that might lead to flirtation, which might lead to dancing and kissing and a whole lot more.

That was part of the problem with taking care of Ellie like he had for the past few years. He hadn't been interested in other women.

At first he'd put it down to grief. He didn't like the taste of food. Why would he want sex?

But as the sharpness of the loss faded, he'd started to realize it had to do with the proximity to Ellie.

And that was one of the things that had spurred the purchase of the ranch.

He needed something else. He needed his own life.

The fact that he hadn't had sex in four years—nearly five—was getting a little bit ridiculous.

And the fact that he'd finally realized that made him a little bit less of a sad sack. Maybe.

"Hey," Gabe said, nodding and pushing a beer bottle to the center of the table.

Caleb sat down and pulled the bottle toward him. "Thanks."

"No problem. I see you got Amelia home safely."

"No," he said. "I left her in the truck. Told her to play with my air freshener."

"Well, I know you're lying, because your truck doesn't have an air freshener."

"Why would I cover up the glorious scent of work boots and sweat?"

"Why indeed," Gabe said, taking a sip of beer. "So, what's on your mind?"

"How do you know something is on my mind?"

"Because sometimes we happen to get a beer after work. But you rarely make an appointment with me to grab a beer."

"Yeah, there's something I wanted to talk to you about," Caleb said.

"Fire away."

"I'm leaving the school." He cleared his throat. "I'm leaving the ranch."

"Oh," Gabe said.

"What? You sound…"

"I don't know," Gabe said. "I just thought it was kind of a family thing. Especially with West coming…"

"West isn't family. I mean, he is. Genetically. But he hasn't earned a place with us as family."

"That's not how that works," Gabe said.

"Yeah, it is. We had Clint. Clint was like family. Because we knew him. Genetics is about the thinnest link I can think of in family. And it's definitely not necessary."

"I'm not…trying to replace Clint with West. It has nothing to do with Clint."

"I didn't say you were," he said.

"I guess not. But it sounds to me like you're worried about it."

"It's just that from my perspective, having West on the ranch will give you the help that you need. It doesn't make it…some family thing we all need to be involved in."

"Are you…avoiding involvement with West?"

"Nope," Caleb said honestly. "I don't really have any feelings one way or the other about the half-sibling stuff."

"Why not?"

"Because. Because we have a full life. I have a full life. They're adults. It's not like they're children that need to be taken care of."

"Are you upset about the idea of them getting a piece of the inheritance when Dad dies?"

Caleb drew back. "No. I don't care about money. I have my own. I might not be rich like Dad, but I had enough to go out and buy my own ranch. That's what I want. I want to make my own way. I don't need to take any of Hank Dalton's fortune."

"I'm sorry," Gabe said. "I guess I'm just having a

hard time figuring out why you and Jacob are so disconnected from all of this. I can't be. You love McKenna…"

"I know," Caleb said. "And it isn't that I'm not going to make an effort to get to know West. It's just… I've got a new ranch that I want to run, and you know, Ellie will probably still need my help…"

"Is this about Ellie?"

"Why would it be about Ellie?" he asked.

A little disingenuous because he'd just been thinking about the link between her and his celibacy. But it was complicated.

It always had been.

"This is about *me*," Caleb said. "You went out and did the rodeo, and now this…this school, this is what you want. Jacob is happy there, too, because he's with Vanessa. You guys went out, you made your own thing. Why wouldn't you think that I'd want that?"

He did want it. More than that, he needed it. Needed to prove to his dad that he could make something of himself.

Needed to prove that he tried, and that his best was good enough. Damn good enough.

"I guess because Jacob's plans ended up aligning closer with mine."

"Yeah, I know that seems surprising."

Jacob and Caleb had been the hellions. Irish twins and always in scrapes together.

They had gone into the rodeo at the same time, and gotten out at roughly the same time, too. They had decided to get into fighting wildfires along with Clint, because the money was good, and it had seemed like an adrenaline high. Which was something the three of them were all very into.

Of the three of them, it had always been very hard to

say which one was the instigator. They had been equal partners in crime, for all of their lives. And losing Clint had been a blow. One that had changed things. Even between him and Jacob. It changed the dynamic. Because they had been the Three Musketeers, and they had become two, and right between them had been a deep, intense sense of mortality that hadn't existed there before.

Jacob had closed himself off, guilt nearly destroying him, until he'd met his wife, Vanessa. And as for Caleb…

His purpose had become Clint's memory. Had become his legacy. Caring for Amelia. Caring for Ellie.

But Ellie was getting back on her feet. Ellie was teaching at the school again, back in the saddle of her dream. Building a life that didn't revolve around what she'd lost. He would always be tied up in that loss. It was inescapable. Utterly and totally.

That was just one of many reasons it was best to take a step back. Perhaps take a step into something else. A different kind of life.

"Not about you, Gabe. I know that might be difficult to understand."

"It's not difficult for me to understand."

"Sure it is. You're the oldest. And a lot of things happened to be about you. And us following you. But we're grown-ass men now."

"Christmas tree farming," he said.

"*Cattle ranching*. But I would be a fool not to make the most of the revenue that's on my land."

My land.

That made him feel something good. Because he was going to have something. Something that was his. He wasn't going to work on his father's ranch. He wasn't going to follow in his brother's footsteps in the rodeo.

He wasn't the disappointment. The son who'd barely graduated high school.

The least of the three. Soon to be the least of more when they found the others, because he was sure he'd find a way to pale in comparison in Hank Dalton's eyes, even put up against the kids he'd just met.

But now Caleb had something that was *his*. And it might be a Christmas tree farm.

But from where he was sitting, the idea of being out there, in one of those large flat fields, surrounded by evergreen trees...

Silence.

Yeah, it didn't sound so bad.

"I want you to have the boys work at the Christmas tree lot," Gabe said finally.

"What?"

Gabe rolled his eyes as if Caleb had been demanding he rephrase. "Can the boys work at the Christmas tree lot this season? It would give them something else to do."

"Yeah, I guess it would."

As much as this whole school thing wasn't his ideal—hell, that was an understatement; anything to do with school was his nightmare—he did have a soft spot for the boys. Maybe because in some of them he could see himself. Kids who were struggling to do what was so easy for seemingly everyone around them.

And if he could help them out, give them something to do outdoors, show them there were plenty of vocations and passions out there for people who found sitting and reading to be exercises in torture...

Well, that was fine by him.

"Sure," Caleb said. "How much do you suggest I pay the little devils?"

"Fair wages," he said. "It's been good. Physical labor. You know it's helped."

"Yeah," he said. "I know." He sighed heavily. "I may have other work, too. If you have a kid that is keeping up with his schoolwork, and who might benefit from a little bit more time outdoors."

"I think Aiden might be a candidate," Gabe said.

A kid who had come at the beginning of the school year, along with the rest. He was a tough nut to crack, and last month when Vanessa and Jacob had been going through some things, the stress of the tension sent Aiden over the edge. He'd ended up running away from the school.

Jacob had rescued him, because somehow he'd fallen off the trail and ended up halfway down a cliff.

He was an angry kid, and he'd been through the kinds of things that could destroy people who weren't half as strong. He was a brat.

And they all loved him.

"Yeah," Caleb said. "That would be good."

"Well, why don't I make up a schedule and send it to you? We can debate the logistics of Christmas tree farming. Maybe I can enlist Calvin to paint some signs for your lot. With Vanessa's oversight, of course."

Calvin was another kid at the school. One who had discovered he had a little bit of an affinity for paint.

Caleb sighed. "Yeah, yeah. I'm still part of your bleeding-heart project."

"Good." Gabe shook his head. "We are family. You can't get rid of us that easily."

"I wasn't trying to get rid of you."

It had less to do with his brother than he'd ever understand. It was about him, carving out a path for himself, a life that he'd built. Where he would have something to be proud of. Something to shove in Hank Dalton's face.

It was easy for Gabe. He'd become a champion in the rodeo. He'd not only denied their father's desire that they "do better for themselves" by going to college instead of working with the land, but he'd excelled, too.

Jacob had never cared what anyone thought. He'd brushed off their father's expectations with a cocky grin and extended middle finger.

But then their father had offered to pay for college for Jacob. It had been his choice to refuse it.

Hank hadn't offered it to Caleb.

But Clint, who had been an effortless straight-A student, had gotten an offer from Hank. And Clint had deserved it.

There was no call for Caleb to be angry that he hadn't been offered something he didn't want. But he would show Hank now.

"Let me buy another round," Gabe said.

"What?"

"To celebrate. Your Christmas tree farm."

He grimaced. "Don't say it like that."

"There's no other way to say *Christmas tree farm*."

As his brother got up to get that next beer, Caleb leaned back in his chair and wondered if he really was insane.

Actually, he knew he was insane. He had a decade of proof on that subject. But oh, well. Insane he was, then.

And apparently, now he was a crazy Christmas tree farmer.

When Gabe brought back the beer, Caleb knocked it back as quickly as possible.

It was going to be a very interesting holiday season, that was for damn sure.

CHAPTER THREE

ELLIE WAS FEELING a bit like a badger by the end of the next school day. Restless, cranky and unsettled.

And she was in the mood to badger Caleb. Because it was the only thing that might manage some of the emotions that were clanging around inside her.

She'd been thinking about his move, and not only the move, but what that meant for her, for nearly twenty-four hours now.

She was still a bit ashamed of herself, and the general possessiveness she felt over him and his life.

The fact that it seemed to shock her that he had dreams and aspirations.

She had never thought of him like that.

He had existed, for so long, to serve her.

And that wasn't fair. Not really.

He hadn't come by her classroom today, either, and she wondered if she had made it so apparent that she was a selfish jerk when he had spoken to her yesterday, that he was a little bit mad.

Of course, the other piece of having a male best friend. He often didn't pick up on subtext, which meant that he usually wasn't mad at her when she thought that he might be. Because he hadn't realized she had done anything that should make him mad. As soon as school ended, she left her classroom, wandering out toward the barn, hoping that she might find Caleb.

She stepped into the structure where it was dim and cool, and heard the sound of mucking stalls. The unmistakable smell of shavings, and the musky odor of horse urine, mingled with dust.

It was a strange smell to feel any sense of nostalgia about, she supposed.

But it was indelibly linked to her joining the Dalton family.

Which she had done the moment she had become involved with Clint.

With that, she had inherited this whole scope of life that she hadn't even realized existed before.

She'd never ridden a horse, not till Caleb had taken her out on the trails one day nearly eight years ago. There had been something defining about it. Something in the memory that still made her stomach feel tense with anticipation. She could remember it clearly. The exhilaration of riding the horse along the rugged trails, the way they had broken through the trees and come out at the top of the mountain, at a clearing. And the look on his face as he took in the beauty in front of them.

He was a man connected to the land in a way that just seemed to be a part of him.

Of course he wanted a ranch. That was who he was.

His brother Jacob wasn't like that. Didn't seem to have the same affinity for it. No, it was more than an affinity. It was like it was in his blood. He was more than a cowboy. He was a rancher. Through and through. A man who needed to spend his life doing this kind of work.

She was the keeper of Caleb's biggest secret. She should have known all along he would want something like this, knowing what she did.

She'd figured it out a year or so before Clint had died, and she'd felt bad it had taken as long as it had.

She'd realized it watching him fill out a DMV form, of all things. And so many moments from the years had suddenly crystallized.

He was dyslexic.

She was the first person to put a name to what he'd struggled with all of his life. And she offered to help him. They'd sat together in her apartment, on the couch she still owned, and had gone over information about a host of different learning disabilities, piecing together his struggles, and ways they could combat them.

And she'd devised a lesson plan. She was a teacher, and it was what she did. And it had been such a great thing for her, to be able to use her passion to help someone she cared about so much.

The relief in his eyes as he'd learned about those things. As they'd found names, diagnoses and reasons for his struggles. Reasons that weren't: "I guess you're just stupid."

He'd confided in her that he'd been afraid he might be. That there was no other explanation for why he couldn't learn what everyone else seemed to be able to.

Caleb was intensely private and intensely proud. And he'd never wanted her to tell anyone, because he'd told her he hadn't wanted it to be seen as an excuse.

She'd honored that. She couldn't do anything but honor that.

He was the only person she would have kept a secret for like that. So perfectly she hadn't even told her husband.

She'd always cared very deeply for Caleb, but that experience had brought them closer. Until it hadn't.

The lessons had ended abruptly one day. Caleb had

just cut them off, with no real explanation. And she'd
gone from seeing him like clockwork three days a week
to not seeing him at all.

And then Clint had died and it hadn't mattered anymore.

Even during that time he hadn't been speaking to
her, she'd known who he was. And somehow in the
past few years she'd lost that sense of knowing him,
wrapped in her own grief.

But she knew him. Of course he needed this. Of
course.

She walked forward and looked into the door, and
was not at all surprised to see him, turning shavings
with a shovel, his tight black T-shirt stretching each
time he flexed his broad shoulders, the muscles in his
arms shifting, corded from the hard labor.

There was something about seeing him like this that
made her heart swell, made it trip over itself.

She was selfish. So selfish to not want him to have
his own ranch. Selfish to consider what it meant for
her at all.

It didn't matter. All that mattered was what it meant
for him.

"Hi," she said, leaning in the doorway.

He looked up, the brim of his black cowboy hat still
shading part of his face. "Hi, yourself," he said.

"I haven't seen you today."

"I know," he said. "I haven't seen you, either."

"Are you busy today?"

"A bit."

She leaned forward, still clinging to the doorway
with one hand. "I want to see your ranch."

He didn't pause in his shoveling. "Really?"

"Yes." She cleared her throat. "I'm sorry that I was ridiculous yesterday."

"Were you ridiculous?" He asked the question without looking at her.

"Yes, I was. I'm happy for you... Change hasn't exactly been my best friend. So you coming to me and telling me things are changing... It freaked me out a little bit. I've gotten into this place in life now where it all feels a little more in my control, and you reminded me today it isn't. I can't control everything around me, which is fair and fine. But it hits me in a sore spot."

"Right. I guess that's understandable."

"So anything changing makes me a little bit nervous. But I know we're friends. Even if we don't work together. Even if we haven't worked together all that long."

"It will be different," he said, propping himself up on his shovel. "You're working here now. I'll be on the ranch. Before you weren't working and I was just doing the wildfires. So I was either there all the time or gone."

"Yes. I used you shamelessly as a babysitter, and a shoulder to cry on and any number of other things. And I appreciate that. But... It's different now.

"You're my best friend," she said. "And I'm really happy for you. And I want to see the place."

"Sure," he said. "When?"

"Right now," she said.

"Right now," he repeated, his brows lifting slightly. "As in right this second?"

"Yes," she said. "Your mom was planning on staying with Amelia for another hour and a half anyway. And that way I can look at things without answering questions. And then, when we finally do go with Amelia, I can look at things and answer questions for her."

"You know, you don't have to go today so that you can convince me that you're excited for me."

"That's not even why," she said.

"Then why?"

"Because I am excited," she said, perhaps a little bit too brightly.

"All right, Ellie, let's go." He sounded a little too long-suffering for her liking. But she supposed she might deserve that.

"Are you going to have horses?" she asked, following him as he ditched his shovel and walked out of the barn.

"Yeah," he said. He opened the passenger-side door to his faded red truck and she climbed in, realizing as she did that she took those kinds of actions for granted.

"Thank you," she said once he was settled inside and had the truck engine turned on. "For everything. I mean, for things like opening the car door."

"That's nothing," he said.

"It's you," she said. "You're the most... The most helpful person. The most loyal. Caleb, I don't know what would have happened to me if I hadn't had you for all these years."

"Why are you being mushy?" he asked.

It was a good question. But she definitely felt a little mushy. "Christmas? Change. There's a lot of change happening right now. The new school, you leaving, West coming."

"I doubt West being here will be a very big difference to you. In fact, it may all be the same. One cowboy is basically the same as the next."

"Oh, that's where you're wrong," she said. "Nothing is the same as you."

She grinned at him, and he shifted, visibly uncomfortable as he pulled the truck out of its spot by the barn, and headed down the paved road that led out to the highway.

"How far away is the new ranch?" she asked when they were on the road.

"About ten minutes off this way," he said, turning left, away from town.

"What's the house like?"

"It has seen better days," he said. "In other words, it's a bit rustic. But I'll be building something new once I get around to it."

"I don't mind rustic," she said. "The farmhouse is a bit that way."

"This is more of a log cabin," he said.

"Well, I like log cabins."

"Good," he said. "That's good."

But he didn't really sound like he thought it was good, and she couldn't quite figure out why. Also, though, she didn't really want to ask, and she wasn't sure why that was, either.

"Tell me more about West," she said, digging for a subject change.

"I don't know anything about him," he said.

"Nothing?"

He sighed heavily. "He rode in the rodeo for a while, but Gabe doesn't know him. Bull rider, I guess. And stayed more regional. Mostly in Texas."

"So you do know some things."

"Yes. Some things."

"I would think that if he were any good Gabe would know who he was," she said.

"That's what I said," Caleb responded. "But Gabe said that wasn't necessarily the case. I wonder if he was just being kind, though."

"Oh, that's not like Gabe," she said.

"Yeah."

"I heard that Jamie was going to start riding pro next year."

"That's the word on the street," he said. "By which I mean, at the ranch."

Gabe's fiancée, Jamie, had been wanting to ride professionally in the rodeo for years, and everything was finally coming together for her.

"Do you think that Gabe is going to leave the school?" Ellie asked.

"I can't imagine he wouldn't. But he'll be back and forth."

"It will be interesting to manage things without them," she said.

"Well, you're doing a great job."

"I'm going to need help with the manual labor and stuff."

"Yeah, I expect you will."

"I guess I'll have to ask West," she said.

"You can still ask me," he said, something in his voice getting hard.

"Okay," she said. "Good to know."

She fiddled with the radio for a while after that, turning up Dierks Bentley and giving thanks it was one of his party songs, and not one of his sexy songs, because that would just make it a little bit awkward.

She wasn't sure why. Only that she knew it would.

Mostly because when you were looking for silence filler, you didn't want that silence to be filled with sincere lyrics about erotic acts.

As if she could even remember what *erotic acts* were like.

It had been so long…

She swallowed hard and turned the music up louder

as she watched the pine trees melt together, a whiskey blur of green out the car window. And up ahead of them were the mountains, rising above wooden telephone poles that created a strange man-made grid with their wires as they zigged and zagged on the uneven roadway.

Caleb hung a sharp right, onto an even narrower paved road with a faded yellow line down the middle. Eventually, the asphalt faded away into gravel, which carried them up a mountain, winding around until they reached another turnoff.

This went back, the land flat suddenly, and a wooden cabin came into view.

It wasn't as worse for wear as Caleb had led her to believe, two stories and with a charming porch that spread out wide, wicker chairs and a love seat right there.

"I think it's lovely," she said.

"It's okay," he said.

"I think it's a little better than okay."

The place he lived in now was much smaller, but he'd said many times that he didn't have use for a big house. It was just him, and he wasn't one for throwing parties.

"Let me show you where the trees are," he said.

"I don't think I have ever been to a place that grew Christmas trees," she said. She looked out the window again. "Of course, all the mountains around us kind of grow Christmas trees."

"Yeah, that's Charlie Brown–looking shit," he said.

"It's God's own handiwork, Caleb," she said dryly.

"Okay," he said.

"Don't tell me that Hank Dalton got his Christmas tree from a tree lot," she said.

"Oh, I wouldn't tell you that." He chuckled. "We never had a real tree when I was growing up."

"You didn't have a real tree?"

"Hell no. The tree was Tammy's domain," he said. "She prefers pink and tinsel."

"I have yet to see a pink or tinsel tree in your mother's living room."

"She's calmed down over the past few years. But when we were growing up, and we first had money, she went flashing it all around. And let me tell you, she didn't spare any expense. She would do themed trees. Buy new ornaments every year, a whole new color scheme. It was tacky as hell. I will never forget her Las Vegas Cowgirl Christmas tree. You know, with a bunch of mini versions of that neon cowgirl in Vegas? But this was all light-up cowboy boots and all of that. It was insane."

"Okay, that sounds a little bit much."

"What about you?"

She realized that they never exactly talked about her childhood Christmases.

"Oh, we didn't really do anything always. It depended. On where we were living. Who my mother was dating. When I was thirteen I found a small fake tree in the dumpster in our apartment building once. Like a tabletop tree. I put it up in the kitchen and decorated it with some old ornaments I found, with a paper chain I made. My mom threw it out."

"Your mom threw your tree away?" he asked.

She shifted, the incredulity in his tone making her uncomfortable. Yes, it had been a mean thing for her mom to do. And yes, Ellie didn't have a relationship with her mom. But she'd also spent a lot of time sitting with the things her mother had done. They hurt her, but she'd also seen them as...normal. Because she didn't know any different.

Caleb being shocked threw into sharp relief the fact that it wasn't normal. Not at all.

"She said that we couldn't have Christmas because it wouldn't be right without Dave. He wasn't even… He hadn't even been around that long. He was just the boyfriend of the season. But every man was so important to her. So much more important than anything else. And I…" She swallowed. "I told her I wanted to have Christmas with her."

She could remember it so keenly. That deep, desperate need to be loved. And that the tree—homely and broken and bedecked with homemade ornaments—felt like a piece of her heart.

"She said I wasn't enough. To make it Christmas." She cleared her throat. "So we didn't have it that year. I got up early and wrapped myself in a blanket and ate cereal. I watched *A Christmas Story* on TV with the sound down."

And she'd decided then she'd have to be enough for herself. That anything she did would have to be for her. And if she was happy, then that would have to be enough.

Thank God, too. Because if she hadn't determined to find that inner strength, who knew where she'd be now. Who knew how life would have crumpled her up.

She'd figured out how to love without opening herself up the way her mother had. Without laying herself bare. Anyway, in Ellie's mind that was obsession.

Ellie had found a brighter side to it. Companionship.

Sadness swept over her and she took a breath.

"Sometimes, I don't think I'm a whole lot better than her," she said, feeling miserable as they pulled up to the field with its rows and rows of trees.

"Why don't you think you're better?" he asked. "As far as I know, you've never done something like that to Amelia. You're a great mother, El. You've certainly never told your child she wasn't enough for you. And damn, you've lost. And still…"

She took a breath. "I know. But we always go to your parents' house for Christmas. And I love it. Your mom has definitely refined her whole Christmas thing." She swallowed. "But we don't have Christmas things that we get out. I just… I haven't wanted to do it."

"There's nothing wrong with that."

"I don't know. I always felt like my mom was the Grinch. For not letting me enjoy Christmas. For making it all about her. Well, I don't really do anything different. It's all about me and what I don't want to do. And what I don't want to deal with."

"It's different," he said. "You lost Clint."

"Yeah. And my mom was often in a state of grief over men. And yes, it was different. But was it to her? It's weird. Sometimes I think about my mom and I get so angry. I think of all the things that she put me through, and how I would never, ever in a million years put Amelia through any of that. And then sometimes I just… I get tired. I get sad. I don't want to do a damn thing and I wonder… Is this what she felt, too? Did I just not know how hard it was sometimes? Because sometimes it's hard. Really, really hard. To put a smile on your face when you just feel crispy inside."

"Crispy?"

"Yes," she confirmed. "Don't you ever feel like that?"

"Define it."

"I don't know, like your insides are dry. And if you're not careful, they might just break. That's how I feel sometimes."

Silence settled between them like an itchy blanket. Heavy and uncomfortable.

"He was great," Caleb said, finally. "The best. I can't imagine growing up without him. He was my brother."

Her heart twisted. It was so easy to forget Caleb's grief in hers. In her worry about Amelia growing up without a father. But Caleb felt it right along with her. More than anyone else.

"I miss him," Ellie said. "I miss him every time Amelia has a birthday. Every time she asks me questions about daddies. Sometimes I get really tired of missing him." Her eyes felt scratchy, but there weren't any tears. She cleared her throat. "Okay. Let's look at your Christmas trees."

She nearly stumbled out of the truck, not waiting for him to open the door for her, and into the crisp late-afternoon air.

There was something about it that helped cut through the cloying sadness that had threatened to overwhelm her just a moment ago.

Wasn't that an awful thing to admit? That she was tired of grief. It didn't seem fair.

Some days she felt like she *owed* him her lifelong grief. Because he'd died so young. Because she loved him, and his parents didn't love him enough. And in many ways it seemed like the best thing to do was for her to carry an eternal flame for him.

But the very idea of that made her feel like she was trudging through a swamp, and in reality she wasn't sure she could bear it.

She walked across four rows of trees, looking down at the endless paths that were forged through the middle. "How many trees are here?"

"Thirty thousand."

"No way," she said. "Thirty thousand trees?"

"Yes," he said. "All in various stages of growth. But

there's about five thousand that are ready to go this year. The next year there will be twice that amount."

"Do you have enough room to have cattle and the Christmas trees on the ranch?"

"I should," he said. "If the trees arc lucrative enough, I may never quit doing it. It's all lined out to keep going for the next four more years, even if I didn't replant."

"It seems like a pretty smart venture," she said.

"You sound surprised."

"No offense. And you know that I say this with a great amount of love. But you're not only a former bull rider, you're a current firefighter. And you fellas have a screw loose."

"True enough. Although, once I'm doing this full-time, I won't be doing the fires anymore."

"I…" Her heart twisted, did free-fall through her chest. "I'm actually really relieved to hear that. I tried not to be psychotic about it. But it really… It's always scared me that you did that still."

"I know."

"What happened to Clint was… Well, it wasn't even a freak accident. It was the result of neglect and poor safety standards on the part of the helicopter company. The odds of it happening again are so low. It was such a specific thing. But still, what you do is dangerous. And it… It scares me."

She couldn't fathom losing Caleb. She didn't want to. Ever.

"Yeah, well, I won't be doing it anymore. I don't really think you have to worry about any of these Christmas trees going rogue."

She smirked, happy to lighten the conversation a little bit. "I don't know. I seem to recall some late-night TV show. *When Christmas Trees Attack*."

"That seems legitimate."

She grinned. "Right?"

His lips turned up into a half smile, and he looked out over the field. There was pride there on his face that resonated inside her. His eyes looked so blue in the late-afternoon light, pale though it was. He walked down one of the rows, and she watched him, his long stride, the way his broad shoulders filled up her vision. Everything inside her felt warm.

Just looking at him made her feel… Calm. Happy.

He was the safest of spaces. Her port in the storm, and even if he was here, that wouldn't change.

It wasn't going to change between them. He would be here for her. Because he always was. The very thought made her heart feel slightly too big for her chest.

Caleb Dalton was one of the few things she could count on in this whole world.

"You know Amelia is going to love this," Ellie said. "She could dress as an elf at the lot."

"Well, I imagine that would bring in business," he said, turning and grinning at her.

"During the day it could be a family-friendly affair, and after dark…you could sell the Christmas trees with no shirt on."

The idea made a funny little zip race through her midsection, up and then disconcertingly back down. She squeezed her thighs together.

He arched a brow. "It's going to be the dead of winter."

"Sure," she said. "But you know, it's not for you. It's for your female clientele."

He snorted a laugh. "Should I ask you to come and wear a miniskirt, be my sexy elf?"

Another little shimmer radiated through her, and she

looked away from him, feeling slightly pinned down by the clarity and his blue gaze.

She sucked in a sharp shot of the cold air and looked down at the ground, trying to clear up some of the heat that had flooded her cheeks.

She looked back at him. "I don't think me in a sexy elf costume would work. It's well documented that women do most of the Christmas tree shopping for the household."

"Well, there are some women who may want to see it, Ellie."

"Okay, how about we don't sexualize the Christmas tree farm," she said.

"Possibly for the best." He pulled a face. "Gabe wants me to have the boys working at the lot anyway. And I don't want them around you if you're to be dressed as a sexy elf."

"No," she said, wrinkling her nose. "I am their teacher."

"Yeah, which means you know they already have inappropriate fantasies, but we don't need to encourage it."

"Yeah. Really no." His blue eyes were somehow just a bit too blue right then. She swallowed hard, confused by the dryness in her throat, and wandered down the same path that he was on. "I can't believe all this is yours."

"That's why I kept doing the fires," he said. "I was able to bank most of my money. Combined with the meager winnings I still had saved up from the rodeo."

She laughed. "Did you ever win in the rodeo?"

"Yes," he said. "I might not have been a champion like Gabe, but I did win some."

"You didn't stay at it very long."

"Yeah, Jacob was done. Clint had a wild new idea in mind…"

"Firefighting."

"It seemed good. And hey, we got to travel around quite a bit. See the United States. I mean, mostly see the mountains of the United States on fire, but nonetheless."

She stepped into the next row, peered around the pine tree and smiled at him. "Well, I like the Christmas trees. They are impressive."

"Thank you," he said. "Want to see the rest of the place?"

"I do," she said.

The rest of the tour went easily, smoothly. No more strange pickups, no more moments of extreme sadness.

And all of it served to comfort her further.

Things might be changing, but Caleb was staying the same.

Because that was who he was.

Her comfort. Her safety.

No matter where he lived, that would be true.

She knew that she could count on that, of the many, many things she couldn't.

With her intent to start moving forward, changing certain things, knowing that he would be ever constant, never changing, was one of the only things that brought her real comfort.

CHAPTER FOUR

IT WAS STRANGE the way it happened. Mostly because Caleb was expecting some fanfare. And he really hadn't expected that he would be the first person to run into West. Not when Gabe was the one coordinating everything; not when Gabe was the one who had been in touch with their supposed half brother. But there he was, standing in the middle of the barn on a Friday afternoon, looking like a disturbing mirror of Caleb himself.

He had darker hair and a slightly broader build, but he had those Dalton blue eyes, and even Caleb could immediately see all the similarities in their features.

"Well," Caleb said. "You must be West Caldwell."

"And you're a Dalton," West said.

"That I am," he responded. "I didn't think you were getting here today."

He shrugged. "Don't think I gave a time."

"I'm not Gabe," Caleb said.

"I didn't figure."

"I'm Caleb. Caleb Dalton."

He stuck his hand out, and the other man took it, shaking it hard.

At least he had a good handshake, so there was that.

It would've been a shame to be related to someone who had a weak grip.

Caleb didn't need to be best friends with the guy, but it would be helpful if he could respect him.

"I don't know what… I don't know what Gabe has told you about the place. But it's not like this is a job that pays well."

"I'm not here for money," West said. "I'm here to see what the hell all this is about. Imagine my surprise when I got a letter from a guy claiming to be my half brother. Saying that Hank Dalton was my father. My mom never told me that."

"She never told you? Because you know she tried to extort money out of my dad."

"Did it work?"

"Not exactly. I guess my mother paid her off. Sent her away, and the other women, too."

"Yeah, Gabe mentioned something about that. That there are other women. Others like me."

The silence that fell between them wasn't uncomfortable, but it wasn't entirely free of tension, either. Caleb felt the urge to defend Hank, and he couldn't for the life of him figure out why since his father's behavior was pretty indefensible.

And honestly, he'd probably been avoiding this because it forced him to contend with just how indefensible head-on.

"Our…our father," Caleb said, "has a checkered past."

"Going back more than thirty years," West said dryly.

"Yeah," Caleb agreed. "So why is it you're here? Hank is in good health, so he's not kicking the bucket anytime soon, and your presence wouldn't be required for you to get a cut of the inheritance even if it did. And this gig at the school doesn't pay that well."

"Believe it or not, Dalton, I don't need your family money. Even if it's mine, too."

"Then forgive me, but what is it you're after?"

His mouth quirked into a half smile, and he rocked

back on his heels, his arms crossed over his chest. And Caleb realized they were standing with the exact same posture. "Would you believe it if I said a family?"

"I don't know. I don't have a reason to disbelieve you."

He lifted a shoulder. "I'll be honest. I'm curious about you. But to an extent… I kind of just want to watch Hank Dalton twist in the wind."

Caleb couldn't even begrudge West that feeling. Not really.

"Well, I don't mind someone being bloodthirsty. Especially when there's a reason behind it. But you know, these boys here at the ranch, they don't deserve to get entangled in the middle of that. If you're going to be working with them…"

"Hell, I am them," he said. "Petty criminal, and general no-good who did all right for himself for a while. I had a decent life. Big house, big ranch. Gorgeous wife. Too bad she turned out to be a liar."

"Yeah?"

"I just spent two years in jail. She implicated me in an embezzlement scheme that it turns out she and her lover were actually involved in. I wouldn't screw with white-collar crime. I never have. I'm blue-collar through and through. If it comes down to it, I'll get my hands dirty. But I'm not about to get them stained with money. I don't steal, not from people who are out there working hard. It's not in me. I don't have a lot of scruples, but that's one of them."

"So you're a convict. And you're here to…help with troubled youth."

"Yep. That's about the size of it." He laughed. "I mean, if I'm honest, it was a good time to get out of Texas, as much as it was anything else."

"Well, that might just be perfect."

"Excellent."

"Welcome to the Dalton ranch."

ELLIE WAS SWEATY. And she was surrounded by open boxes. She had decided to tackle item one on her list.

Her Christmas wish list.

It had been weighing heavily on her the past few days.

And even after she had been soothed by the time spent with Caleb at his ranch, she still wanted to go ahead with it.

Item one: buy a new dress, was where she had begun.

So she had made the most of the varied and brought options and online shopping, and rush-delivered a great many different dresses to her door, and now that Amelia was asleep, she had wine, and she was wiggling herself into fabrics and shapes she hadn't touched since well before she'd given birth.

She was currently wearing a red dress that forced her to walk like her thighs had been taped together.

The shoes didn't exactly help.

They were the kind of shoes that were best worn when horizontal, and not when standing.

She hadn't had occasion for shoes like this in a great while, either, and she'd actually gotten rid of most of her heels years ago.

And there were new styles now.

She'd seen these shoes while online shopping for the dresses and hadn't been able to resist.

But she felt like an impostor now, standing there in this red…bandage that was more likely to fit the Elf on the Shelf than it was to fit her.

She meandered to the mirror in the entryway of the farmhouse and stared at herself.

She was not used to seeing this much of her breasts. Or her legs.

Or wearing anything that might outline the width of her hips to this degree. She turned and eyed her rear end critically. Then poked at the line she could see just above her underwear.

It wasn't…bad, she supposed. It just didn't use to be…quite so prominent.

She turned to the side and curled her lip. Her stomach was not flat. Not even close. She supposed it was a triumph that her ass stuck out farther.

Still, she did not think this was the kind of dress that would lead men to want to dance with her.

The very idea made her stomach feel like it was withering, falling.

Going out and dancing?

She would probably be…six years older than half the women in there. And she had a sudden vision of herself, looking tired and frazzled in a too-tight dress, being passed over for women just old enough to drink whose dresses molded over their bodies with nary a fat bubble in sight.

She had stretch marks.

She could not imagine this going well.

Granted, she had not had a very long time in her life of even trying to date. But from what she remembered, it seemed the kind of men who were out on the prowl were either overconfident and smarmy, or under confident and incredibly nervous.

And she honestly didn't have the patience for either. Not now.

Clint was the only man she'd ever been with.

And she'd known him well when she got naked with him. Very well.

Their connection hadn't been an explosion. It had been sweet, and he had been patient with her. Kind and deferential to her virginity. He'd waited to sleep with her for a whole year after they'd started dating and he'd never pressured her into anything.

Not that she hadn't done *stuff* for him.

She had, of course.

She'd been scared, though, and she'd wanted to be sure she was in absolute control of herself and her life.

What he'd shown her about sex was the same thing he'd taught her about relationships in general: they could be fun.

It had been revelatory to her. That closeness could be sweet and light. That you could laugh while you were under the covers with someone. She missed that. She wanted to find it again.

Not a relationship. But maybe…maybe that physical closeness. A little bit of light fun. A little bit of pleasure.

Okay, she wasn't going to jump into bed with someone immediately.

She wanted… Well, first she wanted to find a decent dress. Then she wanted to dance.

She wanted to feel *pretty*.

She was not sure the stress was going to accomplish it.

There was a knock on her front door, and she straightened, holding the wineglass up and freezing on her very tall shoes. A second later her phone buzzed.

She walked over to where she had tossed it on the couch and picked it up.

It's me.

The message was from Caleb.

She suddenly felt ridiculous, standing in the middle

of her living room wearing a cocktail dress, drinking wine by herself. Especially now that she'd been caught.

She jerked the door open. "Yes?" She peered through a crack in the door, not opening it any wider.

"What are you doing?" he asked.

"What are you doing here?"

"West is at the ranch."

She forgot herself for a moment, holding the door open all the way. "What?"

Caleb jerked back, his eyes sweeping her up and down, his lips thinning into a firm line. "What the hell is that?"

"What?"

It only took a moment for heat to flood her face, realizing she was in the very brief dress still. "It's a merlot, Caleb," she said, holding the wine in front of her and jiggling the glass slightly. "Would you like a glass?"

"I'll take a *bottle*," he said, pushing in past her.

His manner was strange, his posture stiff as he maneuvered himself to the far end of the room away from her.

"So?"

"No, let's talk about your dress first," Caleb said.

"I *hate it*," she said. "In fact, if you're here, you're about to be subjected to a fashion show."

She might as well. After all, Caleb was a man, but he was more of a safe space than any of the men out there in the bars would be.

"Okay," he said slowly.

"I'm putting on the next one now."

"What's wrong with that one?" he asked.

"What do you mean *what's wrong with that one*? It's like a size too small, first of all."

He looked her over, his blue eyes darting back and

forth, the expression on his face that of a man trying to do a very difficult math equation. "I..."

"You don't think it's too tight?"

"I don't think that's a question you can ask men," he said, his expression blank.

"Why not?"

"I don't think such a thing exists, as far as we're concerned."

"Oh, please," she said, patting her stomach. "No one wants to see this." She picked up one of the other boxes and squirreled it away to the bathroom that was just down the hall. She peeled her dress off, pulling out the navy blue velvet garment that was still inside the box.

She wiggled into it and looked at herself critically. It had a wide, deep square neck, and also showed off a fair amount of boob, but it didn't cling quite so tightly to her amplified curves.

She began to exit the bathroom again and froze.

Caleb didn't think the dress had looked too tight on her. Which meant he had liked the look of her body.

And she had no idea what to do with that.

You like the look of his body. He's a good-looking man.

True. She had made a joke earlier today about him selling Christmas trees with his shirt off. It wasn't any different.

They were aware that each other was a man and a woman. Even if their relationship was platonic.

She took a breath and emerged.

He was sitting on the couch, having helped himself to a glass of wine.

"Well?"

He frowned. "What are you buying a dress for?"

She decided not to answer that. "Give me your opinion on the dress first. Then tell me about West."

"The red one's better."

She squinted. "Why?"

"Because it's red. And it's tighter."

"Are men really that simple?"

"Yes," he said easily, taking a sip of his wine. "West is a convicted criminal."

"Really?" Well, that was interesting.

"Yes. I mean, I guess he was cleared of his last few charges. But he was convicted of a few things in high school that he definitely did."

"So he should fit right in with the Daltons."

Caleb laughed, the sound containing a bit of an edge. "I guess."

"Do you like him?"

"I don't know."

"Don't say it like that. Like it was a stupid question. It's not a stupid question."

"Of course it's not a stupid question," he said quickly.

"Then don't look at me like I'm stupid."

He huffed out a frustrated breath. "What's the deal with the dresses?"

She didn't want to lie to him. But she didn't want to tell him, either. But it would be dumb not to tell him. "I…I'm working on my Christmas list," she said.

"What?"

"I… Look, you're making some changes. And the more that I thought about it the more I realized I'm a little bit jealous of you. I want to change things. I want to change…me. I want an excuse to buy a dress. I want to go out. I want to… I want to dance."

"That's on your list?" he asked, clearly dumbfounded by the concept.

"Yes," she said.

His expression was impossible to read, his face blank.

"But first I have to buy a dress. I have to pick one. And I'm having trouble because I haven't worn a dress and gone out since I was twenty-three years old, and hadn't had a baby. And even then I had a husband, so I wasn't trying to look…good for other men."

"You're trying to look good for men," he echoed.

"*Yes,*" she said. "I would really like to look good for men, so that I can dance. And if I don't look good, no one will ask me to dance."

He narrowed his eyes. "It may come as a shock to you, Ellie, but women can ask men to dance, too."

"I know that," she said. "But I don't want to be some sad widow accosting men, trying to get a pity lap around the dance floor to the tune of 'Bubba Shot the Jukebox.'"

He only looked at her. His eyes neutral, his lips pressed into a grim line. "The word *widow* is not stamped on your forehead," he said, his voice hard.

That comment, dry though it was, made her pause. Because she realized that a part of her had imagined it might be.

That *widow* was stamped on her forehead, and *mother* was perhaps written boldly across her arms.

Well, definitely her stomach.

All kinds of things that would make men want to avoid her or lend weight to something she just wanted to be light.

"I just want to go out and have fun. I don't want to talk to anybody about my life. I don't want to…have anything serious happen. I just want… Christmas is beautiful. And they're going to start decorating town, and the bars are going to be packed full of extra people that came in to see the big Christmas celebration. I just want to be with that. In that."

She realized that that probably sounded stupid. That it sounded sad.

Well, she was a little bit sad. Sometimes.

She sighed heavily and sat down on the couch next to Caleb, a wedge of couch about the width of her hand between them. She rested her hand in that space for a moment, and the heat from his thigh seemed too warm. She moved it back on her own leg, and it still felt fuzzy. Strange.

She swallowed. "Don't you ever just want to pretend that...your life doesn't exist?"

"I don't..." He looked over at her, his brows knit together. "What do you mean?"

"I don't mean that I'm not alive. I mean, sometimes I want to pretend to be someone else. Just for a couple of hours. Like I'm the kind of person who could go out and have a drink. And dance. And wear a pretty dress. I never really did any of that. I met Clint, and I don't regret that. But... Now this is my life. It's shaped mostly by not having him. And I want to be able to do things...

"Like someone who didn't lose someone. Just for a couple of hours. Someone who doesn't have a mountain of baggage and a thousand responsibilities. Not forever. Just for an evening." She let her head fall back against the couch, and turned her face so that she was staring at him. "Am I ridiculous?"

"No," he said, his voice rough.

"I have another dress," she said.

"Okay," he said, his voice cautious now.

She pushed herself up off the couch, and suddenly a tightness in her chest eased just a little bit.

She grabbed the last box and went down the hall,

closing herself into the bathroom and taking out a green dress that she had chosen because she thought it might enhance that color in her eyes. They could go gold, blue or green depending on what she chose to wear.

She shimmied out of her current dress and put the new one on. It was somewhere between the red and the navy, the neckline more of a narrow V, but lower than the other two.

It clung to her curves, but it didn't make her feel quite so much like a lumpy sponge with rubber bands wrapped around her.

She walked out slowly, her heels clicking on the floor, and lifted her hands, doing a short turn and then continuing to walk toward Caleb. "What about this?"

He only looked at her for a moment. And then he looked away. "It's fine."

"Just *fine*?"

"Keep it," he said, the words short.

For some reason he was very clearly no longer here for the discussion and she didn't know why.

"Okay," she responded, a little bit disappointed by the reaction.

She didn't know what she had expected. Something. A little bit more of a reaction, maybe.

"Then I will wear this one," she said.

"When are you going out dancing? Tonight?" he asked, his tone very neutral.

"Tomorrow night," she said, lifting her chin. "I figure Saturday night is probably a pretty good…prowling night. For dancing."

"Yeah," he said, the word clipped. "I don't think you really have to prowl to get a dance."

"Great. Well."

"Did you need me to babysit for you?"

That question was definitely a little bit hostile.

"No," she said. "I have a babysitter. But thank you."

"Great," he said.

"Great," she responded.

He stood up. "I should go."

"You don't have anything else to tell me about West?"

"Not really."

"I feel like you came over to talk."

"I did. And apparently ended up the victim of a fashion show."

"The *victim*? I'm so sorry to *victimize* you with my body."

That was all she needed. Really, she'd been feeling so good about herself, and he had used the word *victim* to describe having to sit and look at her.

His face did something strange. A muscle in his cheek twitching, a vein in his neck standing on end.

"I'll see you later."

He left his barely touched wine sitting on the coffee table, and walked out the door of her house.

She huffed and sat down on the couch, then looked over at her phone.

She picked it up and called Vanessa.

"Hello?"

"Hey, pregnant lady," she said, sounding as grumpy as she felt. "You want to go out with me tomorrow night and go dancing?"

"No," Vanessa said. "I don't want to dance. Are you kidding me?"

"Will you go to the bar with me?"

"Well, I could stay home and read one of the Panic books you gave me. But yeah, I can go to the bar with you."

"I want to dance," Ellie said.

"Okay," Vanessa responded. "With anyone in particular?"

"Well. With anyone, in point of fact. Anyone male. In my age group."

"Okay," Vanessa reiterated. "I think we can make that happen."

"Unless we can't," she said, knowing she sounded a little bit hysterical. "Maybe men will feel victimized by my very appearance."

"Are you...okay?"

"Yes," she said. "I think I'm okay. I think I'm very okay."

And when she got off the phone with Vanessa, she determined that she was going to be very, very okay.

She picked up her glass of wine and his, and headed back toward her room.

She didn't need Caleb to give her affirmation. She could get it all by herself. She wanted to do this. And she liked her dress. That was all that mattered.

And if she ended up keeping the red dress, too, it had nothing to do with him.

Nothing at all.

CHAPTER FIVE

"I MEAN, I GUESS the good news is it won't be difficult for you to be my designated driver."

"Yeah," Vanessa said, turning off her car engine. "Since I'm pregnant, and sober even when I'm not pregnant."

"Yeah," Ellie said.

Ellie wasn't much of a drinker, but she had a feeling that tonight she might need a little bit of liquid courage. She had ended up in the red dress. And she didn't even know how that had happened. Because she didn't even like it. But she just kept remembering the way that Caleb had responded to it.

The way that his face had gone all hard, the way that his jaw had turned impossibly square.

Of course, then he had been a jerk.

But he had expressed a clear preference for the red dress, and he was a man. That had been—after all— the point of asking him in the first place. Not that she would have asked him if he had never shown up at her home unannounced, but he had. And since he had, she had figured it was probably a good idea to take advantage of him and his maleness.

If she didn't take his advice, his top pick, then really, she was just dressing for herself. And there was certainly a place for that. At her age, she was much more inclined to dress for herself as she was to dress for anyone else.

She was through with trotting around like a pretty pony and trying to impress men, or, even worse, other women.

Except, tonight the point was a little bit to impress a man. So that he would dance with her.

And maybe kiss her.

And maybe… Maybe eventually…

That last item on her list was the most ambitious. And it terrified her in no small amount.

She took a deep breath and got out of Vanessa's car.

They had parked across the street from the Gold Valley Saloon. It was dark outside, and she could see through the windows that the bar was packed.

The neon sign that hung above the door was lit, the old gold pan on it like a beacon for those looking not for gold, but a drink. A strange emblem for a bar, she had always thought, but not really a strange one for a town famous for its place during the gold-rush era.

Not that any of that was relevant to her current situation. But it took her mind off the reality of it all.

They got out slowly, and Vanessa looked her up and down. "It's a good dress," she said.

For her part, Vanessa was wearing a dress that was dark purple and hugged her curves. Including the baby bump one.

"It's very tight," Ellie said.

She had found a pair of underwear that went decently with it, and smoothed out the lines that had been irritating her earlier. Of course, it was not *sexy* underwear. But then, she hadn't planned on anyone seeing her underwear. Not tonight. Baby steps.

She had to take baby steps, because her heels were so high, and she wasn't accustomed to the way they fit anymore.

"Tight is good," Vanessa said. "Even my dress is tight." She rubbed her hand over her stomach.

"Yes, and you look charming. I'm afraid that I look like I'm trying too hard."

Vanessa laughed. "I think it's pretty safe to say that men like it when women try too hard."

"Okay. I can take your point there. It's just been...so long since I actually wanted to get a man's attention."

"And...that's what you want to do?" Vanessa sounded so skeptical that Ellie felt oddly dented.

"I don't know. It's more complicated than that. I just want to... I want to have fun."

"I have never seen anyone look so grim about the notion of having fun."

"I'm not sure I know how to have fun anymore."

"Well, there's only one way to find out. We have to go in that bar. We have to go in that bar, and see if we can find some men to dance with us."

"You're going to...dance?"

"I don't know," Vanessa said. "I might. But then, I'm dancing for two."

"Also, Jacob might have an issue with that."

Vanessa laughed. "I'm not actually going to dance with another man. Honestly, Jacob trusts me, but if another guy put his hands on me..."

Vanessa didn't look upset, marinating on her husband's jealousy. If anything, she looked pleased.

Ellie was pretty sure Clint wouldn't have cared if she'd danced with another man. And she wouldn't have minded if he'd danced with someone else. They just weren't like that.

For a moment she wondered what it would be like. To have a man be...possessive. The idea made her uncomfortable. But along with the discomfort came something else. Something that spread like a deep ache.

To be wanted so much that a man couldn't stand it if someone else touched you…

She didn't like the feeling it created in her. It reminded her too much of that intensity she'd felt as a girl. Wanting her mother to love her, not the string of men she brought into their home, into their lives.

Wanting her mother to have Christmas with *her*.

Wanting to be enough.

What would it be like to have someone care so much he couldn't stand it if someone else even looked at her?

Bad. Very bad. That was all stuff she'd put away. Unhealthy nonsense that she'd worked hard to get rid of. She wasn't going to go…longing for it now.

"Ready?"

"As ready as I'll ever be to enact my own plan."

They looked both ways, and the two of them tottered across the street quickly, and pushed their way into the bar. Immediately, Ellie found herself enveloped by warmth, the smell of beer and country music. It was loud and so full of people that she actually felt better.

She felt anonymous in here. Like the atmosphere itself had wrapped around her like a cloaking device, making it easy for her to slip through the crowd and find a little table in the corner.

Plenty of people were out on this small dance floor, swaying to the beat of Tim McGraw, laughing, smiling. Some clearly more interested in each other's bodies than in moving to the beat.

Suddenly, she was very glad she was here. Because it looked… It looked fun. And she wanted to be out there.

She was about to stand, go over to the bar and get herself a drink when a man came to the table, a cowboy hat on his head, a smile on his face. He was cute, no doubt about it. Probably a couple of years younger than she was, though it was hard to say. But he still had that slim build of a guy in his early twenties rather than his late.

"Can I buy you a drink?" he asked.

"I… Sure," she said.

"And…a soda for your friend?"

"Thanks," Vanessa said, grinning widely. "The friend would like a Diet Coke."

"I'll go get that with you," she said. "I'm Ellie."

He turned and grinned as they made their way across the bar. "Todd."

"Nice to meet you," she said.

Not a terrible name. Kind of reminded her of a cartoon fox. But foxes could be cute. And anyway, his name didn't matter that much. She didn't really want to make friends with him. She wanted to dance. And maybe have dancing turn into item three on her list: kissing under the mistletoe.

Which could easily become item five: sex.

She looked at the man, tried to imagine him without his clothes. She couldn't.

Her brain immediately got stuck on her being out of hers. And that sounded terrible.

She looked straight ahead, and not at him, because for some reason she was afraid he might be able to read her mind.

He ordered them a couple of bottles of beer, handed hers right to her and smiled at her. "What brings you out tonight?" he asked.

"Dancing," she said.

That she had some other aims was her business and hers alone.

"Well, then I think we should dance."

The bartender brought Vanessa's Diet Coke and Todd took hold of it, carrying it back to the table and offering it to her. He was terribly polite, which was lovely, and when Ellie set her beer on the table he took her hand and led her out to the dance floor.

His hand was warm, and it felt nice to be touched by someone. It really did. He grinned and tugged her up against him, one arm around her waist, the other holding her hand as they swayed to the mellow song coming from the jukebox.

This was fun, and she felt marginally exhilarated when the tempo of the song picked up and he spun her, pulling her back up against his body.

It was fun, which she'd been after.

But she was not…into him.

Not like that.

She blinked, smiling to herself. She was a little bit… pleased that it was so easy for her to identify that. That she wasn't just desperate for any man's touch.

Of course, it might have been a little bit more convenient if she was.

Easier.

She tried to imagine it, though. Tried to imagine letting him take her back to his place and peel her clothes off her. The red dress that she knew would be a whole project, because getting it on had nearly necessitated the use of Crisco.

She did not feel excited. Not even the slightest bit turned on.

Which meant he wouldn't fulfill items two and three on her list. Which meant coming here again. And finding a new dress. And trying to find a man she did want to get naked with. Be skin to skin with.

She looked up at Todd again, trying to see if maybe—
maybe—she was into the idea of trying one of the other
things on her list with him. The idea made her feel…
Well, it was not an enjoyable thought. How did you
choose a man for a hookup? How could you know it
would be good? Or even okay?

She'd known Clint so well before they'd had sex for
the first time. And he'd known she was a virgin, so
he'd been sweet. As funny as it sounded, he'd made her
laugh. He'd made it all okay.

He'd always made it all okay, and she didn't have
him now to make it feel…safe.

But she and Todd could dance. Dancing would be
fine. In fact, Todd proved to be a very good dancer, and
that made him perfect for the purposes of tonight. The
rest of the numbers on her list could wait. And they
would have to.

He twirled her, and she laughed, coming to an abrupt
halt when she looked up and saw Caleb.

Their eyes collided and she froze, feeling like she
was pinned there to the spot.

He was standing a few feet away from the dance
floor, and yet, even in the crowd of people, she spotted
him unerringly.

He was dressed all in black. Black hat. Black T-shirt.
Black jeans. Black boots.

And his eyes were a storm.

This is it.

She didn't even know what those words meant, not
for a moment. And then realized…

It was what she and Vanessa had been talking about
earlier.

What it would be like for a man to see you with
someone else and look…

Well, just like that.

But it didn't make sense. She and Caleb weren't like that.

Her heart thundered hard, and she didn't know why she felt…like she might be in trouble. A huge adrenaline rush washed through her, leaving her feeling suddenly weak and shaking.

And then he was walking toward her, cutting through the crowd. And he stopped, just behind Todd, who hadn't seen him yet, and hadn't noticed Ellie's distraction.

"Mind if I cut in?"

Todd turned, and his affable manner went slightly cold. "I don't know," he said. "I suppose that's up to the lady. But she and I were having a pretty good time."

"It's okay," Ellie said. "He's my friend."

The storm in Caleb's eyes seemed to get more intense.

"I'll be over there," Todd said.

"Okay," she replied.

And suddenly, she was being pulled into Caleb's arms. His grip was strong, his hands somehow so much warmer than Todd's. They were like an inferno. His whole body was. And he did not have the slight build of a man in his early twenties. No. Caleb had always been built like a mountain, but she had never been quite so aware of the intensity of his strength.

Possibly because while he'd certainly hugged her and offered comfort, held her even in those early days while she'd wept a river onto his shirt, he'd never held her quite like this before, and she couldn't say why it felt different.

"How did you know I was here?"

"Your accomplice," he said, his voice rough.

"Vanessa ratted me out?"

"No." He looked over her shoulder for a moment. Then back at her. "Her husband."

"Right. Who is your *brother*." She sighed. "There really isn't a safe space around here."

Caleb's hands shifted, the one on her back drifting lower, and it made her feel…aware.

Caleb was a man.

Caleb was a man who appreciated how she looked in this dress.

She wondered what Caleb would think of her *out* of the dress.

A sharp pang hit her in the stomach and nearly turned her inside out.

Well, *that* was a new thought.

The song changed and got slow, and she waited for Caleb to let go of her. But he didn't.

He tightened his hold on her, his eyes intense on hers. "Your list is successfully fulfilled?"

"No," she said, the response tumbling out of her mouth before she had a chance to think it through.

"No?"

"No," she repeated. "There was more on the list."

And she didn't want to tell him any of them. Not a single one.

He shifted his hold on her and looked down. And it was like being held safe in the shadow of the mountain. Yes, dancing with Todd had been fun, if absent of spark. But she felt… She felt utterly and completely secure with Caleb holding her. She didn't feel awkward about her dress. She didn't feel uncertain.

He was safe.

He was someone she could trust. With anything. With all of herself.

She stumbled, her limbs still a little bit numb from

that first appearance of his, from the ensuing adrenaline, and she found herself completely pressed against his chest, inhaling that scent of his that she'd never noticed on quite this level before. Skin. Sweat.

Pine and cedar.

She put her hand on his chest and pushed herself backward. But left her hand right where it was. He was solid like a rock. But she could feel his heart. Could feel it thundering beneath her palm like he'd just run a marathon.

She looked up at him and found herself completely lost in that blue storm.

And she felt like maybe she was going crazy. Because suddenly everything seemed to make sense, and nothing in her life should make sense. Absolutely nothing. So something had to be wrong with her if it seemed right.

The very idea of taking the next step on the list with Todd seemed… The very idea terrified her. And not just because she didn't feel a spark of electricity with him. But the idea of getting naked with another man… She didn't think she could do it. Who could she trust her body with? Who could she even trust her…her lips with?

Suddenly, in Caleb's arms, the answer seemed clear, if only because the word *trust* seemed to impress itself upon her entire body and warm her completely.

And it hit her then, that if she did come to this bar every night for the next…well, every weekend until Christmas, she wasn't going to find anyone that she felt safer with.

This was her first.

And after this it would be… Well, maybe she would be able to just go out and find a fun hookup. Maybe.

But not the first time.

Not the first man after Clint.

She thought of getting naked with Caleb. Of seeing him without his shirt. Without…everything.

Her heart rate sped up and she didn't know what to do. Should she let go of him? Hold on to him?

He would be…he would be appalled if he knew what she was thinking. If he knew she was thinking about him being naked. And her being naked. And them being naked together.

They had never, *ever* had anything more than a platonic friendship.

And yes, he had appreciated her in the dress last night, but he was a man. And he was just being the way men were. Men liked women's bodies. They liked boobs and were often not very discriminating about who the boobs were attached to.

She found she was discriminating, really, and that was the problem here.

She didn't want a relationship.

She wanted sex.

But she also hated the idea of being with a man she didn't know. Felt horribly vulnerable just thinking about it.

Caleb never made her feel vulnerable. He never made her feel unsure.

He made her feel safe.

Protected.

And right now he was making her a little warm.

"Caleb," she said, swallowing hard. "Can I…? Can you help me with my list?"

THE MURDER IN Caleb's blood had cooled slightly. But only slightly.

When he had walked in and seen Ellie in the arms of another man…

He had seen Ellie in the arms of another man for a decade. A man he cared about. A man he loved like a brother. Who deserved her. Her beauty, her grace, her smiles.

That random-ass *weedy* cowboy did not deserve her.

Clint had been the best man in the world. The best man Caleb had ever known. Hank Dalton had offered Clint money to go to college, and he hadn't taken it. Not knowing how Hank made Caleb feel. He'd rejected the money. He'd stuck with Caleb.

She'd had the best man. And now she was dancing with this…

This *douchebag*.

When Jacob had told him where Ellie and Vanessa had gone, Caleb started walking out the door almost before Jacob had finished his sentence. Because he remembered, clear as day, the dress she'd had on the night he'd come over.

That dress had fired up a hell of a lot of feelings he'd rather not have. Rather not remember. But he had. It had hit him like a punch to the jaw. That body…a body he'd fantasized about late at night.

Until she'd gotten married. Then he'd put a stop to it.

And if things had gotten tense inside him again during their reading lessons, well…

He'd put a stop to that, too.

But God almighty, then she'd been dancing with this…this *boy*.

And when he'd walked in…

There she had been. On the dance floor. A wide grin on her face, and that red dress wrapped around her curves.

Now she was in Caleb's arms, his arms and not someone else's. She had stumbled against him, that delicate hand on his chest, and he'd been certain that he was going to explode. That his heart was going to burst straight through his chest.

And she looked up at him, her eyes blue, fathomless.

And had asked him about her list.

His brain was having an impossible time sorting through everything because his body was caught in the jaws of an intense adrenaline rush. Desire that he'd fought against for so long warring with that cooling rage, the desperate urge to hide all that need he was feeling.

But they'd never touched like this before. They'd never danced.

It felt right. The way she fit in his arms.

That rightness scared him down to his soul.

"Your list?" he asked.

"Yes," she said. She swallowed hard, and he could tell that her mouth was dry. He could also see her pulse drumming softly at the base of her throat.

He was so attuned to everything about her. A slight change in her breath, every shift of her body against his. If she was even half as aware of him, she would know beyond a shadow of a doubt that he wanted her.

Good thing she wasn't. Because no one was as aware of another human being as Caleb Dalton was of Ellie Bell.

"What would that entail?" he asked.

"I can't… I don't want to talk about it here," she said.

"Okay," he said slowly.

"So…can we…take a walk?"

"Sure," he said, looking back at the table where Vanessa was sitting, tapping on her phone. But when she looked up at the two of them, her gaze was laser focused, and he had a feeling that she was either reporting the exact goings-on to Jacob, or was only pretending to be on her phone so that she wasn't just staring at them.

He supposed they did make a little bit of a spectacle. The man dancing with his best friend's widow.

She let out a breath and suddenly peeled herself away from him, walking back over to her table and grabbing her purse. He just stood there watching her, frozen for a moment as she spoke some hasty words to Vanessa.

He walked across the space slowly, watching as her movements became more and more tense.

And for some reason, he walked even more slowly. He didn't know what was going on with her, but his being away from her seemed to be creating a small amount of torture, and he was...

Well, he was kind of enjoying that.

Given that the past twenty-four hours had been a study in torture for him.

"Hi," Caleb said as he approached the table, addressing Vanessa.

"Oh," she said, almost as if she was surprised by his presence. "Hi. Just going for a walk?" she asked, her dark eyes very keen.

"Apparently," Caleb said.

"Yes," Ellie said, grabbing hold of his arm, the casual touch sending a streak of lightning through his body.

She tried, with her very petite frame, to propel him out the door. But since he had no reason to resist her, he just went.

A moment later they were outside in the cold air. And Ellie had her arms wrapped around her slim frame.

"Didn't you bring a jacket?"

"No," she said, her teeth starting to chatter as they walked down the sidewalk.

"Here," he said, taking his coat off and draping it

over her shoulders, because he couldn't stand for her to be uncomfortable. Not even for a moment.

She stopped walking, touched the edge of the coat and let her fingertips drift along the zipper.

He felt that as if she had touched him. As if she had run her fingers along his skin.

Her eyes met his. "Thank you. I mean…really, thank you. I don't think I have fully appreciated everything you've done for me. The kind of man you are. I… You're always there for me. Things like this. Anything. You're always there."

It was his turn to freeze; any words he might want to speak freezing in his throat like a knot.

"I need you to…" She fumbled for her purse, which was now underneath her jacket, and pulled out a small, folded square of paper. With shaking hands, she gave it to him.

He unfolded it and saw her very familiar handwriting, along with the doodles that she often put on any paper she had been tasked with writing on.

She even put little doodles on her whiteboard in her classroom. It was just what she did. On this particular piece of paper were holly, presents and what looked like a string of lights wrapped around some of the letters.

He wasn't going to shame himself by asking her to read it to him. But he hated having people watch him read, too, since it always took twice as long as it did anyone else. Though Ellie knew that.

She was the one who knew why. And he'd actually read out loud in front of her, so there was no reason to get uptight about it now.

He let his eyes drift back to the page, and he pressed his thumb beneath the first line, using it to help him keep focus.

❧ Ellie's Christmas List ❧

1 - get a new dress 🎁

2 - go dancing in the dress

3 - get a kiss under the Mistletoe

His vision started to blur.

4 - make out by the fire

5 - ~~sex?~~ <u>sex</u>

Well, he had no trouble at all reading that last word especially, but he was having a hell of a time *comprehending*.

He looked up at her. "*This* is your list?"

"Yes," she said. "And I thought… I thought maybe he—*Todd*—could help me. I mean, he did dance with me. But then I thought about… I thought about the rest… And I…I didn't want him."

That was the biggest damn relief Caleb had ever experienced. She didn't want that guy. But on the heels of that came a rush of blood, roaring through his ears, roaring through the rest of his body.

She'd asked him for help with *this list*.

He stared at it, then looked back up at her, the rock in his gut glowing hot and red and evil. "Are you…? Are you asking me to help you find a guy to fuck?"

He didn't talk to Ellie like that. Not ever. He was

careful with her. Chose his words cautiously. But he could not…

The very idea of her finding a guy, some random guy to sleep with…

He couldn't breathe around it.

"No," she said. "I'm not asking you to do that. I'm not asking you to…"

She took a deep, miserable-sounding breath, rubbing her hand over her forehead. "*You.* I think that… it should be *you.*"

It was like tipping over the edge of a cliff. One he'd been teetering on for over a decade. And once he'd taken the plunge… It was taking every ounce of his self-control not to grab her and propel her down the side street, push her up against the brick wall and show her everything he'd tried not to fantasize about for the past ten years.

It should be you.

The murder had burned itself out of his blood completely. Replaced by a roar that was drowning out thought. Drowning out reason.

The roar of a beast that had broken free of its chains.

For one blinding moment, he didn't care what her reasons were. Didn't care what had changed to make her want this.

He just wanted to have *her.*

So many years spent pretending he didn't. Pushing it down. Protecting her. Honoring Clint.

But he'd forgotten himself one other time.

During those reading lessons. A year of them, at her house, in secret, while Clint was on shift at the fire department in town.

It was fine because they were friends.

So their sharing a secret was okay.

He'd never do anything.

Neither would she.

And then... And then she'd told him she was pregnant. Her eyes shining bright with joy. Pregnant with Clint's baby. And his first reaction hadn't been happiness for them, no.

He'd been enraged. On some animal, biological level that he couldn't begin to think around.

It was then he'd realized what he'd been doing.

Creating secrets and time alone with his best friend's wife. Something had been changing inside him, but not her. Thank God.

Because Caleb Dalton was not the best man in the world, not even close. So much so that the beast in him was sharpening its teeth and getting ready to take a bite out of her.

But thankfully, the man who'd sworn to do right by her, the man who'd sworn to honor his friend, had enough control to pause for a moment.

"Why?" He managed to grind the word out through his tightened throat.

She blinked, her blue eyes unreadable. Her throat worked. She hesitated. And the moment seemed to stretch on for an eternity.

"Clint is the only man I've ever been with," she said. "And I...waited a long time before I was with him. I don't know how to be with a stranger. I don't know how to be with someone I don't trust. Not the first time. Not when it feels significant. Like I'm...basically losing my virginity all over again. Because that's how long it's been. And that's how foreign it feels to think about figuring out how to do this with someone else. When I was writing the list I thought it might be exciting. And then I realized it was a little bit terrifying. But I still thought...maybe it was exciting to be with someone new. But I didn't want him. And the very idea of trying to figure out how to kiss someone that I don't even like… I don't think I can be with someone I don't trust. And I trust you. Look at you. Giving me your coat. Opening your truck door for me. Showing up when I was going out dancing, being a backup in case no guy wanted to dance with me."

He was not here to be a *fucking backup*.

But he didn't know what to say. He didn't have any words. She was looking at him with utter sincerity and telling him that she wanted him because he was safe.

And he felt anything but *safe* right now. He felt close to tearing this entire street apart. Brick by brick. Bending the streetlamps in half, just to make the point that he was nobody's lapdog. He wasn't some easily tamed gentleman, or a boy that she could make demands of.

But that wasn't even what she meant. The sincerity in her eyes was absolute, and she had no idea that what she was saying was about the most offensive thing she could have possibly chosen to say.

He had held all this down for years. And now she was playing with it. Taunting him. Treating him like he was toothless.

She wasn't overcome by desire for him.

She was afraid of her other options.

And he made her feel safe.

And he… He couldn't breathe around how much he wanted her right now. Years of holding it back and now she had unleashed it with a dress and four simple words.

Now he was standing there being honest, he didn't think he had breathed right since the day he'd seen her in a wedding gown walking toward another man. Just thinking about it now made his bones ache. Made his body physically hurt. He had stood there beside the groom, so close to where he wanted to be, and so impossibly far.

That was the thing about a wedding.

If you wanted to be the groom and you weren't, proximity didn't exactly help.

She wanted him because he was safe.

And he wanted her... It wasn't because she was safe. His heart hadn't been safe from the moment that Ellie Bell had walked into his life.

He'd never experienced more pain. More fear. More guilt.

He'd never denied himself half as much as he had these past years.

She wasn't a safe space for him, and she never had been, and he was here anyway.

"Oh..." She pinched the bridge of her nose. "Have I horrified you? I thought... You're a man, Caleb, and you like the way that I looked in the dress, so I thought that..."

"Do you think I don't *want* you?" he asked, the voice sounding like a stranger's. So gritty and flat and pained.

"You look like I just stabbed you in the stomach."

He felt like she had. He felt it down to his bones.

"I don't want to ruin things between us," she said. "You're my best friend. You're my best friend in the entire world. But don't you see? That's what makes it perfect. I... You take care of me. And I know that it would be... It would be nice between us. Don't you think?"

For the first time, he fully understood why being damned with faint praise was actually worse than being maligned.

He would rather she be filled with the disgust at the idea of being with him, because at least then it was picking a position. This muddy, milky description of how she thought it might be when their bodies came together…

He couldn't handle that. This obliviousness.

"You want me to help reintroduce you to sex."

"I mean, we can start with kissing," she said. "That *is* on my list."

"No, cut through the bullshit." Because he had to. Because it was all he could see. "You want to have sex. With me. Because you think it will be easy."

"Well," she said, her voice small. "Yes."

"Buy a vibrator, Ellie," he said, the words so rough they scraped his throat raw. "Because I'm not a damn sex toy."

He turned and started walking back toward the saloon.

"Caleb," she said. His name spoken, so soft and small, hit him between the shoulder blades like a bullet. He stopped. But he didn't turn. "I didn't… That's not what I meant. I…I want to be with someone. I miss being close with someone. I miss sex. And skin-to-skin stuff, not just orgasms. And I thought that maybe I could go out and have it with a stranger, but I can't. I don't think I can. How can I relax and… I wouldn't be able to have any fun. And I don't want a relationship. I don't want anything like that. But wouldn't it…? Doesn't it make sense?"

"No, it makes sense on your end, and you can't for the life of you understand how it sounds to not consider my feelings on it all."

"I'm sorry," she said, sounding close to tears now, and he hated to be the cause of that. He really did. But she had just torn his heart bloody, and he hadn't thought it was possible for her to shred that any more than it already was.

"I didn't mean to offend you. I'm attracted to you," she said.

He closed his eyes, taking a deep breath.

"I mean," she continued. "I…I felt something when we were dancing. Maybe you didn't."

"I felt it," he said, laughing at the way he said it. As if it was no big deal, and as if maybe it was new.

"So… Would it be so bad?"

And he realized that he was caught between a rock and a damned hard space, because there was no real way to explain to her why getting offered this was… Was a slap in the damn face. Not without revealing himself in a way he wasn't willing to do.

Safe.

He was safe.

But she wants you…

No. She wanted sex, and she thought sex with him would be fine.

That was different than wanting someone.

And he knew it well.

Because he'd had sex with women over the past decade; of course he had.

And he'd done it while he'd wanted Ellie. No matter that he'd told himself he didn't; he had. The whole damned time. And her standing there staring at him with luminous blue eyes made all his internal claims to the contrary seem laughable.

He'd had good sex, where he'd thought about only the woman he was in bed with, but he still hadn't wanted them. Not in a specific way. He'd wanted sex, and an attractive woman to have it with.

But it was different. It was different than this. Than this craving that overwhelmed everything you did, that flavored everything.

Does it matter?

He didn't know. He honest to God didn't know.

He turned then, saw her standing there looking like every damn fantasy he'd ever had.

"No," he said.

And he wondered where the hell he got the strength to say that word. He wondered why the hell he was saying that word even as he did.

He knew how to *not* have Ellie.

He knew that well.

And so, going on not having her seemed to be the easiest thing.

"Well, will you help me find someone else, then?" she shot back.

And it hit its mark.

"Sure," he bit out. "I'll find you a guy you can trust. A guy who matches up to Clint. You think you can do that on short notice? Should I conduct interviews? Do a drawing?"

"Why are you making fun of me?" She drew back, wounded. "This was really hard for me. I…I hate my body right now. I hate it. Putting on this dress makes me feel…horrible. The last time I slept with someone for the first time I was nineteen years old and had *not* had a baby. Everything was tight, and up where it was supposed to be. And now I'm…I'm sad, and my body is weird, and everything about this makes me want to cry, and you're just…"

But he couldn't even feel bad for her. Not now. Not when she was playing a particular kind of torture game with him without even realizing it.

And her ignorance didn't make it any better.

In some ways, it made it worse.

He breathed in deep through his nose. "Did it ever occur to you it's not a comfortable subject for me?"

She drew back. "Caleb. I'm sorry. It's because of

Clint, isn't it? I forget sometimes. I know that sounds really stupid. But I forget that he was *your* friend. I forget that you weren't my friend. Because these last few years you've been... You've been so much of my world. And I didn't even think what it would mean as... I guess I'm your best friend's wife to you."

Dammit, he wanted to turn a car over. That had *just occurred to her*, that this might be about Clint. Oh, he'd lived with that guilt.

Lived with the guilt in the early days of their relationship and at the end, right before he'd died, when Caleb realized what an utter fool he'd been with those reading lessons. Hanging on to doomed and sinful fantasies that weren't actually dead.

And he was having to face it again now.

Of course it was about Clint. Everything between them was, and always would be.

"It wouldn't be betraying him," she said. "I think... I mean, I think he probably would've preferred it to me...finding a stranger. He trusted you and...I'm sure he would've trusted you with me."

That *did it*. "I'm done with the conversation, Ellie," he said, walking away.

"Well, then you better help me find someone else," she shouted after him as he walked straight back toward his car.

"Fine," he shot back.

"What about your coat?"

He stopped. He didn't give a damn about his coat.

"I'll get it from you another time. Maybe when we talk about where to find you a sexual partner."

And then he got in his truck, and he drove away. And it wasn't until he was halfway home that he realized he hadn't taken a breath since she had told him what she wanted from him.

But then, that was just how it was. Ellie made it hard for him to breathe.

And apparently, no matter what she asked of him, it was going to be that way.

Now he just had to figure out how to forget this night had ever happened.

ELLIE FELT VERY SMALL, very foolish and thoroughly scraped raw as she walked back into the saloon. Vanessa was sitting there waiting, her eyes comically wide, and then she looked down at her phone as if she hadn't been giving herself whiplash looking at the door.

She blinked furiously and walked back over to the table. "Can we go now?"

Vanessa scrambled to get her things. "What happened?"

"How do you know something happened?"

"Because you look horrible and like you want to die."

She would have laughed but she was incapable. "Yes, that is accurate."

"What happened?" Vanessa whispered as soon as they got outside.

"I propositioned him."

"You what?"

"I asked Caleb if he would help me finish my list. I have sex on my list." She realized perhaps she needed to give Vanessa some context. "There's a list. It's why I'm here."

"So you just…asked him if he wanted to have sex with you."

"Yes."

"And he didn't say yes?"

"No, he didn't. In fact, I think I ruined our friendship."

Vanessa sighed. "I doubt you ruined your friendship. You've been through a lot worse than a failed proposition."

"Yeah, I suppose that's true." But Vanessa hadn't seen the way Caleb had reacted. It had been awful, and she felt like she had done something unutterably horrible, and she couldn't even figure out why it had been so horrible.

But she was so embarrassed. There weren't words for how embarrassed.

"Do you…? Do you *want* to sleep with him?" Vanessa asked.

"I mean… When we were dancing I…I suddenly realized… I actually can't imagine myself with anyone else. Not right now. When I thought about sleeping with Todd, the idea… It didn't appeal to me at all. And maybe I'm just not attracted to him. But when I think about being with Caleb…"

Suddenly, she really thought about it. Not just in a vague way, but thought about touching him like that. Thought about kissing him.

"He's always been there for me," she said. "He's always been so good to me. And I just think that he would be… I trust him. And I can't imagine being with a man that I don't trust."

"Yeah, but you can imagine how that came a little bit out of the blue for him."

"Yeah. I know." They got in the car and she rested her head on the seat. "He got really mad."

He'd been angry at her once before. At the end of their reading lessons. The ones he'd ended. And she'd had no real idea why he'd been angry. He'd just suddenly gone distant. But of course she hadn't randomly propositioned him last time. This time… Well, this time she had probably earned it.

"Did you actually say to him that he would take care of you?" Vanessa asked.

"Yes. I said that he's the one I want to be the first one since Clint. Because I feel safe with him."

"I don't really feel like men prize that as a descriptor."

"No?"

"Not when it comes to their penises, no."

Oh. *Oh.* She'd called Caleb's penis *safe*. And now she was thinking about his…and she wasn't even really upset by it. And everything was wrong. "Right. So I messed that up."

"I think so," Vanessa said sagely.

"Well, that makes me feel slightly better, because I was a little afraid that he was just that horrified about seeing me naked. And I don't think my ego can handle that."

Vanessa looked hesitant.

"What?" Ellie asked.

"I just think this is part of the problem."

"What?"

"I understand that for you this is a reclamation of some things. And a healing. And there's nothing wrong with that. But Caleb isn't a new dress. You can't just decide to put him on because you're in the mood to feel something exciting. He's a person. And there are going to be two sides to this kind of thing. Buying a new dress…that's just you. Sex?"

Heat lashed Ellie's cheeks. Because nobody liked to be scolded like they were a child, but when Vanessa repeated all that back to her, she could see that she sounded like one.

"I do know that," Ellie said. "It's just that… I guess…

I figured for him sex probably isn't that big of a deal. I remember going out to bars with him all the time when Clint was alive. And he rarely left alone."

"And since Clint died?" Vanessa pressed gently.

Ellie blinked. "Well, I don't go out to bars anymore. So… I don't really know what he does at them."

"Isn't he usually with you at night? Helping you with things?"

"I guess so," Ellie said, feeling increasingly uncomfortable.

"I'm not trying to be mean," Vanessa said. "I can completely see how you're thinking about this. I just think that… You have to realize how it may have sounded to him."

"It's funny," she said. "You and I have only gotten to know each other recently. But of course we've talked about our sex lives."

"Mostly because I got pregnant," Vanessa said. "That made it difficult to ignore mine."

"Yeah, but still. And Caleb is my closest friend. He has been for years. But I don't really know anything about his sex life."

"On the flip side, you also haven't propositioned me. So. Yet another difference."

Ellie laughed. "Well, you're married to Jacob."

"Yeah. And the thing is, also, he's a man and I'm not. And that means your friendship is different. Maybe not even because he's a man, but because *apparently* he's a man you wouldn't mind sleeping with. If that layer exists on your end, it must on his, too."

"You don't think that kind of thing is simpler for men?" Clint had been with quite a lot of women before her, and it hadn't really bothered her. She hadn't been with anyone, because she hadn't been able to imagine giving herself over to someone like that when the risks were so high. When she'd watched her mother get destroyed emotionally again and again by the men she dated.

Men who walked away not destroyed at all.

"I think they pretend that it's different," Vanessa said slowly. "And maybe for some of them it truly is. But I don't know—look at their dad. And the way that he behaved. I don't think he did it because he was the world's most well-adjusted person. I don't think he went and had a ton of affairs because everything was all right inside him. And even if for him, it's nothing more than a handshake, the repercussions are not the same as a handshake."

"Well, I was going to have safe sex with him," Ellie huffed.

"I know. But… You know, a disastrous handshake might result in a flesh wound or something. A little bit of embarrassment. Disastrous sex…" She put her hand on her stomach. "I mean, this didn't end up being a disaster, but it wasn't like Jacob and I were planning on having a baby."

"I actually kind of agree with what you're saying," Ellie said. "Sex isn't casual, even when we pretend that it is. And I think we have a lot of layers of pretending in our world. But even if we decide that emotionally it's not that big of a deal, it's physically a potentially very big deal. With consequences. And all of that. I know. And that's why I feel like I'm stuck. Because I want to do it, but in the end I think I need a little bit of emotional closeness. Trust. I think I'd need that for it to be sexy."

"You know, that sounded a lot nicer than saying he was safe."

"So you're saying I need to change my approach?"

"I'll tell you what. Let's talk again in a couple of

days. I have a feeling this is going to sort itself out naturally," Vanessa said.

"Why? Why do you think it's going to sort itself out? I have no similar confidence that it will sort itself out either way. In terms of our friendship, or in terms of me having sex." Ellie huffed a laugh. "Also, I might die of embarrassment. So there's that."

Would anything ever be simple? She felt fifteen and also one thousand years old at the same time. Like a stupid, immature child and single mother with the weight of the world on her shoulders.

Young and old in all the worst ways.

"I think…" Vanessa spoke slowly. "Actually, the biggest issue with all of this is that you're assuming he's never thought about having sex with you before."

"I don't think he has." She laughed because crying was the only other option. "He was horrified."

"I don't know," Vanessa said, maneuvering the car up the dirt road that led to Ellie's house. "If he really never thought about it, don't you think he would've asked you…if you were joking? Or…something? Was he shocked and appalled? Or was he angry? Because I think that tells you something."

"Oh," Ellie said, looking out the window. The car stopped, and Ellie remained motionless. "I don't think he thinks about me that way," she said finally.

"I think he does," Vanessa said. "And I feel guilty saying anything because that's all stuff that I've observed being part of the family. And Caleb is intensely protective of you. I think more than anyone on earth, he wouldn't want something to jeopardize your relationship."

"Well, he should have said that to me instead of getting angry at me," Ellie said, feeling stirred up and resolute.

She felt slightly guilty for the way she'd talked to

Caleb, but her feelings were still hurt, and she didn't want to let go of that, either.

"Maybe," Vanessa said. "But he didn't. And you should have handled things differently, too. But like I said, you two care about each other, and that means it's going to sort itself out. You know, when one of you sorts it out."

"That sounds like work," Ellie said. "And not like it simply *handling itself*."

"Oh, well," Vanessa said cheerfully.

Ellie sighed, unbuckled her seat belt and got out of the car. "Good night."

Vanessa's good-night was muffled by the closing of the door. Ellie trudged toward the house, pausing for a moment because she wasn't sure she was ready to deal with bidding farewell to the babysitter.

She was so confused. She'd gone out. She'd gone dancing. And she'd felt something a lot like desire for another person for the first time in years.

But it hadn't been for a stranger.

And it hit her then how much she wished it could've been.

How much she wished she could be different.

Whatever it took, a little more denial, a little less self-awareness… God knew she was damaged. But maybe it wasn't damage she needed to have anonymous sex.

Maybe it was more self-confidence?

She closed her eyes and saw Caleb's face in her mind's eye. The way he had looked at her.

Fury.

There had been fury in his eyes when he had walked into that bar, and she hadn't identified it until just now.

Maybe the real problem was just him. That he had shown up, and that suddenly not a single man in the room had looked remotely appealing.

Who was the most attractive man she knew. And really, what was the point of being with somebody that she found less attractive?

Ease. Simplicity. Not ruining your friendship.

Hell, she might have already ruined their friendship.

Because if he hadn't ever thought of sleeping with her, and she'd just thrown that into the middle of the table, now it was there. The thought was there. It was certainly in her mind.

And if he had thought about sleeping with her before?

Well, she was going to have to sit with that.

And she could only hope that what Vanessa said was right. That it would sort itself out.

She and Caleb had been through hell together.

This was just a blip on the radar.

She would have to make sure of that.

CHAPTER SIX

CALEB HAD SLEPT terribly last night, and now he was in a helluva mood. And sadly, this morning he had an audience for that mood.

West was meeting with Hank and Tammy this morning, and all the brothers, plus McKenna, were assembled in the kitchen waiting to see how it had all gone. They hadn't planned this. They'd just all shown up.

"Why are you guys at home?" he asked, feeling grumpy as he lifted his coffee mug to his lips. He knew the answer already. It was the same reason he was here. But he felt spiteful.

"We're offering emotional support for West," Gabe said.

"Are you?"

"And eating Mom's cookies for breakfast," Jacob said.

"Why are you in such a mood?" McKenna asked.

"Not in a mood," Caleb responded.

"Yeah, you're in a mood," Jacob commented.

"*You* were in a mood for four years."

"And you called me out on it," Jacob said.

"No," Caleb said. "I didn't really. I let you have it."

"How's your Christmas tree farm?" Gabe asked.

"Good," he responded, surprised that his brother had asked about that.

"I want details," McKenna said. "I love Christmas. Officially and forever now, thanks to my new family and my upcoming Christmas wedding. So a Christmas tree farm—"

"Is not my ultimate goal. But if you'd like to adopt my Christmas trees, McKenna…"

"Grant would love that," she said, exceedingly cheerful.

"Made any progress on the place?" Jacob asked.

"No. I don't close until next week."

"Well, that should be enough time," Gabe said.

"Time for what?" Caleb asked.

"To figure out if West is going to work out or if we have to find someone else."

"Am I being kicked out of the family already?"

Just then, West appeared in the doorway of the kitchen. Tammy and Hank were standing behind him. Hank looked grim, and Tammy's face was pale, her eyes red.

"No one is kicking you out of the family," Hank said.

"I was kidding," West said.

The strain and tension, the toll this was taking on his parents' marriage, was obvious. West didn't seem at all affected by it. But then, there was no real reason he should be, Caleb supposed. He didn't have any ties to this family beyond blood. But even if Caleb knew that both of his parents had a stake in this situation, he couldn't enjoy watching them have to contend with it. He had thought they'd been through the worst of it.

They'd had a volatile marriage for years. It had made Caleb certain that he didn't want any part of the institution from an early age. The screaming, the fighting, the betrayals. Yeah, they hadn't exactly sold it. But then for the past decade or so everything had been good. Tammy had finally threatened to leave, and she'd meant it. And Hank had promised to stay faithful—which he had.

When their McKenna had come into the picture a

year ago it had created a small wave, but it was all sins of the past.

That Hank had been unfaithful wasn't a surprise. It was just the appearance of an illegitimate child that had been somewhat of a revelation.

But this… That there were more children. And that Tammy had known and hid it… It was testing things.

Caleb didn't think it was fair.

His mother had been faithful. For all of her sins, and she certainly had committed them, she had never once violated her marriage vows. And in his mind, she had done the best she could to protect the children that she had by sending the women who had come to get money from Hank Dalton far, far away.

For Hank, it had taken his sins and compounded them. Because not only had he been unfaithful, now he was a negligent father, too.

And that was something he was struggling with.

Caleb had a feeling that if he were Tammy he would have told his father that he didn't get to struggle.

He made morally unacceptable decisions for years. Tammy had done this one thing.

She'd forgiven him, over and over again, and given him a chance to change.

He didn't think Hank had the luxury of hesitating on his own forgiveness.

But it wasn't Caleb's marriage to fix.

And these weren't his sins to atone for.

Maybe one of these new kids would be the one Hank had wanted all along. One who was smart and went to college and did something other than ranching.

Someone who wasn't Caleb.

"Well," Tammy said finally. "Isn't this some sullen family meeting." She sighed heavily. "West, you're family."

West turned and looked at Tammy. "I'd have done the same thing," he said finally. "You didn't owe me a damn thing. You certainly didn't owe my mother a damn thing."

"Thank you," Tammy said. "But I don't require absolution. We don't like to sit with our sin for a while. And we are not afraid of anger." She looked over at Hank, and then back at the boys. "Did you want some coffee?"

"Got it," Gabe said.

"I'd take some more," Jacob said.

Topped off with coffee, and sent off with doughnuts, they exited the house, heading out toward the area of the property that housed the school.

"So you're leaving," West said, addressing Caleb.

"I'm not going far."

"Provided I work out as a… What exactly do we do?"

"We're mentors," Jacob said. "Which is hilarious, because we are all pretty marginal characters."

"Good to know," he said.

"I'll walk you through the paces today," Gabe said. "But a lot of it's farm work. And we're helping guide the boys in it, to an extent. Because we believe that a little blood and a little bit of sweat makes for a better man."

"Well, I do believe that," West said. West and Gabe went off toward Gabe's office, and McKenna bid them all a farewell so she could get back to Get Out of Dodge and get started on her workday there.

But Jacob lingered with Caleb.

"Vanessa said that last night got weird," he said.

"I knew you were waiting to comment on that," Caleb said. "Your wife needs a lesson on keeping things to herself."

"My wife tells me everything. And I tell her everything. So you had better be aware that I'm going to tell her you said that."

Caleb sighed. "Ellic and I had a fight. Not a big deal."

"Yes, it is. Because you never fight."

Jacob wasn't going to leave him alone unless he just told him. And anyway, why not? If Vanessa hadn't already, she would. "Well, she asked me to sleep with her."

Jacob nearly snapped his neck, turning to face him. "She *what*?"

"You heard me. I'm not repeating it."

"And you said no."

"Damn right I said no."

"You said no," Jacob repeated.

"She is Clint's wife," Caleb said, and not even he believed that bullshit excuse.

"Clint is dead," Jacob said. "And you want her. We can pretend that you don't. But you lectured me on grabbing hold of a woman who wanted me when I was nearly dumb enough to let Vanessa get away."

Caleb felt like he'd been slapped. "Whatever I felt for Ellie…that was a long time ago. When I talked to you about women I meant…not waiting till the moment passed. The moment passed for Ellie and me when she became Clint's wife."

Jacob looked at him for a while. "And you've never wanted her since."

He thought back to the lessons. To the dress.

To the dance.

It should be you.

"I didn't say that."

"Well. If you want her, why not?"

He blew out a harsh breath. "She's Clint's wife. I can't…"

"I thought all this stuff…the Christmas tree farm and all of that… Isn't it about changing things?"

"Change for the sake of it isn't exactly good."

"Yeah, but there's a few different kinds of change. And also, you can't stop change. It will happen. But some change you can take a little control of at least."

"I'll keep it under advisement."

"Speaking as a man whose entire life is different now than it was a few months ago… I might know what I'm talking about." He cleared his throat. "And if it's not you it's going to be someone else. She's on the path now. She won't just…stop. You know Ellie. Think on that."

Jacob gave him a half wave and wandered off. As far as Caleb was concerned, it was all easy for Jacob to say.

This was stuff Caleb had wrestled with for years. And Ellie had stirred it up again, easy as a shimmy into a tight red dress and a careless request.

He'd been willing to let it lie.

But she hadn't left well enough alone.

Jacob was right about one thing; if it wasn't him it would be someone else. Todd from the bar. A guy named Todd. What the hell.

And if not him someone else.

Some other guy who wouldn't take care of her the way she deserved. Who wouldn't appreciate what she was.

And just going out and getting it over with was…

She deserved more than that.

He continued to walk across the property, and suddenly, there she was, a light shining down on her golden hair, illuminating her like it was a halo.

It made him think far too keenly about the first time he'd seen her. And the way it had torn him up inside.

She saw him and ducked her head, her cheeks turning bright pink.

He let out a long, slow breath and began to cross the space toward her.

"Hi," she said. "I left Amelia with a different babysitter today. Your mom mentioned that this morning they were going to be dealing with some family things."

It struck him that it was interesting she led with that comment about her daughter. He cared very much about her daughter. He had been there when she was born.

He avoided sometimes thinking about how close he felt to her. Because there was something sharp about it. Something kind of painful. About what might've been and wasn't.

But she had definitely led with that to avoid talking about what was really on her mind. And he could tell from the color of her cheeks exactly what she was thinking about.

"West was meeting with my parents this morning. With…our dad."

"Do you think that Hank and Tammy are going to be okay?"

Ellie hadn't known his parents during the most intense time in their relationship. She had really gotten to know them after they patched things up between them, and it had been smooth sailing for quite a few years.

"Honestly, they've been through a lot worse things than this. Personally, I think my dad owes it to her to let it go."

"Do you think you could let it go that easily? Finding out that you had kids you didn't know about?"

That question seemed tangled up in what he'd been

thinking earlier about Amelia. No, he didn't have children, but he had been helping take care of another man's child for a long damn time. And if he had children of his own, and they were kept from him for any reason…

"Yeah, I'd be angry. But the thing is, Hank hasn't earned the right. I think he has to give it up, basically. Because he did a lot of things that hurt my mother. A lot of them. He did a lot of things that hurt Gabe. The kids that he had. How can he be rigid about someone else's mistake?"

"Well, feelings aren't fair," she said.

And that statement felt loaded, too.

"I guess not," he said.

"I guess I better go set up my…my classroom for school tomorrow."

She turned and then paused, standing in the doorway of the barn, and it was the damnedest thing. Right there in the doorway was a sprig of mistletoe, with a red ribbon tied around it.

He looked around for the first time and noticed that there were some Christmas decorations up in a few places around the barn. Probably because Tammy had hired someone to do it. It wasn't even December yet.

But there it was. Mistletoe. Like a beacon. Like a sign.

And suddenly, everything just seemed to fit. Right there, in that spot where she stood.

Like all along the way, since last night, he had been collecting jagged pieces, and in this moment he had figured out how they all went together.

Ellie. He wanted her.

He'd always wanted her, no matter what he'd told himself. And the first moment he'd seen her, she'd been with another man. And if it had been any man other than Clint he'd have said to hell with it and seduced her right into his bed.

But it had been Clint, so he hadn't.

So he'd pushed it down. He'd crushed it.

And for the past near five years he'd crushed his whole damn libido. For Clint, he'd done that. He'd do it a thousand times over.

But not for someone else.

And now it would be someone else. She'd been desperate enough to throw her proposition out to him, so there would damn well be *someone*.

Being a security blanket, safety. Easy. That was all unacceptable.

Her being with another man was *unlivable*.

He'd walked away last night.

He wouldn't walk away now.

He took a step forward, and he wrapped his arm around her waist, his blood roaring hot through his veins, his heart thundering hard. And he couldn't believe that he was doing it. That he was holding her in his arms.

This was no lapse of control on his part. His control was made of iron. And he had proved it more times than she would ever know. So many times that the moments faded into memory, had become nothing more than a dull pain, a downpour beating against the tin roof. Dull, continuous. And he had learned to let it wash away into the background.

Not now.

Now it was sharp. Hard.

It wouldn't be denied and neither would he.

It wasn't for her. Not anymore. All that mental dancing he'd done a moment before was a lie. This was for him.

Because he'd damn well earned it.

He was going to kiss Ellie Bell.

And he wouldn't be rushed.

Her eyes were wide, her lips parted slightly, and she was looking at him like he was a stranger. But maybe that was for the best.

For his part, he couldn't pretend that she was. Not now. Not now that he held her in his arms like he had wanted to for so long.

She was soft. Even now with his hand resting on the small of her back, he could tell that. He raised his hand and cupped her face; the lightning conducted between that space where his palm met her cheek, and immobilized him for a moment.

Then he let his thumb drift over her skin there, looked at the faint freckles that scattered across her nose. And he let his eyes drop to her lips. Pale pink and full, turning down slightly at the ends like a little pout, and he'd always found it unbearably sexy. He had the shape of her mouth memorized, and he'd never touched it. Never pressed his lips to it, no matter how much he wanted to.

The need to do it now was like a prowling, insistent beast. Clawing at its cage. Demanding to be let out.

So he did.

He leaned in, closed the distance between them.

And his world became fire. Nothing could have prepared him for this. Not a decade of anticipation, not charts and graphs, nothing.

Because this went beyond a kiss, deeper than how she tasted, more than how soft her skin was against his, more than the sigh that she made when he parted those lips with his own and slid his tongue against hers.

His knees nearly buckled. It was more than the blood roaring through his veins like a lion, more than the instantaneous hardening of his body. It was something beneath his skin, something in his bones. In his veins.

In him.

In the way that he breathed. The way that he was knit together. From the beginning of time, maybe. As if he had been created for the purpose of kissing Ellie.

And she kissed him back.

She raised a trembling hand and pressed her fingertips to his chest, the move causing a feral growl to rise up inside him. It was intimate, that touch. As much as her lips against his.

She let her fingertips drift down slowly, and he lowered his hand from her face, grabbed her wrist and propelled her back, pinning her hand to the doorway of the barn. Because God knew if she pushed it too hard he was going to lose control. Absolutely. Completely.

He pressed himself to her, his chest against hers, and he could feel those high, firm breasts against him, and it was nearly his undoing. Holding her hand steady was hardly going to keep him from losing it. Not now.

This was how it would be between them. This.

Heat and fire.

It wouldn't be soft. It wouldn't be easy, and he did his best to communicate that with every pass of his tongue over hers. This wasn't safe. It wouldn't be. It couldn't be. Because it was years of denied need—*years*—poured into one moment, and it could never be something as benign as safe.

When he pulled away, they were both breathing hard. Ellie looked stunned, like she had been electrocuted by a live wire.

"There's number three on your list for you," he said, his voice like gravel. "And let me tell you, if you want to move on to those other items you wrote down, we need to get a few things straight. You're not in charge. I am. I can't guarantee you it's going to be nice. I can't guarantee you it's going to be easy. You don't get to say when, you don't get to say how. You want something more than a sex toy, that's what you're going to get."

She said nothing. She only stared at him with shocked blue eyes. Eyes that had never looked at him like this before.

Like she was scared of him. Betrayed by him.

Like she wanted him.

"You know how sex toys work, Ellie? *You* control them. They don't have a say. You hold them in your hand, and you use them how you want. That's not me. You want a man, that's damn well what you're gonna get. On my terms. My way." He pressed his thumb to the indent in her chin, just beneath her lip, and tilted her face up so she was looking at him. "Do you think you can handle that, baby?"

He didn't know what he expected. But he did not expect her lip to tremble. And he did not expect her to turn and run away.

But that was exactly what she did. And she left him standing there with a raging hard-on and a gut full of regret.

CHAPTER SEVEN

ELLIE FELT LIKE a kid on a sugar high for the rest of the day and into the next. A constant, sustained kick of energy that left her light-headed and with shaking hands.

Over a kiss.

One that she'd asked for.

But it was her first kiss in four years. And her first *first* kiss in more than ten.

Her first kiss with Caleb.

Without thinking, she put her hands up and touched her mouth, and was then thankful that her classroom was empty, and that school was done for the day, because if she was going to sit there pressing her fingers to her lips like a giddy schoolgirl, she didn't need an audience of schoolboys.

She had successfully managed to avoid Caleb for the rest of yesterday and today. Although, given the fact that she was largely stationary in her classroom throughout the day, it was probably Caleb who was avoiding her.

But then, she had run away from him.

He had kissed her, and she had run away. But she hadn't… She hadn't known it would be like that.

She hadn't known he would be like that.

The way that he had advanced on her, the way that he had kissed her.

She had been expecting something sweet when their mouths came together, in the very limited amount of time that she had allowed herself to imagine it, but this had not been sweet.

She swore she could still feel the burn from his whiskers on her cheeks, and if she thought about that too hard she could definitely still feel a pulse throbbing between her legs.

That was what had scared her the most.

In those crazy, heady moments when she had allowed herself to imagine what it would be like to sleep with Caleb, her imagination had gone soft and fuzzy.

She'd imagined feeling close. Warm. Had imagined being held in those strong arms of his in a different way.

She loved those arms. She loved the feeling of being pressed up against his chest, and she had loved it in both good and bad times.

But it had never been sexual, and she had been fascinated by the idea of that sense of warmth and caring, of safety, being translated to something sexual.

But this hadn't been a translation of that hug. It had been like an entirely new language.

The most disturbing thing was, it hadn't been like any contact she'd known from Caleb before, and it also didn't feel much like any kiss she'd ever had before.

There had been a wildness in it, an intensity, and she had felt something begin to stir inside her that she'd never really felt before.

And that was why she'd run.

The creature of her own creation had turned into a monster that she didn't think she could control.

And hadn't Caleb said as much? That if she did this, if they did this, it wasn't going to be all about her. And she wasn't going to be able to control what he did when he did it.

That, she didn't like very much.

She looked at the clock inside. She needed to go get Amelia from Tammy. Maybe Caleb had gone home. Although, she didn't imagine he had. It was early still, and the two of them usually lingered around the ranch until sometime after four.

Which meant that she could still run into him, and she didn't know what to do or say.

She had made an idiot out of herself. Making demands of him, and then… Well, and then when he gave her what she asked for she'd run away like a baby.

He did not give you what you asked for. You asked for nice.

She imagined the way it had felt again, his lips sliding over hers, his tongue…

Pleasure cut through her midsection like a knife. No, it wasn't nice. Nothing about it was nice.

It was too sharp and too bright for that. It hurt. She pressed her hand to her stomach and gathered her things, shrugging her coat on as she walked outside, then putting her purse over her shoulder. She shoved her hands in her pockets and began to walk across the property, toward Hank and Tammy Dalton's house. The grounds were beautiful, well manicured and restrained.

The house itself was…like a museum of Western kitsch dipped in gold.

Hank and Tammy were proud of their redneck roots, and proud to call themselves gold-plated white trash. They didn't even try to pretend they were sophisticated, old money or restrained in any way, and that was something that Ellie really liked about them.

When she had been growing up, that sense of feeling different, of being the poor girl with no father, one winter coat—three years old and too short in the sleeves—and

a pair of boots with a hole in them, had made her an odd-
ity. An outsider.

And she had learned to be ashamed of that feeling.

Hank and Tammy seemed to own that. To take what
was different about them and make it bigger, make it
brighter.

Of course, they had money, so they might have kept
that sense of being low-class, but they didn't have any of
the precariousness that came with being poor anymore.

She and Clint had always been okay. They both worked
and during their marriage hadn't had any children. They'd
been in a stable position by the time she'd gotten pregnant. Everything so much more planned than life had
been when she was a child.

She had been able to stay home with Amelia for the
first four years of her life. While she got on her feet,
while she found her strength again.

Because the last gift that Clint had given her was a
life insurance policy he had been responsible enough to
go out and get, and then there had been the settlement
with the helicopter company.

It was a terrible thing to think of, the money.

Because money was terribly cold comfort when you
lost the man you loved.

But Clint had known how much she'd wanted their
children to have stability. How important it had been
to her that there would be no uncertainty about where
the next meal was coming from or where they would
live if they got evicted.

The security that she had all around her—the house,
the clothes that Amelia had, the winter coat that she
had just put on to keep warm that did its job so well—
was him keeping his promises to her even though he
wasn't here.

She blinked, her eyes feeling scratchy. It felt weird to be thinking about him so much. But then, he was never far from her thoughts. He was such a huge part of the foundation of the life she lived even now. Even though he wasn't here, he was a cornerstone, and he always would be.

He was Amelia's father, and nothing would change that.

She frowned, standing there on the front porch of the house, waiting to knock.

Was she going over all of this because of the kiss with Caleb?

She thought she had sorted through all of this before she had even gotten to a place where she wanted to go out and be with another man. But maybe because it was Caleb it made it…

She'd always been with Clint while she'd known Caleb, until Clint had died.

But he was gone. He wasn't her husband anymore. She didn't have a husband.

He mattered. So much. She would always see him when she looked at Amelia, sparkling through her eyes. He would always be the man who had taught her how to smile. To have a little bit of fun. Not treat everything like it was so grave.

But he couldn't be her husband.

He couldn't hold her at night. He couldn't kiss her.

She *really* needed to be kissed.

Right now kissing only made her think of Caleb. And that brought her right back full circle to where she didn't know what to do, and she was still standing on the front porch like an idiot.

The door opened, and of course, it was the devil himself.

"Have you been standing out there for like five minutes?"

"Yes," she said, feeling awkward. She looked over his shoulder and didn't see anyone else. "Should we talk? Or…"

"I don't have anything to say," he said. "Leastways not more than I already did."

"But I…"

His jaw turned to granite. "Ellie," he said slowly. "I'm not having this discussion with you. Because it won't be a discussion. Don't play with me. You have two choices. You go back and forget that ever happened, or you put your hands on me. But once you do, that's it. So you better choose. I'm not going to do it for you."

She felt the air go out of her in a gust, like sails on a ship losing their wind. It left her flat. Listless. And vulnerable.

Because she realized that she had, in fact, wanted him to make that choice for her. Part of her had been avoiding him because she had been certain that he would. That he would rail at her and tell her she was an awful friend and that anything happening between them was off the table forever.

Or that he would grab her and pull her into his arms and say this was his show now and she had started on the path that it was too late to go back.

"I…"

"It's your list, Ellie. Not mine."

She nodded and pushed past him, careful not to make any contact with him, and made her way into the kitchen, where Tammy and Amelia were washing their hands, having just finished mixing what looked like biscuit dough.

Tammy smiled. "Just getting ready for dinner," she

said. "Do you want to wait around and take some biscuits home, Ellie?"

Tammy reminded her a bit of Dolly Parton mixed together with Miranda Lambert. A little glitter, a little gunpowder and a whole lot of fight. Ellie had liked her instantly.

And she knew that right now Tammy was between a rock and a hard place in her marriage and family. The fact that she had concealed the existence of three of Hank's children, paid off the women who had come seeking out money and kept all of it from Hank had opinions divided in the family.

But in a way Ellie could understand.

She could understand defending your turf. Could understand protecting what was yours.

She felt a kinship to Tammy in that way.

She knew what it was like to be poor. To have nothing. And this house, this family, her boys... That was Tammy's kingdom.

You would defend it at all costs. And sometimes there were casualties. But what wouldn't you do for your own children?

On that same note, Ellie knew that if she'd had a child the way those other women had...she would have been camped out on the man's doorstep herself. Making sure that she had the resources to raise her child in the way they deserved. Because there was no way in hell her baby should be poor, no way her baby should be living hand to mouth if its father and half siblings were living well.

Basically, she could see herself behaving as any of the women in the scenario had.

To her mind, the only person with true fault here was Hank. If he hadn't cheated, there would never have been secret babies to deal with in the first place, and none of the women would have had to make these choices.

But what wouldn't you do for your children?

Ellie knew that the answer was…nothing. There was nothing she wouldn't do for Amelia.

In all the things that had been confusing, difficult and awful over the past few years, that had always been clear.

She'd been gray for months after Clint had died. Her entire pregnancy had passed in a fog.

She'd cried when she felt Amelia move inside her for the first time, because Clint wasn't there to feel it.

Because he never would.

Wouldn't see his baby girl, not ever. The baby he'd wanted so much.

She resented the life inside her in so many ways because Clint's life had been snuffed out. She hadn't been able to connect to the joy of it, hadn't been able to seize on to the hope.

New life meant nothing when she was mourning the passing of her old life.

Until Amelia was born. And in that moment Ellie had found purpose. A purpose that she would never take for granted. With that had come a whole gamut of emotions that she thought had been lost to her.

Including joy.

Even in the middle of her grief, looking at Amelia's face had brought her joy.

So as far as she was concerned, Tammy Dalton didn't have anything to answer for.

"We're probably just going to go home, Tammy," she said softly.

"Is everything okay?"

The other woman was more a mother to Ellie than her own had ever been.

And that had been a difficult thing for her to sort out. For all the same reasons she was so resolute in her understanding of Tammy, and in her sympathy for her, she felt more distant from her mother than ever after the birth of Amelia.

If Ellie had been able to care for her daughter after her husband had died, surely her own mother could have done more.

Though since then, in moments of quiet guilt, she had been afraid that she understood the things her mom had done.

"Everything's fine," Ellie said, lying.

It wasn't fine. She needed to get away from Caleb as quickly as possible, because he had just issued an ultimatum in a space where she could do nothing about it, and she needed to get away from him and think.

"Mommy!" Amelia closed the space between them and wrapped her arms around Ellie's legs. She embraced her daughter, that true, simple love erasing some of the confusion rocking around inside her. For a moment.

Caleb walked into the kitchen and stood in the doorway, crossing his muscular arms over his broad chest, his blue eyes level with hers.

"Come on," she said, patting Amelia's back. "We should go. We'll get burgers from Mustard Seed."

"Yay!" Amelia dashed off to gather her things and Tammy looked between Ellie and Caleb.

"I just need to go to the powder room," she said, far too astute. "I'll see you tomorrow, Ellie."

Ellie stood there, regarding Caleb closely. The moment seemed to stretch between them like an elastic band. Tight. Impossible to breathe through.

But then Amelia returned, her arms full of coloring pages. The tension didn't break, but neither of them could stand there and indulge in it, either.

"Okay, let's go," she said.

She passed by Caleb, who didn't move, in the doorway.

And then she stopped, unable to help herself. Her breath froze in her chest like a ball, her heart fluttering like a trapped bird.

"Let's talk later tonight," she whispered, the words getting stopped up in her throat.

She lingered near him for one breath.

Two.

Then she put her hand on his bicep, dragging her fingertips down the deep valley in his muscular forearm.

His blue eyes collided with hers, his nostrils flaring like an angry bull.

But he said nothing. And neither did she.

But she touched him.

And with that touch she'd made a promise to them both.

It wasn't until she got in the car that she started to question what the hell she'd done.

CHAPTER EIGHT

THE QUESTION THEN became whether or not he would come.

She thought about that all through the dinner she didn't eat, and all through reading Amelia her bedtime story.

She didn't know if she should change into her pajamas...change into a dress?

Change into sexy underwear?

That thought froze her for a whole minute, standing in the center of her bedroom.

What kind of underwear did Caleb like?

It was weird. It was weird to think about. What would Caleb want to see her in? What would he want to see her out of? What did he *like*?

She had been thinking about this from such a one-sided point of view, and that was really why the whole thing had freaked her out so badly. Because he had made it clear that this wasn't something she could think of only in terms of herself. This would be about him, too. About his...his pleasure.

She was very new to thinking of Caleb in those terms.

But if they... If they...

She had put her hand on him before she'd walked out of the house. And he had said that if she touched him again...

She had done it. She had made the choice. She had made the choice because somehow the idea of going back seemed impossible.

Because something about that kiss had thrilled her as much as it had terrified her.

But maybe he wouldn't come. Maybe she had abused his friendship way too much in the past few days for it to...

She didn't know if she wanted him to come or not.

And now that sounded dirty. She had thought enough times that she could only think of it in terms of... *sexually coming.*

She would really like to come.

Did she want to come *with him*?

Yes.

The answer hit her decisively. She did. She wanted him. And that was terrible, because he was the last person that it should be in many ways, and also the only person that it could be. And what a terrible tangle to be caught in. That sort of two-edged nightmare where she would be cut either way.

But strangely, she didn't worry so much about it ruining their friendship. If she had, she never would have asked him for it in the first place. Really, her asking him at all... That was the thing that she worried might ruin their friendship. But if they got on the other side of it, if they actually did have sex... Everything would be fine.

She wasn't sure why she wasn't afraid it would ruin them.

They'd had one hiccup, and she'd never discovered what it was about. But when she'd needed him it had all been forgotten.

He'd been the one to tell her. He'd come to her door, tears in his eyes. He'd folded her into his arms. He'd wiped away her tears and somehow…somehow she knew he'd helped her shoulder that grief and that without him she'd be crushed by it.

Their friendship had been forged in something worse than fire.

It had been in grief and loss. She had been broken, and she was in the process of being remade. And he had been an integral part of that process so far.

More than that, he had shared her grief with her.

He had loved Clint like a brother, and they had wept together. He'd been the one to tell her she was a widow. The one to let her cling to him in the aftermath of that. He hadn't left her side that whole horrible day. He'd slept on her floor in the living room after she'd fallen asleep on the couch. And in the morning he'd held on to her again while she'd cried more.

He'd been the man who held her hand and wiped the sweat and tears from her face as she'd brought her daughter into the world.

He'd seen her in pain. The deepest emotional pain. The sharpest physical pain. He'd been through it all.

Maybe that was why this felt right.

She had fallen apart with him in the worst of ways. Why not *this* way?

It was right.

But weird. Frightening.

And maybe he wouldn't show up.

If he didn't, they could forget it ever happened, and she would go on this part of the journey by herself. She would find somebody else, and they could go back to their expected roles with each other.

Except, it would be different anyway, because he was moving. Because Christmas tree farms.

That was the root of this in the first place.

If there was an evolution happening, then she wanted to make one, too.

And it felt like it wasn't wrong for there to be a slight evolution in their relationship. And then when it was time for it to be over, it just would be, naturally. Because they had shifted and bent and broken and filled spaces in each other's lives for years now, and in many ways she just felt confident that they would keep on doing it.

While she was standing there pondering these things, her doorbell rang.

Caleb always showed up.

That was the thing.

She never should have doubted.

She cursed, and she didn't know if it was terror or relief that brought the word to her lips. But she was out of time to debate the finer points of her innerwear or outerwear.

She took a breath and scampered out the door, down the stairs. Then she slowed her pace so that he wouldn't hear frantic footsteps and opened the door as casually as possible.

"Next time, maybe send a text," she said slowly. "So that Amelia doesn't wake up."

"Right." He made his way into her living room and looked around. "You have firewood?"

"Yes," she said slowly. "It's stacked around back. Did you…?"

He walked past her and went through toward the back door. She heard the screen door swing open and shut, and she just stood there, watching the space where he had been a moment before.

She wasn't sure what he was doing. He came back in a moment later with an arm full of wood and kindling.

Then he went into the living room and knelt down by the fireplace.

"What are you doing?"

He looked at her, those blue eyes boring into her. She shivered.

"That's number four on your list," he said. "You want to make out by the fire."

Ellie blinked. "I thought we were going to talk."

He looked up at her. "And I told you that if you touched me there wasn't going to be anything to talk about."

And she had done it. She had.

But she didn't know what to do with this man. This utterly different version of her friend.

This man wasn't holding her and soothing her. He wasn't offering her a safe space to land.

He was pushing her. A challenge lit his blue eyes as if he expected her to back down. As if he expected her to run away again.

And part of her expected she might run, too. But what if she didn't?

He pushed the couch back, dropping her little throw pillows onto the floor, the items looking absurdly feminine and small in his large hands. Then he took the throw off the back of the couch and put it down over the rug before returning to his task of starting the fire.

"I... To be honest, I thought we would just skip to the sex," she said.

For some reason, the idea of kissing him—*just kissing* him—made her feel uncomfortable.

More intimate.

She wanted to skip to darkness, and bed and nakedness. Hands skimming over each other's bodies and the rush of release.

She didn't want to be down here, with the lights on.

"You have a list," he pointed out.

"I know. But that was when everything was very hypothetical. And this is not very hypothetical. Plus, we know each other. I thought it might be…you know, a guy I didn't know. Or maybe more than one guy or…"

Something about the sharpness in his blue eyes cut her words right off.

His movements were efficient and he had the fire started quickly, much more quickly than she could ever manage.

He had done this for her many times. Because she didn't know how, and she had loved the fact that her little farmhouse had a fireplace, but she didn't know how to actually light a fire when she had first moved in. And even now that she did know, thanks to Caleb, she wasn't very good at it. Certainly not as quick as he was.

But all the times he'd done it before it had been a caregiving-type gesture.

This was different.

"I'm not going to make this quick and easy for you," he said.

"Why not?"

"Because I'm not a Band-Aid you can rip off, Ellie. I already told you. You have to decide what scares you less. A man who doesn't know you, who's going to take you to bed and not care about your pleasure, because he's just out to hook up. Or a man who knows you. Who knows what you like. Knows what you want. A man who will make it his mission to make it feel as good as possible because God knows if he doesn't it'll be awkward later when he sees you at work."

It all sounded scary, quite frankly. Though, to be

perfectly honest, the idea of being with a stranger suddenly sounded easier.

It all seemed so simple when she thought of it in terms of trust. But now she was thinking it in the way that meant her friend was going to actually see her entire body. Touch her body. Kiss her body.

And she would do the same to his.

Yeah, everything seemed so simple in theory.

"I'll tell you what," he said. "Why don't you quit thinking? You made the list. And the minute you asked me to be the one to help you fulfill it, you put me in charge of that list."

"I did?"

"Haven't I always taken care of you?"

"You told me it wasn't going to be easy."

"I did. But I didn't say I wasn't going to take care of you. But I'm going to give you what you need. It just may not be what you are thinking."

His words sent a shiver through her body.

"Caleb…"

But her words were cut off as he grabbed her wrist and pulled her toward him, lowered his head and kissed her, deeper, harder, more ferociously, than he'd done at the ranch.

But then he slowed it down, every taste, every pass of his tongue, becoming more leisurely as if he was on a long, slow walk, savoring the journey rather than trying to reach a destination.

Heat rushed through her, making her limbs feel tingly, like they were on fire, making her whole body feel like it was.

His hands were large and heavy where they rested, on her lower back, on her face. He folded her against his body, his chest hard and muscular, his thighs against hers, his…

He was hard. Hard for her. She could feel it.

She rolled her hips forward, gasping as she confirmed that, yes, that was his cock.

He was hard already, just from a kiss.

And she was wet.

For him.

Her breasts felt heavy, her stomach hollowed out.

She wanted Caleb, and she wanted to weep with the relief of that. Because part of her had been afraid.

So afraid that she didn't know how to want a man other than Clint. That missing sex was just about missing him, and if she finally was able to find a man to sleep with, she would only picture her husband the whole time.

But she wanted Caleb.

She was clinging to Caleb. And she knew that she was. He slid his hands down, over her butt, down to her thighs, and he lifted her up off the floor, wrapping her legs around his waist.

Maybe he would just carry her to bed, after all.

But instead, he lowered her down to the floor, onto that blanket on the pillows that he had left there, in front of that fire.

She was restless. Each and every kiss drove her arousal up higher and higher, and created an ache in her chest that started to build, matching the one between her legs.

He settled between her legs, kissing her deeper, harder, and she arched against him, gasping as his hardness made contact with the most intimate part of her.

Even through their jeans, it was intense. And it was glorious. She cupped his face with her hands, loving the feel of his rough whiskers against her palms, and her eyes met his and held. He rolled his hips forward, a spasm of need rocking through her. And he didn't kiss her. Instead, he just pressed his forehead to hers and rocked his hips back and forth.

She clung to his shoulders, biting her lip as he ratcheted up that desire inside her.

He just needed to finish it. To answer this ache that had built inside her. To do something to quiet the insanity that was making her behave this way.

If she could just take the edge off, then maybe it wouldn't feel like so much. Maybe it wouldn't feel so desperate.

Maybe she would be able to get to nice, and safe.

Maybe she would be able to laugh. But that was the problem; none of this felt fun or funny. There was something dark to it, something intense and wild that terrified her. And they still had their clothes on. But the sex couldn't be quite so intense, could it? It couldn't live up to this promise. It was just prolonging it.

She pulled at his shirt, and he grabbed hold of her hands, caging her wrists and pulling her arms up over her head. "We're just making out, Ellie. Don't get excited."

She was breathing hard, and she barely recognized her voice as her own. "We are not, you jerk. Let's just..."

"I," he said, nipping her lower lip, "am not," he continued, licking her, soothing away the sting, "something that you can just get over with."

He pinned her there, to the floor, his chest pressed firmly to her breasts, his hard, flat stomach against her much softer one, his powerful thighs holding her down. And then he kissed her again, kissed her until she was trembling.

Her hands were restless, and she didn't know what to do with them.

So she ran them down his arms, felt the heat and muscle there, down his back and, eventually, to his butt. She parted her thighs wider, grabbing him and holding him firmly as she sought to soothe the need between her legs with her own movements.

He separated himself from her, wrapped his arm around her hips and pulled her to the left so that the hard ridge of his desire was no longer right there where she wanted it. She wiggled, but he had her right where he wanted her, and there was no fighting it.

He pushed his fingertips beneath the hem of her shirt, those calluses so shocking and rough against her skin. The heat of his touch so much more than she had even imagined it could be.

Suddenly, tears prickled her eyes, and it was so unexpected she could hardly breathe through the shock.

It just felt so wonderful to be touched.

Like she was beautiful.

Like she was a *woman*.

And what she had underrated while she had been thinking of Caleb touching her, while she had been thinking of the trust between them, of the way that he was so careful with her, was that he had held her while she was grieving. But he had not held her because he desired her. And now…

Right now he was caressing her like a man did when he wanted a woman, and she had needed that.

Right now his fingertips were skimming over the silvery stretch marks on her stomach, that bit of extra skin that she had now, that kept her stomach from being as tight as it used to be.

And the sound he made… A guttural sound of pure,

male satisfaction left her in no doubt that he did not find her wanting.

And as much as she had hated her body two days ago when she had been thinking about making love to a stranger, she loved it now, because this man growled when he got his hands on it.

Slowly—torturously so—his hand migrated upward, his thumb skimming just beneath the bottom of her bra, up to the curve of her breast.

The calluses on his fingers made a rough sound against the smooth satin of her bra, and she suddenly cursed the slight padding in the undergarment, because it kept her from feeling his touch as keenly as she might.

Suddenly, it seemed like he broke his own rules, his hand moving more than just the small fraction he'd been teasing them with this whole time. He cupped her breast, that large hand engulfing it completely, and he squeezed her, bucking hard against her body as he did. She gasped, digging her fingernails into his shoulders.

He relaxed his hold slightly, moving his thumb over her cloth-covered nipple, and then she was grateful for the padding, because even with it, his touch was creating a sensation so sharp and keen she wasn't sure she could withstand it.

And still, he was kissing her. Slow, deliberately slow, maddeningly sweet.

He pulled his mouth away from hers again, brushing their noses together before he went back to her, consuming her. The fire suddenly seemed too hot because his body was like an inferno, above hers, around her somehow, hard and uncompromising, a living rock that seemed to have been pulled directly from a flame.

She kept waiting for him to remove some of her clothes, or his, but he didn't. He pushed both hands beneath her shirt, his thumbs working in tandem over her breasts, bringing her arousal up to levels she had never before achieved with clothes off, never mind with them on.

She didn't know who she was.

She didn't know what she was.

But somehow, she still knew who he was. She could see his face, whether her eyes were open or closed.

Her world narrowed, centered on this moment. On his hands, his big body, that hard ridge between her legs. She arched her hips rhythmically against his, in time with the stroke of his tongue against hers, her breath coming in short, sharp bursts.

He nuzzled her neck, peppering kisses down the tender skin before moving back up to her mouth, kissing her deep again.

"Please," she whispered against his lips. "Caleb, please."

He lowered his head, clenching his eyes shut. His teeth gritted as he stilled his movements. Then he looked at her and shook his head, but as he did, he moved his hand to the button on her jeans, undid them, brought her zipper down partway. Her heart hammered in anticipation, and his fingertips dipped down beneath the waistband of her panties, and then found that place between her thighs, sure and certain, slick and rough.

He fused his mouth to hers, rubbing his thumb over her clit, her orgasm breaking over her like a wave. She arched up off the floor, his lips capturing her cry of pleasure as wave after wave of sensation battered her like a lost sailor cast adrift. It wasn't gentle. Or easy. It didn't flood her with a sense of warmth.

It made her feel broken.

Shattered. Spent and storm-tossed and barely able to breathe.

And not finished.

Very much not finished.

She lay there, breathing hard. Every sip of air containing shattered glass.

But then Caleb got up and moved away from her. His face was like a stranger's, the expression there that of a man who had been on a torture device, and not just kissing her.

"I think that fulfills item number four," he said, the words jagged.

She swallowed hard, suddenly very aware of the fact that her jeans were open, and her shirt was pulled up halfway, exposing her very plain and unremarkable bra.

She looked silly.

She hadn't cared a minute ago, but she cared a lot more now.

Arousal was like a fogged-up mirror. And now that the passion had cooled, she could see things just a bit too clearly.

She tugged her shirt into place and began to work at buttoning her pants.

"Why don't you come upstairs," she said, the words coming out in a rush.

He got down on one knee in front of her, grabbing hold of her chin with his thumb and forefinger. "Because you're not ready," he said. "You're not ready for it to go that way."

"I am," she said, reaching out and putting her hand on his chest, wondering if the intimate touch was acceptable now that they weren't kissing. That was something of an unexpected snag.

She felt a certain level of entitlement to his body now.

He had just touched her...there.

The second man to ever do that. Surely, she could

touch his chest, even if they weren't currently making out.

He moved away from her, though, and it made her feel like she had done something wrong.

She wasn't used to that feeling with Caleb, but it had happened a lot over the past week or so. Starting with that Christmas tree farm, and her selfishness, and ending here.

"You're turned on," he said. "Not the same thing."

"Yeah," she said. "I am turned on. Very turned on. And I would really like…" Something wicked slid down her spine, created a hollow base of need in her sex, completely unexpected considering the orgasm she'd just had.

"I want you to fuck me," she said, biting her lip after, embarrassment coming on the heels of the boldness that she'd felt only a moment ago.

His eyes went blank, dark, and suddenly she found herself being lifted from her position on the living room floor and brought up over his body, where he crouched on the ground, her thighs on either side of his hips as he pushed his fingers into her hair and brought her face down for a searing, intense kiss.

He was shaking.

She could feel it.

Could feel that he was on the edge of his control. Could feel that he was on the verge of losing it completely. And then he lifted them both to their feet, and set her apart from him. He was like a wild thing, and suddenly she had the strangest feeling that she had been keeping a lion as a pet when all this time she thought he was a house cat.

Safe, only because he allowed her to be.

"No," he said, his voice rough. "Not tonight. Because

that's not what I'm going to do to you. Do you understand me? Fucking is fun. Make no mistake. But it's hard, and it's quick. And what I want to do with you is not quick. And it's not just hard. I want to go fast, and I want to go slow. I want soft and hard, and I want you to beg for it. Do you understand me?"

"I think what I did was pretty close to begging," she said, shivering slightly.

"You don't want it bad enough," he said. "I need you to want it badly enough that you realize the list was a bad idea, because it could never be anyone but me."

And with those rough words still hanging in the air between them, he turned and walked out of her house, leaving her there both satisfied and aching for something she didn't even have words for.

CHAPTER NINE

YEARS LATER CALEB would still wonder where he got the strength to walk away from Ellie Bell with those words on her lips.

Hell, as he got into his truck, his hands shaking, he wasn't even entirely sure what he was trying to prove.

He had her beneath him. Had felt her desire for him, slick and ready between her legs.

Dammit.

He wanted to charge back into the house, drag her upstairs and finish it.

But that was the problem. She wanted to finish it fast, and he didn't like that, any more than he liked the idea of her going off and being with a stranger.

Any more than he liked being an easy substitute for that.

No, he wasn't going to let that happen. Guilt churned through him. Guilt that he was finally doing this. Guilt that he had denied her instead of giving her what she wanted.

Which was worse?

That he was finally fulfilling the long-held fantasy of being with Clint's wife? Or that Ellie had come to him for something, and he was now taking it, twisting it and using it for his own satisfaction?

He did not the hell know.

He found himself driving to his parents' ranch, and God only knew why.

No. He knew too.

He needed to go for a ride. Even in the dark. Needed to do something to cleanse this raging, ridiculous need that was consuming him like a monster.

He pulled up to the barn and sat there for a moment, gripping the steering wheel tight. He closed his eyes, and he remembered.

Remembered what it had been like to watch Ellie walk toward him in a white wedding dress.

Knowing that she was walking toward the man standing to his right, and not to him.

It had nearly destroyed him, but he had stood upright.

All those years had been difficult, but he had stood upright.

And in his mind, he had Ellie more times than he could count, and according to the Bible it was all the same. If he'd even lusted after a woman in his heart, he'd committed adultery with her, per the scriptures.

But to Clint…it wasn't the same. And to Caleb it sure as hell wasn't.

He had never touched his friend's wife.

He had wanted her, but he would never have betrayed him like that. But what was this?

What did he want?

To step into Clint's life? To take his wife and his daughter?

It was so close to things he had thought of, to things he had wanted, before Clint's death, that it made him feel like doubling over.

His feelings for Ellie were part of another time, tied up in a whole lot of things.

Maybe this was the perfect way to let it go.

To finally draw a line under it.

She wanted him physically, but she didn't want him emotionally.

And what he wanted...

Well, what it all came down to was that he couldn't be the man she'd had. And he never would be.

And she deserved to have everything she wanted, not an approximation, a sad replacement that existed just because of proximity, and not because of feeling. What he knew about her was that she had never intended on getting involved with anyone while she was going to school, but they had met, and he had demolished her defenses.

He was just here. And he hadn't actually managed to eradicate his desire for her; that much was clear.

So why not have it?

He got out of the truck and headed toward the barn, shocked to see that there was a light on at the far end. He heard someone moving around and he froze.

"Hello?"

A man appeared in the doorway of the tack room, his broad frame filling up the space. "Caleb?"

"Yeah," he said.

It was West.

"Sorry. Hank said that I could come by and ride whenever I felt like it. So..." He shook his head. "I don't sleep well."

"That's why I'm here, too," he said.

"Because you don't sleep well?"

"To ride."

"Well, what are the odds that we would both deal with things by going out riding late at night?"

"Apparently decent?"

"I guess that kind of defeats the purpose of going out and finding solitude."

For some reason Caleb didn't mind. Maybe because West hadn't been here the whole time. Maybe because West didn't really know Ellie, or him, for that matter.

"It's all the same to me. Anyway, you don't know the terrain. You should probably follow me."

"I assume the horses know the terrain well enough."

"True. Do you have a headlamp?"

"Yeah," he said.

Caleb fished one out of the tack room, and the two of them set about to getting horses ready to go. They worked in silence, and Caleb was overcome by a sense of strangeness. That you could be so like someone you had never met. They even finished tacking up at around the same time.

"How did things go with my parents? I only saw the aftermath."

"Good," he said. "I mean, as good as can be expected."

"You said you were looking for a family."

West paused, holding on to the horse's reins, his expression obscured by the relative darkness in the space.

"I've never really had one before, so I can't be sure about it. I made it a long damn time without one. And then everything kind of went to hell in my life. I never cared about anyone or anything. Except for my wife. She screwed me over worse than anyone else ever has. Prison's not fun, if you were wondering."

"I didn't figure."

What he did wonder is if it was the reason that West didn't sleep.

They led the horses outside the barn, and then slipped their headlights onto their cowboy hats before mounting up.

"How did you grow up?" Caleb asked.

"With my mom," he said. "Some of the time. I was in and out of foster care. And by the time I was sixteen I was on my own. I moved to Texas because I thought that was the Wild West."

"Oregon is farther west," he pointed out.

"True. But you know, with a name like West Caldwell, I figured I was born to be a cowboy. I found a hell of a lot there. More than I bargained for. Made some money doing things I shouldn't have done. Underground fighting, things like that. Made some money doing some okay things. Bull riding. And then found out I had a decent head for numbers. I set up some investments. Then I figured, why not do it for other people? My primary focus was agriculture and livestock. Farm implements. All that kind of stuff. But I started expanding. Got well versed in a whole lot of up-and-coming industries. I learned as I went. That's what I've always done."

Caleb grimaced, thankful his half brother wouldn't be able to see him. "You know, Hank would've been thrilled to have you. He never could get the three of us to want much more than ranching, and he hated that. He had money. But… Jacob and Gabe didn't want college, and me? He didn't even bother to try and talk me into it. Anyway, we Daltons can't be told."

"Somehow that doesn't surprise me. So tell me about Hank," he said.

"Well," Caleb said. "He spent the majority of his marriage cheating on his wife. That's not a secret. What was a secret was the consequences of all that cheating. McKenna came first. Well, we thought McKenna had come first."

"I never knew my mom hit him up for money," West said. "I wasn't even living with her back then."

"Well, maybe she wanted money so that you could."

West chuckled. "Maybe. Or maybe she needed money to bail herself out of some jam or another. I send her money now and again. I've done well for myself, so there's no reason not to. She gave birth to me. I suppose for that I owe her a little something, because she didn't have to. But I don't send her too much money, because she didn't really raise me, either."

"I wonder if any of you fared all right."

"McKenna was in foster care, too?"

"Yes. She never knew her mother at all."

"Could have been worse, I guess. For me."

"McKenna came here for money," Caleb said. "At least, that's how it started. But I can't rightly figure out what it is you want."

Caleb felt like a hypocrite saying that to the other man. Caleb had no idea in hell what he wanted. Well, he did know. But he didn't know what the end of it was. Didn't know what the point of it was.

"I proved that I could be successful on my own. I spit in the eye of everybody that ever told me I wouldn't be anything because I was nothing more than a bastard kid from nowhere. I made my way. Forged a path. Well, I reached the end of that. It came back and fell down on me like a ton of bricks. And I guess sometimes a man has some questions. About what would have happened if his foundation had been just a little bit different."

Caleb wondered that. He wondered that a lot.

Because one thing he wondered was that if his foundation was different, if he had come from a different family, if he had been shown different things, if he would have been a man who could have loved Ellie right.

Could have loved her like she deserved.

As it was…

A dyslexic cowboy with toxic roots in his family tree…a man with more anger in his chest than love. Yeah, he wasn't the man for her.

She'd had the best.

He would be a piss-poor consolation.

"I expect those are questions that sometimes need asking," he said.

"How about you? What things do you question?"

"What makes you think I'm going to talk to you about that?"

"Well," West said, "my very appearance required an explanation. So now you know more about me than anyone at home does."

"My appearance here doesn't require an explanation," Caleb said.

"Your appearance at the barn tonight might have an interesting one."

"I'm the youngest," he said. "There's nothing impressive about me. I'm not a rodeo champion like Gabe. Didn't save lives like Jacob. Didn't get good grades like Clint."

"Clint?"

"An honorary Dalton. He was a good friend of ours, practically grew up at the house. Dad offered to pay for him to go to school."

He was deliberately bringing Clint up now. Because apparently, West could have benefited from Hank's tuition offer that he gave to Clint. And it was all a sore subject where Caleb was concerned.

"And he didn't offer to pay for yours?"

"Nah. He knew wasted money when he saw it." Caleb didn't like to talk about any of it. His skills didn't lie behind a desk. They never had. Reading made his head hurt. The way the letters jumped around on the page and seemed to turn themselves backward. Hank always said he didn't apply himself, and maybe that was true.

"You have a wife? Serious girlfriend?" West asked.

"No," Caleb said, gritting his teeth.

"Love is overrated," West said.

"Yeah, well, I'm going to be the only one that agrees with you on that."

In his world, love just held you down on the ground and kicked you a bunch of times until you begged for mercy. And then it didn't give any.

And what Ellie wanted from him now was a strange, pale shadow of a thing he'd wanted back when he was young enough to believe he might be able to have it.

But not now.

"See, I thought maybe it was a wife or girlfriend that brought you out here," West said.

"I didn't think you were here for family," Caleb bit out.

"So it *is* a woman."

"Isn't it always?"

West chuckled. "Yeah. I mean, in the end, I suppose it is. It's why I'm out here. A few different women, actually. Tammy Dalton, my mom. My ex." He paused for a beat. "You know, you could always tell me, because I don't know who anyone is. More to the point, sometimes talking to someone who doesn't know you is easier."

"Why do you care?"

"Because you just listened to me for a while."

"You're not going to pretend it's brotherly bonding?"

"Hell no," he said. "I'm not big into bonding. But I am big into listening. You never know what information comes in handy later."

"You're not even going to pretend you're being helpful?"

"If you knew me at all you would know why that's not remotely believable."

"Just got a woman in my head," he said. "That's all."

"Quickest way to fix that is to get her in your bed."

"Normally, I'd agree," he said. "But that's what she wants. And then it will just make it too damned easy for her to be done."

"You want more than sex?"

He paused his horse and maneuvered it so that he was facing West.

"No. But I denied myself for a long time where she was concerned. Fourteen years. I'm not burning it out in a few days. I don't want more than sex, but I want a hell of a lot of it. And on my terms."

"That's a hell of a long time to carry a torch, man."

"You're telling me. It starts to burn."

"Only solution is to put it out."

"Yep. But again…that many years of lust deserves more than a few days, don't you think?"

"I would imagine. I've never wanted anything that long in my whole life." He chuckled. "Except for money."

"Well," Caleb said. "It seems to me you have your money now. So I can't say as I'm really sure why you're here."

"Seems to me you could have your woman if you want. You're here, too."

Caleb gritted his teeth. "It's not that simple. She's not my woman. She's never going to be."

"Well, I've never yet had a woman be mine permanently. That hasn't stopped me from enjoying what I could get."

"It's complicated."

"Because you're making it complicated."

"Haven't you ever done anything that you are ashamed of?" For some reason, even as he looked up at the sky, at the stars, that moment when Ellie had told him that she was pregnant was looming large in his vision.

He remembered it clearly. Sitting on her couch where they had done their lessons for nearly a year. Where she had helped him with his reading and writing like he was a child. And he had let her.

It was the only time he had ever enjoyed a lesson in his life.

They had never touched. They had never done anything remotely untoward. But Caleb—who had imagined that he had buried his feelings—had had to confront the fact that he had fallen in love with his friend's wife all over again when she told him that she was pregnant.

Because he'd been angry. Because it had burst into the bubble that was this secret world they had built together. And had been forced to confront the fact that it wasn't that for her.

And thank God.

He'd congratulated her, stone-faced, he was sure, and then given an excuse to leave. After that, he had told her they couldn't meet anymore, making excuses about his work, and about her needing extra rest. And when she had pestered him, he had told her to just leave him the hell alone.

They hadn't spoken.

Not for the next month.

And then Clint had died.

"No," West said.

The silence that settled between them was strange. When West finally spoke again, he spoke slowly. "That isn't to say I've been a model citizen, by the way. I should be ashamed of a great many things that I've done, but I can't really muster up the energy to manage it."

"Well, I'm happy to share some around."

"No, thanks," West said. "I'm good. I had a lot of time to sit and reflect in prison." He chuckled. "I'm kidding. I had a lot of time to make sure that nobody ever treated me like their bitch. There is no room for shame in a situation like that. There's no room for shame in a life like mine. You just gotta survive. That's why I am where I'm at today."

"On my father's ranch riding his horse?"

West chuckled. "Alive. In possession of a small fortune."

"What is your game here?" Caleb said.

"You want to keep going around and around with this?"

"Yeah," Caleb said.

"Maybe I don't have a game. Maybe I just want to see where this goes. Maybe you should do the same. You know, there doesn't have to be a game. You can just see how something feels. Go from there."

"Well, I have to say I didn't expect to be getting relationship advice from my ex-convict half brother in the middle of the night."

"And I didn't expect to give it. Because believe me, no one should take relationship advice from me. Advice on how to get laid, on the other hand, I'm pretty good for that."

Maybe that was something Caleb just needed to get used to.

His life was far from ideal. Hell, so was Ellie's.

Maybe *ideal* wasn't the thing to aim for. Maybe what felt good for now would be good enough.

But there was one thing he was certain of, beyond the fact that he wanted her. Beyond the fact that however he had pushed it down, he wanted Ellie.

He would never replace Clint. He could never.

The very idea was laughable.

But that was all about emotion. Not the physical. The physical...

He could make her want. He could make her scream. He could make it good.

But as complicated as it was...

He couldn't replace his friend, not when it came to being a husband. Sure as hell not when it came to being a father.

But he didn't want her thinking of Clint when they finally made love.

And that was the road. He had to be sure.

Had to be sure that she didn't just want this, but that she wanted him.

Maybe West was right. Maybe he wanted to do it the hard way.

But Caleb Dalton had always done things the hard way. Naturally, in many cases.

So he didn't see why this shouldn't be the same thing.

CHAPTER TEN

CALEB WOULD HAVE been perfectly happy to avoid Ellie for the rest of the day. Not because he felt uncomfortable. No, he didn't. In fact, after he had left the ranch last night, he had gone home and relived those moments by the fire, over and over again. The way that it had felt to touch her between her legs, the way that it had felt to kiss her, finally.

No, he didn't want to avoid her out of a sense of discomfort. He wanted to avoid her so that he could preserve that fantasy.

Dark and close and warm. More than warm. Incendiary. The best sexual encounter he'd ever had, and he hadn't even come.

He hadn't let himself come last night when he was by himself, either. Because that wasn't what he wanted.

He wanted to prolong it, in a sadistic kind of way.

Wanted to take this out, examine it and turn it over at his leisure.

Because he had repressed it for so long. It had been necessary. It had been the right thing to do.

But now he was resolute. Because now, taking care of Ellie involved this. And he was going to go ahead and use it for his own gain.

He was going to go ahead and draw a bold line underneath this thing that they shared.

He was going to burn it out of his system.

But first, he wanted to exist here. Poised on a knife's edge, where wanting her wasn't a sin.

Okay, maybe wanting her still was a sin, but a ghost couldn't get into a fistfight with him.

And a ghost couldn't please his wife, either. So there it was.

But there was no avoiding Ellie. And the reason was a little blonde moppet that he couldn't deny any more than he could quit breathing.

"Caleb!" Amelia flung herself off his parents' front porch and into his arms. He picked her up, and she wrapped her legs around him, clinging tightly to him. And then she leaned forward and kissed his cheek. She smacked her hand against his jaw. "Prickly," she complained.

Something in his chest tugged. "Well, you caught me at the end of the day, squirt. I need to shave."

She looked at him and wrinkled her nose. "Am I going to need to shave someday?"

He laughed. And he was surprised how genuinely light he felt in that moment. "Not likely. Your mom doesn't have a beard, does she?"

"No," she said, frowning. "My mom says that you have Christmas trees."

"I do," he said. "At least, they're about to be mine. It's going to be a whole farm of them."

"I didn't know you had Christmas trees on a farm," she said.

"Well, you can. It's where most of the Christmas trees from the lots come from."

"I want to see them."

He hesitated because he knew that if he took Amelia to see the trees, in all likelihood he would have to take Ellie with him. And really, spending time with Ellie

and Amelia in the same space right now was strange
and loaded.

"All right," he said. "But only if your mom's okay
with that."

"She will be," Amelia said, full of confidence.

He set her down, and she scampered into the house.

"What am I going to be okay with?"

He turned around and saw Ellie. The sight of her just
about set him back on his heels. She looked the same
as she always did.

But that was the problem.

"Amelia wants to go out and see the Christmas trees,"
he said. "I didn't figure you would mind. I don't mind
taking her by myself, if you need to go home."

She lifted her shoulder. "No. I don't mind going up."

She started to take a step toward him, and his gut
tightened. Then the door opened again, and Amelia re-
appeared with her backpack from preschool, and another stack of old printer paper that his mother had
given her to scribble on.

"Can we ride in Caleb's truck?"

"Yes," Ellie said.

"I'm sitting in the middle."

A smile tugged at the corner of Ellie's lips, and she
narrowed her eyes slightly. The impish expression making his gut feel hollow, and effortlessly conveying that
she had been hoping for the middle seat.

She was flirting with him.

Now, that, he hadn't expected.

So maybe this whole making-her-wait thing was really
going to work in his favor.

Amelia took his hand and led him to the truck. He
opened the door and lifted her inside, buckling her

into her seat, the one that he kept inside his truck all the time.

Suddenly, the moment felt…unbearably domestic. Even more so when the passenger-side door opened and Ellie got inside while he was still buckling her daughter.

He swallowed hard, and then got into the pickup, closing the door and starting the engine.

"How did you sleep last night?" Ellie asked as he pulled out of his parents' driveway.

He shot her a look over the top of Amelia's blond hair. "Just great," he returned.

"Not me," she said. She licked her lips. "I was a little bit restless."

"Well, that's a shame," he said. "I would have thought you would drop off to sleep like a rock."

She had come. She had come pretty hard, as a matter of fact.

A memory that made him get hard just thinking about it.

"Yeah, you would have thought," she said. "But… I just kept thinking there was unfinished business."

"Ellie," he said, his voice warning.

"I think that owls are the best bird."

Both he and Ellie just about got whiplash looking at Amelia at the center of them. "What?" Ellie asked.

"I've been thinking," she said. "Owls are the best bird." She spoke with the cool authority that only a four-year-old could ever possess.

"I don't know," Caleb said. "I think that eagles are pretty cool."

"They're mean," Amelia insisted.

Amelia continued to extol the virtues of specific birds and malign others on the trip up to the ranch, and Caleb was exceedingly grateful for the random conversation of the avian variety that they found themselves in. Because it was a hell of a lot better than trying to dance around double entendre with Ellie while he didn't have any control of his body and her daughter was sitting there as an audience.

They turned up the winding driveway that led to his new place, and a sense of calm flooded Caleb. This place, this ranch, represented the new beginning that he so desperately needed.

And what he was doing with Ellie represented the last of the old business in his life that needed to be taken care of.

It all made sense. Yeah, for the first time in a long time everything made quite a bit of sense.

He didn't bother to drive by the house, instead going straight to the Christmas trees.

He stopped and got out, helping Amelia get down, too. She took his hand, and he led her over to the first row of green, bristling pines.

"You have a whole field of Christmas!" She darted into the first row, then the second.

"Don't go too far," Ellie warned.

"I won't!"

Amelia started running in circles around one of the trees.

"It would be nice to have that much energy again," Ellie said. "At least half of it. Which would help me keep up with her."

"I have a feeling that it's always going to seem a little like you can't keep up with her."

"Probably," Ellie said, shaking her head. Her expression grave for a moment. "Thank you. For bringing her up here. For helping me keep up. You know, if it wasn't for you…"

"Let's not do this," he said. "You don't need to thank me every time I do the bare minimum. You're my friend. Clint was my friend. My best friend. I want to make sure that his wife and daughter are taken care of."

"Am I still his wife to you?"

"Does that matter?"

"In light of last night it matters a little bit."

He tried to figure out how to choose his words very carefully. "Look, I knew Clint longer than you did. I knew him most of my life. And I'll tell you, I never knew a better man. You couldn't have married a better man."

"He was great," she said softly.

"And I met you when you were already with him."

That seemed loaded, and she couldn't really say why. "I know."

"Yes," he said finally, the words grinding against his breastbone before they rose up in his throat and scraped across his teeth. "You'll always be Clint's wife."

Ellie closed her eyes, the breeze kicking up slightly, her pale blond hair twisting in the wind. "I'm not, though," she said. "And nobody knows it better than me." She looked at him, and he felt like he'd been struck with the green and gold there. "Do you know how I know I'm not his wife, Caleb? Because he can't hold me. He can't kiss me. I can't talk to him, not ever again. I'll never walk down the street and hold his hand. We'll never talk about stupid things like what the craziest potato chip flavor we can come up with is, and whether or not platypuses are a scam."

"That was…actually a debate that you had?"

"Yes," she said. "Because he was ridiculous. And he was fun. And he brought something into my life that I'd never had before. He left some things behind. He left a brightness in me that I didn't have before. And he left Amelia," she said, both of them turning and looking at the little girl darting around the trees. "But I'm not Clint's wife. I'm his widow. And that's just…not something I would have chosen to be. But I am. So please… Don't look at me that way. Because it isn't fair. For you to hold yourself back because that's what you think when I don't get any of the benefits of having him here."

Caleb didn't quite know what to say to that. He felt like there was a rock lodged in his chest. He looked toward her, and he reached out, wrapping his hand around her wrist. "I'm not holding myself back because of that."

"Then why does it matter to you to keep reminding yourself who I was married to?"

"Because it's why I'm here. It's why taking care of you matters. Because it's what he would've wanted."

"Does part of you want to take care of me? Even a little bit?"

"Of course I do," he said. "You matter to me. You always have."

"Except for the couple of months where you didn't talk to me."

He felt like he'd been slapped. "That was nothing. That was just…me going through some things. And when Clint died it didn't matter anymore."

"If he hadn't died would you ever have talked to me again?"

The words hit him hard. And he had honestly never thought of it before. Because there had never been a reason to think about something like that. Their lives had changed. Utterly and completely in the space of a moment.

"Yes," he said, because it was the only answer that could possibly be true. He couldn't imagine never speaking to Ellie. That had never been in the cards. Hell, if it was that easy, he would have done that in the beginning instead of just trying to carve his feelings out of his chest with a spoon. Instead of just suppressing his desire for the better part of the decade.

"Why were you mad at me?"

"Why does it matter?"

"I don't know. Because I keep thinking about it. Because things are changing with us. And because I've made you mad recently, and it made me think about then."

He gritted his teeth. "Because we had a secret," he said. "And when you told me you were pregnant it hit me how stupid it was. Meeting for secret lessons."

"It was a secret because you didn't want…"

"Yeah, but it occurred to me how messed up it was that we had one at all."

Realization seemed to wash through her like a wave.

"Oh," she said, looking away.

"It's okay if you didn't think of it that way. You were married. I'm not. I wasn't. So for me, I was a single guy coming to your house in the middle of the day when your husband wasn't home, and spending time with you that he didn't know about. Hell, outside work I was starting to spend more time with you than I did him. Our…friendship was getting stronger than the one I had with Clint. And I'm sorry that I didn't handle it well."

"Were you…? Were you attracted to me?"

"*Fuck*, Ellie. Why would you ask that?" The words escaped before he could hold them back in.

"Because I want to know."

She was asking expensive questions and she had no idea how much they cost.

"Yes," he grated. "Obviously, if I thought of you as

nothing more than a talking cabbage it wouldn't have been an issue that I was meeting with you by myself."

There was a long pause, and he wanted to grab that line of tension and strangle himself with it. Knock himself unconscious for a bit. Anything rather than being right here in it.

"You didn't do anything," she said.

"Yeah, well."

"And you wouldn't have. It's obvious that you wouldn't have. You cut off lessons with me. So…"

"Don't absolve me of it."

"I'm not," she said softly. "I'm not doing anything with you, or to you, when it comes to…whatever you felt back then. It's not… Life is really complicated. And it doesn't matter what you felt for a minute. What matters is what you did. You were there for me. You've always been there for me." She put her hand on his chest, and for a moment it seemed like a comfort gesture. But then her hand slid upward an inch, and the mood shifted, the tension between them becoming sexual.

He let go of her wrist and pressed his hand over hers. "But I was never as safe as you thought."

She huffed a laugh. "My whole life wasn't as safe as I thought. Life changes. That's about the only thing we can guarantee. It will be what it is—that's another thing. I don't want to be safe, Caleb. If I wanted to be safe then I would just keep doing what I was doing."

He looked down at her, and his mouth burned. Her tongue darted out, touching the center of her lower lip, and he ached to taste it. Ached to claim her mouth again the way that he had done last night.

"Caleb! There's an owl in one of your trees."

"What?" He looked over at Amelia.

"You have an owl," she said.

"Those trees are too short for owls," he said.

He had no idea if that was scientifically or…zoologically true, but he barely knew his own name right now.

"Not these," Amelia said. "That one."

She pointed to a tall, scraggly pine on the edge of the curated rows. And indeed, there was a white, moon-faced barn owl up at the top, gazing down at them with no small amount of judgment.

"That's great," he said. "Just great."

"Kids have an unerring sense of timing," Ellie whispered.

"And it's a good thing she does," he said. "Because there's no way anything can happen with her twenty feet away. And also…you're not ready yet."

"Why am I not ready?" she asked.

A teasing response hovered on the edge of his lips, but for the first time he wondered if it was he who wasn't ready. It was weird, the way that he had ended up confessing about the reading lessons.

He certainly hadn't anticipated that.

Exposing his tarnished soul to her wasn't exactly on his to-do list. Just the opposite.

He hadn't expected to put that out there in the open, but it didn't seem to have changed anything. She seemed resolved, and it hadn't seemed to rock her world in any way.

He had to wonder why that was.

"Just trust me," he said. "You're not ready yet."

"I don't know that I do."

"Until you do, you won't be ready. You gotta trust me with your body, honey. And if you don't…"

"How many years of fantasies do you have?"

That hit him like a bullet. "You're not going to find out if you don't behave."

"Then I guess I'll behave."

THE NEXT WEEK was an exercise in frustration, at least for Ellie. Caleb seemed...well, distressingly fine. And Ellie was...

She didn't know what was happening to her. Because the need for sex had shifted into a need for Caleb, and that had happened before they had ever kissed.

But sometime between their encounter by the fireplace and this very moment, it had turned into a sickness.

She was going to die if she couldn't have him.

Him, specifically.

And everything between them was a jumble, a ridiculous tangle that she wasn't sure she could quite sort out, but it didn't change the fact that she wanted him.

"You seem cheerful today," Vanessa said, coming into the classroom with lunch in hand.

"I am...bemused."

"By?" Vanessa pressed.

"My life?"

"That is a lot to be bemused by."

"You're telling me."

"Does it have to do with a certain tall, handsome cowboy?"

"How did you guess?"

"Oddly," Vanessa said, taking a fierce bite of her sandwich, "we live in a place where that necessitates being more specific. Because we are beset by tall, handsome cowboys."

"What a thing to be beset by."

"And bemused by."

"Obviously, it's Caleb."

"Obviously. What's going on?"

"He won't… He…"

She'd been sitting on what had happened between the two of them because it felt very raw and personal. Because her reaction to Caleb was embarrassing.

"He's being a tease. And I have…blue…ovaries? Is that a thing?"

"I don't think so."

"Well, if they were a thing, I would have them. He's torturing me. He… He kissed me. And then…he did more than kiss me. And I want…everything."

"You want to go all the way." Vanessa smirked over the top of her sandwich.

"Yes," Ellie said. "I want…" She sighed. "I wanted to get carried away with passion, the way that you and Jacob did. When you talked about the two of you having sex against the wall… I was jealous. I was jealous because it sounded so intense and wonderful and like an escape."

"Yes," Vanessa agreed. "An escape into motherhood." She put her hand on her stomach. Yes, her impetuous sex with Jacob had had consequences. But still.

"You know what I mean. He's drawing it out. He's not giving me the thing. And the worst part is I…I want him so much I can't see straight. *Him*. It's like a sickness. He is my best friend."

"I'm a little wounded by that," Vanessa said. "But go on."

"You know what I mean. He's been in my life for years. As my friend. And it's like the world suddenly tipped over. And I feel like I've reached my quota for how many times my world is allowed to shift on its axis completely. This isn't something that I wanted, but now… It's happening, and I have never looked at my best friend's ass so many times in the entire fourteen years that I've known him as I have in the past week."

"Well, what are you going to do about that?"

"He says I'm not ready," she said.

"What?"

"He says I'm not ready," she repeated.

"Do you have to…wax on wax off a car first before you're ready to get on him?"

Ellie shot her a baleful look. "He doesn't like that I propositioned him. At least, that's my take on it. And he's making me wait, because he's in charge."

Vanessa snorted. "Oh, what alpha male crap."

"Right?" Ellie said. "I thought so, too."

"I bet he would not be able to stick to his guns if you ambushed him with yours." She gestured toward Ellie's boobs.

"He made it pretty clear," Ellie said.

"So what?" Vanessa asked.

"What happened to considering him as another person involved in this list situation?"

"Well, obviously he wants you. And I never said that you couldn't play a little dirty. Isn't that the point, after all?"

"I guess," she said.

"You guessed nothing. You want him."

"I do. And…"

Ellie thought about telling Vanessa what Caleb had told her about his attraction to her while she was married. But somehow…it didn't seem right. It seemed like something that should be between the two of them. Because it obviously bothered him to admit it.

But attraction was normal, wasn't it? She had always thought he was a good-looking guy. And the fact of the matter was, she never considered sleeping with him because she hadn't considered sleeping with anyone other than her husband. But she had known that he was handsome. And clearly she'd always possessed the ability to be attracted to him, or they wouldn't be in this situation now.

She wondered why he felt so cut up about it.

But then, it probably had to do with the fact that he and Clint had a long relationship, and also that Caleb admired Clint so much.

"I lost you," Vanessa said.

"What?" Ellie jerked out of her drifting thoughts.

"I'm just saying," Vanessa said. "If you want him, make it happen. Honestly, I don't think there's a man alive who wouldn't be pretty excited to have the woman that he wants to sleep with show up at his place half-naked."

"Hmm," she said.

"I can watch Amelia for you. And he's closing on his house, and moving in within the next couple of days…"

"You're enabling me."

"Yes," she said. "And why not?"

And now that it was in her mind, she couldn't let it go. Because these feelings that she had for him were starting to feel a little bit like a drawn-out illness, and she was eager to get in bed, and get it done with.

Then maybe she would magically be on the path to moving on. From all kinds of things.

Of course, she had asked him in the most explicit terms she possibly could have to have sex with her last week, and he had still walked away.

But he was only a man. Flesh and blood. If she took her top off… Well, Vanessa might have something there.

Ellie really hoped that she did, because there would

be no real way for her to get a grip on her life if she couldn't handle this.

She didn't like feeling off-kilter, and she didn't like feeling out of control. And that meant it was time for her to do something about Caleb.

CHAPTER ELEVEN

CALEB WAS HOME. Really home.

The concept of home didn't matter much to him. He took it for granted. He had spent most of his life in the house his parents lived in now. Of course, when he'd been really little, they had lived in a trailer park. But he barely remembered that, and at his age, it felt stable enough. Though he knew that his father resented the years spent in their humble residence, to a little boy a roof over your head was a roof over your head.

But there was something about this. About something that was his. His specifically and not anyone else's.

It wasn't Hank's, and it wasn't bought with Hank's money.

It was his place. His ranch. His land.

And in his estimation, a man wasn't no kind of man if he didn't have some land.

The place was a little bit weathered—inside and out—but it would give him something to do, fixing it up. Yeah, it would make for a nice project.

Something that he could do. He'd always been good at working with his hands. He might not have been able to ace a test, every essay he'd ever written might look like chicken scratch, but he could build things. He'd done the sets for the school play, and that kind of extra credit was about the only way that he'd managed to graduate high school.

He took on physical projects that no one else really wanted to do. And he did them well.

You're letting them pigeonhole you.

His dad's voice rang in his ears. A memory from a long time ago.

They think you're just trailer trash. The kind of boy that's only suited for manual labor.

We haven't been trailer trash in a long time, Dad.

It doesn't matter. People remember. Their memories are long.

You only care about us doing well in school because you want to prove that we are not trash down in our blood.

Is that so bad? I worked hard to get us out of there. I worked hard to change our circumstances. You don't care because you don't remember.

I remember well enough. But I thought the point of having money was to get a little bit more freedom in your life.

As far as Caleb could see, it had meant that for his father. It had given him permission to go out and do whatever he wanted, even though he had been doing a bit of it beforehand—as evidenced by the ages of his half siblings.

But Caleb had never wanted to be the fulfillment of Hank Dalton's shortcomings.

And he didn't want to sit around having a constant reminder of his own. So now…this was his place.

It wasn't gold-plated like his father's, but Caleb didn't need all that.

He just wanted what was his.

So maybe… Maybe that was his concept of home.

Thankfully, he had few possessions. He hadn't brought any of his furniture with him—it had been old anyway—and his new furniture had arrived from the delivery service that morning. Otherwise, it had been work boots, fancy boots, work pants, fancy pants, T-shirts and button-up shirts. A few cowboy hats. His TV, which he basically reserved for watching football, and his truck.

He was a man who traveled light through the world.

The new house, weathered though it was, was so much bigger than the cabin that he'd been renting, that he'd gone and gotten himself about the biggest bed he could find. One his feet wouldn't hang off, and one that could easily fit a partner, and accommodate no small amount of physical activity.

It seemed to be a little bit of a mockery right at the moment.

But he'd chosen it. Because he was a masochist, apparently.

He closed his eyes and thought about Ellie. He wanted her.

But for how long? And what did she want from him?

And why the hell did it matter?

He hadn't thought this deeply about sex since he was a sixteen-year-old virgin.

He went and opened the fridge and stared at the contents. Beer bottles, that was basically it.

And as he reached for one of them, wrapped his hand around the cold glass, he froze. Because his own motivation suddenly fell on him like a ton of bricks.

He was testing his control.

Proving to himself that Ellie Bell couldn't tempt him beyond what he could handle.

And he thought back to what she'd said earlier.

It doesn't matter what you wanted to do. What matters is what you did.

It did matter. Both things. But whether or not he was able to be the master of his own body meant something.

Because he didn't have a whole hell of a lot of feelings about what kind of man he was, and about how worthy or good he might be, but he had his control.

He'd never been the smartest. He'd never been the most successful. But he was a man who put his head down and did what the hell he believed in.

He had been a loyal friend, a good brother. And wanting Clint's wife had gone in the face of the one thing he was the best at.

And now... Now it was like he was testing his own mettle.

Dammit, how annoying.

He slammed the fridge shut and pressed his beer bottle lip against the counter and slammed his palm down on the top, separating the cap from the rim.

He lifted the bottle to his lips and shook his head.

There was nothing wrong with making sure his control was rock-solid.

Hell, he'd spent all his school years feeling like his life was out of control.

Every other damn kid in the class just learned to read. Why couldn't he do that?

Dyslexia. He knew the answer to that.

But no one had cared about learning disabilities in a small town all that many years ago, and Hank Dalton certainly hadn't ever considered it.

He was seen as lazy. Disrespectful.

Stupid.

When he'd been trying his hardest. Trying his damnedest.

He felt like he was drowning, and he resented it.

It had only gotten worse as he'd gotten older. Physically, he was strong, and he knew that when it came to hanging out in a group, making conversation, he could do it as well as anyone else.

He could take apart a car engine and put it back together. Could do the same to a tractor. Put something real in front of him, something physical, and he could make it work, make it not work, make it into something shaped like a chicken. Hell, whatever anyone needed.

But sitting down and reading out loud in a room full of people? Hell no.

And so he'd found his way. He found his group. His friends.

His career.

One that required brute strength and brilliance on a physical level, and not all that stagnant book learning that threatened to give him a migraine every time he attempted it.

And the only person he had ever tried to improve that for was Ellie.

Hell, he knew his motivation was tainted during those interactions by the sheer fact that he hadn't done it in the first place. Because nothing else had ever made him *want* to fix it.

Of course, having a name for what he was, for what it meant that the letters looked all kinds of funny, and tended to move on a page, had meant something, too.

Ellie had known. Of course.

Because as little as he could wrap his brain around anything like that, it was what she did. She didn't just understand all that; she could teach it to other people.

She had even managed to make inroads teaching him.

And given the amount of teachers he'd had over the course of his life who hadn't been able to do that at all, he knew what a damned miracle it was. What it meant to be a good teacher.

And how it was a gift and a calling more than it was anything else.

Ellie was that.

Ellie was also a thorn in his side.

Ellie was also the reason he'd kept his dyslexia a secret. At first it had been innocent enough. He hadn't known what to make of having a name for his struggles. He hadn't been comfortable with it. Hadn't liked it.

And slowly it had become something secret, shared with the one woman he craved intimacy with. It might not have been physical intimacy, but it was an intimacy and he'd found some kind of satisfaction in that.

And after that...well, even after he'd put a stop to the lessons, he'd held on to the secret.

It was tangled up in her. In his guilt.

There was a knock on his front door.

Which was weird, because he had only lived here for about twenty-four hours. The only people who really knew it were his family. Of course, it could be a roving band of Jehovah's Witnesses on rotation. That was entirely possible.

He took the wooden stairs two at a time and crossed into the entryway, beer bottle still in hand. He jerked the door open and froze.

Because Ellie was standing there, carrying a very large casserole dish.

Now, normally the casserole dish would not be the first thing he noticed, but she was holding it in a way that covered her breasts, and it was held so high aloft it was right in his face, and she was gazing at him with a strange kind of hopefulness that he couldn't quite figure out.

"Hi," she said.

"Hi," he responded.

"I brought you dinner." She held the casserole up yet more insistently. It was covered with tinfoil, so he didn't know what it was.

"What did you bring?"

She blinked, and then looked up at him like that owl in his tree. "Does it matter?"

"Yeah," he responded.

"Because you have something better in your fridge?"

He flashed back to the fridge full of beer and nothing else.

"No."

She rolled her eyes. "Just let me in."

He stepped aside and she breezed past him. For a second there, the interaction had felt almost normal. The way they had been before the kiss. Before the... Yeah, before the much more than kissing.

She went into the kitchen and started hunting around.

"Can I help you find something, Ellie?" he asked, leaning in the doorway and watching her flutter around officiously.

"A serving spoon."

"What is it?"

"Chicken and stuffing," she responded, making a sound of triumph when she opened the drawer and found a large flat silver spoon. Then she rooted around in the cupboards, taking down a couple of plates. She peeled back the tinfoil, and his stomach started to growl.

"Good thing I came," she said.

"Yeah," he said. "I guess so."

She dished him a heaping helping and handed the

plate to him. Then she squinted as she looked around. "Do you really not have a dining table?"

He lifted a shoulder, following her gaze to the barren dining spot in the kitchen. "One is coming."

"And what were you going to do until then?"

"Eat on the couch. Which frankly is what I'm going to do most of the time anyway."

"Well, then, I guess we should go eat on the couch."

Ellie availed herself of her own beer, and handed him the bottle, which he took care of scalping before he handed it back to her.

Then the two of them went into the living room. The floors were bare, and for some reason, when Ellie crossed them, her feet loud on the wood planks, he had the thought that he needed a rug. Something to make it a little bit more comfortable.

She sat down in the armchair, her feet tucked up under her, and he took a place on the couch. They ate in silence, barely looking at each other.

"Where's Amelia?" he asked.

"With Vanessa and Jacob," she responded. "I thought it might be good practice for them."

He chuckled. "A four-year-old is hardly practice for a newborn baby."

"Hey, their kid will be four eventually. They'll be able to look back on this couple of hours and draw inspiration from it."

"I bet she already has Jacob dressed up in a tutu."

A smile tugged at the corners of her mouth, and he felt an answering tug in his gut. "She's very persuasive that way."

That was true. The little thing was a petite blonde bulldozer. Just like her mother.

Which made Ellie's appearance slightly suspicious.

Ellie was the kind of woman who went right for what she wanted. She'd done it as a young woman, getting into college like she had. She'd done it when she'd established the school at the Dalton family ranch.

She didn't do anything without a plan, and she didn't do anything without a huge amount of strength.

Including making casseroles.

He looked up at her just as she took a bite, and she treated him to a closed-lip grin, which looked as suspicious as about everything else in the moment did.

"When are you going to open up the tree lots?" she asked, her tone a shade too sweet and interested.

It was damned suspicious.

"Well," he said. "We're going to start cutting trees this weekend. I'm going to commission some of the boys from the school. Do you have any thoughts on who might need to get involved in that?"

She nodded slowly. "I'll send over a list. And I'll offer it to some of them as extra credit."

Caleb's heart felt a little bit tangled up, because it reminded him so much of how he'd gotten through school. What he'd just been thinking about.

"It's nice to be able to use the strengths you've got," he commented.

"Well," she said. "I certainly think so. But then, I also like to think that, in general, the size of the school and all of that, that it lends itself to playing to their different strengths. To help them see that they have them."

Caleb nodded and took a bite of stuffing. "It's good to have someone give you those chances. Regular school for someone whose brain doesn't work...regular. Well, that isn't any fun."

"I'd like to say that things are set up a little bit better now across the board," Ellie said softly. "The kids don't suffer the way that you did. But it's only ever as good as the administration allows it to be. It's only ever as good as the education on the funding that the schools receive. And sometimes it's only ever as good as the teacher. So a lot of these boys have been hurt. And sometimes it's because they are their own worst enemy. But the fact remains that it means they need to learn a different way of experiencing school. A different way of interacting with authority. And cutting Christmas trees will probably be good."

"Yeah, and then after that they can work the lot. See it through." He took a breath. "You know, I understand the way that some people view manual labor. With a kind of sneer, looking down your nose at it, like it's less. But I've never found anything more satisfying than going out and making a change with my own two hands. Seeing a project through from start to finish, knowing that what I did…that it changed something. The shape of an object, the landscape. When you're fighting fires, that your hands helped put up the blockade that preserved the wilderness. That you dug those trenches, ran those fire lines that saved houses, trees, animals. Lives. There's no shame in it."

"I've never thought there was," she said softly. "It's the kind of thing I admire, really and truly."

Ellie set her plate to the side and scooted to the edge of the chair, planting her feet on the floor. Then she looked at him, a note of determination in her eyes, and stood.

"Ellie," he said, his voice a warning.

Then she sighed heavily, dropped her hands to her sides before gripping the hem of her top and pulling it up over her head, bra and all, leaving her standing there showing off the most perfect, beautiful pair of breasts he'd ever seen.

"Oh, yeah," she said. "I brought dessert."

CHAPTER TWELVE

ELLIE THOUGHT THAT she might die.

In the space between that moment she decided to remove her shirt, and when it actually came off, her brain had gone entirely blank. And then she was standing there with her boobs out, looking at her best friend's face, which was going through so many shifts and changes she couldn't even get a read on one.

She took a breath, and she took a step toward him. And tension was strung tight inside her like a live wire.

Because the man had given her an orgasm. Only the second man to ever do it. And she was straight-up obsessed with getting near him again. Getting his hands on her, and she didn't know how to function like that. Not even a little bit.

She was thinking about it constantly, and sometimes when she thought about it, it was like a heavy weight that threatened to crush her. Honestly, sexual frustration was the absolute best that it could be.

She had bantered about it with Vanessa yesterday, she had flirted with Caleb in the days in between and all of that... All of that had helped push the larger, heavier something away.

But she couldn't outrun it. Not anymore. So she just needed it finished. Needed it done.

He opened his mouth like he was going to say something but she didn't give him a chance to. Instead, she wiggled herself out of her jeans and her panties before she could think better of it, and watched as the color drained from his face.

He leaned back in his chair, his large hands pressed to his thighs. And she made the decision to just keep going.

She braced herself on the back of the chair, leaning in, the heat from his body radiating from his large frame. And then she put one knee on the chair beside him, the other on the other side, and scooted herself in close, her legs parted, her breasts right at his eye level, and every part of her feeling so exposed it was a miracle that she wasn't shaking like a Chihuahua.

He was frozen, his hands still gripping his own thighs, and if it hadn't been for the slight rise and fall of his chest with each jagged breath he took, she might have thought he was made of stone.

"I'm ready," she whispered, her lips right near his. "And you don't get to tell me that I'm not."

And suddenly, he moved, his big hands gripping her hips, hot and rough and calloused, jerking her down hard onto his lap, the most tender place on her body coming into contact with the hardest part of his.

It was a whole litany of sensation. The rough denim, his erection, hard as steel. Heat and strength, the roughness of his hands.

He just stared at her, those blue eyes never wavering.

Her lips burned, but he didn't make a move to kiss them.

So she did.

She kissed the edge of his mouth, right at the corner, and the growl that rumbled in his chest reminded her of a lion.

And then his hands were in her hair, holding her steady as he consumed her.

This had all the passion of their previous encounters, but there was an edge to it. He didn't seem to have control of himself. Didn't seem to have control of anything. He was shaking. Shaking like a damn leaf as he plundered her mouth, his blunt fingertips digging into her hips. His hold might leave a bruise, and she didn't even mind.

He arched his hips upward and she gasped. The intensity of the pleasure, of the need inside her, shocked her completely.

She had thought that maybe... Maybe what had happened by the fire was a little bit of a fluke. Because it had been so long since she'd been with a man, so long since she'd been touched, that perhaps it led to the intensity that she'd felt. But this was even more intense. Even more overwhelming.

Sex, in her experience, was light and fun. Pleasurable, companionable. She had kissed more smiles off her husband's face than she could count.

But nobody was smiling here.

This felt feral and angry, desperate and on the verge of madness. He let his hands slide up, his thumbs curving around the underside of her breasts as he leaned her back slightly and lowered his head, taking one nipple into his mouth and sucking hard.

It sent an arrow of pleasure down between her thighs, made her cry out. And maybe it would've been embarrassing if she had the access to those kinds of feelings, but she didn't. She was a creature made entirely of fire and desire, and there was no space for embarrassment within that.

It had all been burned away.

His whiskers scraped against her tender skin as he licked and sucked a path over her body, as he teased and tormented her, holding her still on his entirely clothed lap.

"I want to see you," she whispered, fumbling as she pushed her hands beneath his T-shirt and made contact with the muscles there.

She jerked it up over his head, her movements clumsy as she did so.

And then he wrapped his arms around her, crushing her breasts to his bare chest, the heat, the intensity of being so close to him, skin to skin... She didn't think she could survive it.

She didn't know what this was.

She had thought she knew all about sex. She'd thought she'd known what desire was. Because hadn't she felt it hundreds of times?

But it wasn't *this*. Nothing had ever been this before.

But maybe it was because she'd never been this before.

She was a woman who had gone through the fire and, like metal, had been tortured and forged into something else, something harder, sharper, and as a result...

The need was harder. Sharper.

Darker.

Something that belonged to a stranger.

And when she looked up and met her best friend's eyes, he was a stranger, too. Because this wasn't the man that she had known for all these years.

This man was...

Dangerous.

Just like he'd said.

She was never as safe as she'd believed. Because this had existed beneath the surface all that time.

If she hadn't known.

You didn't even know what was in you. How could you have ever known it was in him?

But then all thought was eradicated when he consumed her mouth yet again, using his free hand to undo the buckle on his jeans.

"Wait," she whispered, the word sounding slurred, thick and drunken. "Just wait a moment."

Because she'd come prepared. She'd come prepared for this.

She scrambled off his lap and went back into the kitchen, totally naked, pulling through her purse and retrieving a couple of condoms. Then she returned, and when she did he had shucked his jeans partway down his thighs.

And there he was.

She squeezed her thighs together, pleasure striking her like an arrow. She felt hollow, desperate with need.

He was huge.

And beautiful.

She could honestly say she'd never thought about *that* body part as being beautiful. But he was. All of him. The bit of his muscular, glorious thighs that she could see, that flat, rippling stomach with just the right amount of hair covering it. Up to that magnificently furred chest, well-defined and absolutely delicious.

She tore the condom open and made her way to where he sat. Then she got down on her knees in front of him, wrapping her hand around his body and leaning in.

"What the hell?" he growled, grabbing hold of her hair and jerking her face backward.

"I was pondering a blow job," she said. "I have it on good authority that men enjoy those."

"Later," he growled, pulling her up onto his lap.

"Later?"

"I need to be in you," he gritted out. Looking purposefully at the condom.

She grabbed it, rolling it down over his hard, thick length. She moaned as she did, biting her lip.

She was about to say something about going slow. About being gentle with her, because it had been a thousand years since she'd had a man inside her. But the words were lost when the thick head of his arousal met the entrance to her body, and he began to lower her slowly onto his length.

She gripped his shoulders and he held her hips, and with one last thrust that took her breath away, Caleb Dalton pushed himself fully inside her.

And she couldn't breathe.

Her throat closed, a knot in it, an ache that made it feel like her chest was being crushed. Tears filled her eyes, a heavy, dull pain radiating through her body that threatened to overshadow the pleasure that she felt over being filled by him.

She didn't know what was happening to her. Nothing like this had ever happened to her.

And Caleb wouldn't look away. He wouldn't smile. He wouldn't make a joke. And so it all just built. And built and built and built, while he sat there with him inside her, unmoving.

She trembled, her bottom lip quivering, her internal muscles pulsing around him. And she was sure that she was going to come. Just from sitting there, with him inside her. And maybe cry, and do it again. Again and again. Because there might be no end to this. It was like a fathomless ocean that she couldn't see the bottom of.

She was going to drown.

Thank God she knew those hands. Knew those hands could take a broken thing and fix it, whatever it was.

Just as she had the thought, he pressed his thumb between them right there, stroking the source of her need as he flexed his hips, and then withdrew from her, thrusting back in, and lights burst behind her eyelids. She clung to him, wave after wave of need pulsing through her body as she came and came, in an endless wave of pleasure.

She clung to him, because she didn't know what else to do.

Clung to him, because if she didn't, there would be nothing at all to hold her together. Nothing at all.

But he wasn't done with her.

He wrapped his arms around her, and lowered them both to the floor, the wood rough and cold against her back. And then he thrust into her, harder this time. His movements animal, lacking any kind of rhythm as he drove her to a place that was somewhere past pleasure. In the realm of desperation and fantasy, where she was afraid she might be sliced in half as easily as she found release.

And she couldn't look away from him. Couldn't find a way to breathe. Because it was Caleb, pounding into her like his life depended on it. It was Caleb who made a guttural sound and clenched his teeth, lowering his head and then biting her neck as he found his own release, as it triggered hers.

Every muscle in her body went tight, and she arched up into him, clinging to his shoulders, aware of every pulse of her body, and every answering pulse in his.

She had known pleasure. She had known orgasms. But this was something else. This was like an invasion. And when it was over, she didn't feel better. She didn't feel like it was finished. And she didn't feel like everything would be okay.

And Caleb... Caleb looked like fury.

Fury in the form of a beautiful man who had just ridden her to ecstasy, and now looked like he might destroy them both with the force of his rage.

He rolled away from her, and she cried out when he withdrew from her body.

"Ellie," he said, his voice jagged.

"I..." A tear rolled down her cheek.

"Dammit," he ground out. "I told you it wasn't time yet."

"I don't know what happened," she said. "I don't know what... I don't know... It was time, obviously, because it happened." She finished it lamely, unable to find any more eloquent words, because she was naked, and because her body was still on fire, and because she wanted to curl up in a ball and weep because she didn't know who she was anymore, and even worse, she didn't know who her best friend was anymore.

"It wasn't supposed to happen like that," he said.

"How was it supposed to happen?" She felt thick-headed and sad. And she wanted to go lay her head down on the couch and weep, but she didn't want to do it in front of him, either. One tear was all she would forfeit. The rest were going to have to stay put.

"Are you telling me that was an accident? You bringing me dinner and taking your clothes off?"

She felt so exposed. She had given herself to him. She'd taken a risk. She'd given him sex—damned amazing sex—and he was mad at her now. Afterward, of course. Because he'd been all in when he'd been...well, all in.

How fair was that?

She'd stripped herself. Bared herself in more than one way. And he was angry?

That wasn't fair.

And that conviction heated her sadness until it had boiled over into something much more dangerous.

"Are you honestly going to complain about it?" she yelled.

"I told you…"

"I don't give a damn, Caleb. I don't give a damn what you want. Or what you told me. This was about what I wanted. I got it. I got it, and you couldn't control yourself, so don't be a little bitch at me about it."

He looked like he'd transitioned back into a mountain. "Fine. I guess you got what you came for. I hope it felt good."

"Oh, just the best," she said, getting up and stomping over to where her clothes were. "Just the best. What a great time." She forced out a laugh.

"Is that what you wanted? You wanted a good time?"

"Yeah. Why not. That's what sex is. It's supposed to be *fun*. And this isn't *fun*. And I don't know."

She looked at him, at the fury on his face, and stood there in the pit of her own making for just a moment. The despair that was growing in her chest, weighing her down like an anchor. And for the first time since all this began, she didn't know if they were going to be okay.

Because this didn't feel finished. It felt broken. She felt broken. And maybe she had been broken too many times to be fixed again.

"I'm leaving. I need to go home."

And she wasn't even going to go get Amelia. Vanessa could keep her. It was for the best.

"Ellie… You don't have to go."

"I want to go."

And without another word, she got dressed. "You can keep the casserole."

Then she walked out of the house, and it wasn't until she was in the car that she let herself dissolve completely into tears.

CHAPTER THIRTEEN

CALEB'S WORLD WAS rocked on its axis. Ellie had done that. And then she had left.

She had come into his house and subverted his control. Everything that he wanted to believe about himself, and she had shown him that he was exactly what he had always feared he was.

A breath away from betraying everything and everyone that he cared about if Ellie ever once acted like she'd wanted to taste him as badly as he wanted to taste her.

He could still feel her hair, soft and sifting through his fingers, could still feel her bare breasts pressed against his chest. Could still feel the tight, wet clasp of her body around him.

Like home.

Like heaven.

Like hell.

But she was gone.

She was running.

And maybe she *should* run. He wasn't the man for her. If he had been…well, he would have been. At some point over the years.

She'd had the best man.

And he wasn't that.

She didn't even know the half of it.

But the sex had been…

Yeah. That had been the best. He knew it had been,

for her, too. From the way she had clung to him, dug her fingernails into his shoulders, cried out her pleasure. From the shocked, frightened expression on her face when she had gathered her clothes.

This had terrified her. And he understood why.

He'd had a lot of sex. Well, more to the point, he'd had a lot of sexual partners. A whole lot more than Ellie had had—that much he knew. And he could say, without a doubt, that chemistry like that wasn't common, wasn't accidental.

He'd never felt anything like that before.

And as soon as it was finished, he craved more.

But she was gone. She was just gone, and it wasn't acceptable.

She had done this. She had done this to them both. That night out in front of the bar, when she had said that it should be him. She had done it.

And a better man would let her walk away. He knew that.

But he wasn't a better man. Maybe it was time that he accepted that.

He couldn't be. He was never going to measure up to the ideal of anyone else. Not his brothers, not Clint.

That was something that his father already knew.

After Hank had offered Clint the money for college and Caleb had…well, he'd acted out of spite, was what he'd done.

Stolen Hank's antique rifles and stashed them in Clint's truck.

When the missing guns had turned up, Clint hadn't known how to explain their presence, and Caleb hadn't said a word.

The next day Clint told him he'd refused his father's offer, not because of the situation with the guns but because he knew that Hank hadn't offered the same to Caleb.

And Caleb still hadn't said a damn thing about those guns.

And Hank had tried to believe Clint when he said he hadn't known where they came from. But things hadn't been the same.

Caleb had done what he'd set out to do. He'd put a rift between Clint and his parents, one that was forgotten in the fullness of time, and with Clint passed on from the world.

But the guilt had eaten at Caleb ever since. It had gotten corrosive when Ellie had come on the scene, and mixed up in his desire for her had always been the question of if he just wanted what his friend had.

Since then, he had tried.

He had *tried*. Tried to be the best man he could be. And a lot of that had hinged on the kind of friend that he'd been. To Clint. And since then to Ellie.

Well, tonight he hadn't exactly been the best friend.

But he'd been the best lover. And he wasn't sure he could go back to being the friend.

Which meant they had to go full steam ahead. At least, that was what he figured.

Because she was playing games. Back and forth, hot and cold. She thought that she could come to his house and take what she wanted, exactly how she wanted. No matter how many times he told her that he wasn't her toy, she wasn't seeming to understand what that meant.

He'd told her that she wasn't ready, and he hadn't realized how true that had been, but she didn't know that.

For all she knew, he was a damn psychic.

In reality, *he* hadn't been ready. Not for this.

But it was too late, and that was her fault.

He grabbed his keys and put his cowboy hat on his head, still buckling his belt as he got into his truck and began to drive in the direction toward her house.

It was possible that she was going to pick Amelia up, and then he was going to have to be very careful about the content of their conversation.

But no, Ellie had been upset. She had an evening of babysitting. Plus, going over to Vanessa and Jacob's house would necessitate telling them exactly what had happened.

Though he had a feeling that Vanessa was privy to what was going on, all things considered. Ellie probably would still avoid going back and explaining herself, especially considering how upset she was.

It was a strange realization that he knew that. That he knew it down to his bones, and didn't even question it as he continued on the winding road that would take him to her little farmhouse.

He had never known a woman he was sleeping with to this degree.

He had never wanted to. Not since her.

A pang shot through him, reverberated in his teeth, and he clenched his jaw shut. He didn't like that. Didn't like that all this *stuff* seemed to exist just below the surface.

All these *feelings*.

But maybe it was just because there was no escaping the history.

That moment when he'd first seen her, that had felt a lot like love at first sight. The slow-growing death of that hope, until he finally had to kill it off completely.

The mistake he'd made letting himself get close to it, tricking himself into believing that emotional intimacy wasn't as bad as physical intimacy. That it wasn't moving into territory with his friend's wife that he had no business being in at all.

When he pulled into the house, her car was already there, the light on in the front window of the farmhouse. Yeah. She was home.

He parked and stomped up the porch, and it took every ounce of his self-control not to simply barge in.

But he still had some civility, and he was going to go ahead and employ that. For now.

He knocked.

And he waited.

She knew who it was. He had no doubt about that. It was why it took her so long to come to the door. But she did. Eventually, it cracked slightly, and her wary blue eye appeared through the crack.

"I thought it was you," she said.

"You didn't have to open the door," he said.

"That would be childish."

"Storming out of my house wasn't childish?"

"We had a fight," she said, opening the front door wide and standing to the side.

He pushed in past her, his boots heavy on the wood floor. "We had sex," he said. "And you ran away."

"Because you were mean," she said.

"Because I already told you that I wasn't going to be used by you, and that's exactly what you did."

"No," she said, flinging her hands wide. "I wasn't... using you. It's just that I..."

"You weren't using me? Really? So you didn't get what you wanted then have a fit because you couldn't control the entire thing? Every feeling? You didn't come in and seduce me when you knew full well..."

"Oh, shut up. It's not like you don't have any self-control. You didn't have to let me seduce you. You wanted it."

"Maybe I did," he said. "But I also knew that it would be a disaster, and I tried to warn you."

"Well, I'm not the keeper of the sex. You engaged," she pointed out. "Enthusiastically, I might add."

"And then you got upset."

"I don't know what to do with this," she said, shaking her hands. "I don't know what to do with these feelings. This is not *sex* to me."

"You came, Ellie. That much I know."

"Yes," she said, her eyes widening. "I did. And I… It made me want to cry. It did make me cry. I don't feel normal anymore. I feel like I've been hollowed out, and I just want to be filled. By you. And I don't even mean that in a physical, dirty way. Except, I kind of do. And I don't know what to do with any of this. Because this isn't something that I… I didn't want this."

"What is this exactly that you didn't want?"

"I didn't want to do this. I didn't want to draw comparisons. Because it's not fair. To anyone. Not to you, not to Clint, not to me."

Well, he didn't want her to do it, either, but he couldn't stop her from talking. Because he couldn't think of a damn thing to say. And then she went on.

"But I was a different person than I am now when I met him." She looked up at him, her expression bleak. Sad. "All I knew about relationships was people chasing other people. My mother chasing men, me chasing my mother. She wasn't enough for them. I wasn't enough for her. And I was sick of it. Sick of it as a daughter and determined to never, ever be that as a woman."

She shook her head. "I didn't know how to smile. I didn't know how to laugh. I'd never been on a date because I didn't want to get derailed from my life. I didn't want to fall in love and get married. But he made me laugh. And kissing him made me smile. And he made me want to do things with a man that I'd never wanted to do before. And he made them fun. He made me laugh even when we were naked, and that was a shock to me. I didn't think anything about love could be fun, but he made it fun. And that's what I thought…that's what I thought sex was. I thought for me, it could just be fun. That's what he showed me, that relationships didn't have to…"

"Are you saying that wasn't fun?" *Fun* really was a bad word for it. Nearly getting your head blown off couldn't be described as fun.

"Am I laughing?" she asked.

"No. But it felt good."

"Yes," she said. "It did. I've never felt anything like that. Sex has never been… It's certainly never been all-consuming for me. Not like that. I don't know if I like it."

"Why?" Even though he couldn't deny what she was saying. It was true. What they'd experienced together wasn't like anything else he'd experienced before.

But he wanted it. He craved it. He had been trying to be a stand-in for her all this time. And he had just now become conscious of it. Trying to hang back and be the best man. Trying to take care of her, be solicitous and gentle and caring, and everything that Clint had been for her.

But that had been who Clint was.

And Ellie had needed him. She had made that abundantly clear. Clint had been the man that she had needed in order to fall in love.

But if she wanted to have screaming orgasms and get sweaty in bed, maybe he was the man that she needed.

And maybe she wouldn't end up laughing when they were in bed together, but she would sure as hell come.

"I'm not Clint," he said.

"Yes," she said dryly. "That is basically the thesis of the conversation."

"I never have been. But I've been trying. I've been trying to be what I thought you might need, because he was my best friend and I know that he would have wanted you to continue to be taken care of in the way that he did it. But I can't. But I can give you this. I'm not a particularly good man, but I am very good in bed."

She swallowed hard, and then drifted away from the door, wandering into the living room and sinking down on the couch. "Why don't you think you're a good man, Caleb?"

Because I hated your husband sometimes as much as I loved him. And because I did act on something, not just think it.

But he didn't say that. He couldn't.

"I'm fine," he said. "But like you said. Clint came into your life and he made you laugh. He was the missing piece that you needed right when you needed him, and I am afraid that I might take a whole lot more from you than I can give. Hell, it was you that gave to me, remember?"

"Right. But we just established that you've taken care of me for the past few years. And that is something that a good man does."

"Maybe. But that's also not all of me. This is me. And you're not sure if you particularly like it."

"I'm not sure if I particularly like me. That's different."

"You don't need to compare me to Clint. I already do. I grew up with him. And I loved him like a brother. And my parents loved him like a son. Like a better son than me. It was a different time, and my dad did not understand that I was dyslexic. You know I didn't understand that until you talked to me about it. Until you gave me some information about it. I didn't know. And my dad just figured that I wasn't trying. And I sank right into that. I just… I just quit trying. I did what I could to make those situations mine. I didn't even make an effort to do schoolwork. Not when I knew I couldn't get good grades. And then when… When my dad offered Clint all that money to go to school, and he didn't offer it to me, Clint didn't take it."

Ellie looked down at her hands. "He didn't… He didn't tell me about this."

Caleb laughed, but he didn't feel like anything was funny. "He wouldn't, would he? My dad offered to pay for Clint to go to school. But he didn't take it, Ellie. Because he couldn't do that to me. He sacrificed his whole future because he didn't like the way that my parents compared us. And I was bitter. I was jealous."

And he'd acted on it. Then Clint had turned out to be a better man than Caleb had given him credit for. And for what? So he could go on and fight fires and die?

Even with what had happened, his jealousy had not faded over time. When Clint had shown up with the woman that he had suddenly, violently wanted more than anything else.

And even that… Even that, Caleb had questioned.

Had he really wanted Ellie? Or did he just want something that his friend had?

He knew later that he wanted her. That it was about

her and not Clint at all. But for a while, he'd wrestled with that. Really and truly.

"Well, then, Clint didn't want to go to college that much," Ellie said.

"What?"

"You know him. He was a good guy, but I don't think he was that self-sacrificial down to his core. If he had really wanted something, he would have gone to you and talked about it. He would have made sure it didn't hurt you, but if he'd really wanted to go…"

"It doesn't matter," Caleb said, cutting her off. "He did that for me. The fact of the matter is that I held him back in life."

"You didn't."

"Ellie, he's dead because he became a firefighter and not…a lawyer. Or a doctor."

"Oh, come on," she said. "Do you think that he ever would have become a lawyer or a doctor? He would have hated that. Clint did not want a desk job. He wanted to be out there with you. And I don't blame you. I don't blame Jacob for not taking the call that morning, even though I know for a long damn time he wished that I would. I'm not going to poison my life blaming the most important man in my…"

She cut herself off, her expression softening. "Caleb, I'm not going to blame you for his death. I'm sorry if you want me to. I'm sorry if that would somehow help you come to terms with the fact that you shouldn't be here, and he should be, or whatever twisted, mixed-up game you're playing in your head. But I'm not going to help."

Tension rolled over him, a slow tightening of his muscles, his stomach. He couldn't breathe through her. Through these feelings she created in him. And he got down on his knees in front of her, cupping the back of her head and drawing her down toward him. She gasped, their mouths a scant inch from each other's.

"I fantasized about you. Do you know that?"

She blinked, and then she looked away.

"No," he said. "You look at me. I fantasized about you while you were with him. I knew that he had sacrificed going to college for me. And I wanted you. His woman. I used to think about what you looked like naked. I used to touch myself at night and I thought about you. What do you think that makes me?"

She drew in a shuddering breath. "I don't know."

"Did you ever think about me, Ellie?"

She looked stricken and pulled back, and he knew that he had crossed the line. But something in him felt compelled to do that. Because if they could make it through this, if they could make it out the other side, as friends or anything else, then he would know that she could handle him. Otherwise, it was just going to be all this…crashing into each other and retreating, and *that* he couldn't bear. Not anymore.

"Caleb," she protested, "let's not do this."

"If we don't do it now, when will we do it?"

"Never."

"I can't do never. So," he said, "let's do it. Let's get it out. That's me. That's the ugly inside me, and it's all for you, El. Do you have any for me?"

She swallowed hard, her throat working. "When you took me riding that time. Up on the ridge… I'm not blind, Caleb. I know that you're an attractive man. I thought you were good-looking. But I…I didn't even want to have one relationship, let alone ever get involved with my best friend."

"You mean your boyfriend's best friend?"

"No," she said. "I mean *my* best friend. You became my best friend so fast, Caleb, and yes, part of me didn't quite know what to do with that. That I was dating Clint, and then there was you. And you were beautiful, and I wanted to be around you. But it was different. It was always different. I was with him. And just because I thought about what it might be like to kiss you…"

"Tell me about that," he said, digging his fingers into her hair and keeping his hold tight. "Tell me about wanting to kiss me."

"I told you. On the horse ride. We had known each other for a couple of years."

"Yeah. I remember."

"I just… I had this crazy thought that… I could live a whole different life. If I kissed you, that things would change, and maybe that would be something that I wanted. And then I realized, that's probably what my mother did every time she got in a relationship with a different man. For what purpose? To chase someone who might not even want her? Because something felt stagnant with the other one, because it felt a little bit too deep. Because at that point… I knew he was going to ask me to marry him. I knew he was. And I knew that I should marry him. But it scared me. Because it wasn't what I thought that I wanted for my life." She met his gaze, obstinate. "I'm glad that I married him. And I didn't think about kissing you. Not after that."

"Never?" he pressed.

She looked defiant and then spoke slowly. Softly. "When we used to sit on this couch, and I used to give you lessons, I thought how lucky some woman would be to kiss you. To kiss your mouth. But I knew that it was never going to be me. Because I'd made my choices. I would never, ever have been unfaithful to my husband."

"And I would never have been with my friend's wife. Which is why I had to run away from you. But you're right. You're not his wife. Not anymore. And this is not what you had with him. And it isn't going to be. So I guess the question is… Can you handle it? Because I'm not going to tone it down, and I'm not going to give you that light fun thing that you thought you were going to get. You were lying to yourself, Ellie, if you ever thought that you were going to control me that way. If you ever thought that you were going to turn me into a replacement for him. I'm not him. I'm a different man. And you know it. You sensed it back then."

She lowered her face, her cheeks coloring with shame, and he had a moment's guilt for forcing her to admit that she wanted him before, but that guilt was replaced by a blooming, satisfied heat that flowed all through his body.

"I'm scared," she said. "I just wanted to fill spots on a list. I just wanted to… I wanted to move forward. I wanted it to be familiar. I wanted it to take me back to who I was before he died. But it isn't going to happen, is it? I'm never going to be her. Ever again. I'm stuck being this person who feels all these things, so deeply, and I never did before. Before Clint, I just studied. I was going to change my life. Change my future. I was going to do it myself, and I wasn't going to care about anyone, and then I met him. He showed me this beautiful side to myself. I can't find it. Not anymore. Everything hurts. Wanting you hurts. Loving Amelia hurts. Thinking about the future hurts. And it's all so deep. These feelings. And I don't…"

"It's too late," he said, leaning in, his mouth almost touching hers. "It's too late for us to go back, and you know that."

She lifted her hand, put it on his chest. "But we have to someday. Because this can't…"

"I know," he said. "Right now?" He brushed her hair back, tucking a gold strand behind her ear. "Tell me that you think if I walk away right now you won't think about kissing me ever again."

"I can't do that," she said.

"So there you have it, Ellie. The box is open. And the dark, ugly things are already spilling out. Like you said. This is not what you thought it would be. But it is what it is. You can't go around the dark woods, Ellie. You gotta go through them. You can go through with me if you want."

A tear slid down her cheek, and he expected her to pull away again. And then she closed the distance between them and the flames consumed them.

CHAPTER FOURTEEN

As soon as her lips touched his it was as if she had transferred the control. That moment of agreement between them had been her, giving it over to him. Surrendering.

Because he was right. The box was open.

And she didn't know… She didn't know if she liked any of the things that were being stirred up inside her. But the fact of the matter was the past few years had been like being frozen. She had done things. She had moved on and forward because that was what you had to do. And she had relentlessly looked at as many good things that she possibly could. Because she had to.

She had Amelia.

And that meant she couldn't wallow. Not in her grief, not in her misery and not in her uncertainty about her personal future.

That was what this was. Caleb. This was about her. About her being a woman, and while she had luxuriated in that in part right in the beginning, she also realized now that it was one reason it was so difficult.

Because this wasn't about a greater good, wasn't about doing something she knew she needed to do—getting back to work, raising her daughter, giving her a happy life.

This was about her. All of the extra things in her own life that went beyond survival.

About filling in the holes that her husband had left behind.

Not about replacing him, but about fully and truly acknowledging that he wasn't here.

And maybe that was why it was hard.

Except when her eyes connected with Caleb's glittering blue ones, she knew that it was more complicated than that. And from the blinding moment she was enraged at him for making it more complicated. For forcing her to admit that she'd felt something between them before.

She had rationalized it, justified it and not spent a whole hell of a lot of time thinking about it.

Because of course, he was a handsome man. She had never pretended he wasn't a man. Ever.

And when she had been younger and not married yet, he had been sort of fun and dangerous to be around. Because there was something a little bit exciting about being alone with him, even though she would have never done anything.

There was ample proof that they would never have done anything. Because it had taken them both being single, and years separate from the grief of losing Clint, for them to pursue this simmering attraction between them.

So there was no point marinating in an idea that they might be bad people because of momentary pops of electricity they'd never acted on.

But she didn't want to think about that. Not anymore. She didn't want to think about anything but what was happening between her and Caleb, about how much she wanted him, even though she'd had him less than an hour ago.

This was…not at all what she'd wanted it to be. Not at all what she thought it would be, or even could be.

And for a moment, as their kiss sparked between them, like a dangerous fire getting ready to rage out of control, she wondered if that was the real reason she hadn't kissed him that day they'd gone up riding.

That something in her had sensed it would be *this*.

And oh…as terrifying as it was for twenty-eight-year-old Ellie, nineteen-year-old Ellie would have died on the spot.

What would he have been like *then*? A young man, full of all this intensity.

He could have been that obsession.

And the girl she had been… She would have run away screaming.

Caleb had always been handsome. She remembered clearly how handsome he'd been back then, softer-faced, less hair on his body. Those blue eyes had always been mesmerizing, to every woman who had ever come around him.

But the Caleb he was now…

He was lethal.

And she was woman enough to handle it. She'd walked through some fires, through some trials, and come out strong enough to handle this wrought iron man with broad shoulders, deep chest and beard that left scratch marks on her skin. With strong hands that might just leave a trail of bruises from holding her so tight.

She would've said she didn't want it. Back then.

But she might just need it now.

And she knew. Knew this time going in that she wasn't going to laugh. That it was going to rock her, down to her core. And somehow, it didn't frighten her.

Somehow, she wanted to press on.

She was so glad it was him.

Because no other man could carry her through this dark forest. None but the man who had to go through it with her. The man whose life was linked to hers, to her pain in such a way.

But suddenly, this wasn't about pain. It wasn't about grief. It wasn't about the past or the future. It all burned away, caught up in the passion that was igniting between them.

He pulled her down off the couch and then stood, lifting her up, and she wrapped her legs around his waist in order to keep from sliding to the ground.

A thrill raced through her as he backed her up, pressing her against the wall, rocking his hips forward.

She could remember feeling jealous when—a few months ago—Vanessa had told her that she and Jacob had lost control and had sex against the wall.

Ellie had *never* had sex against a wall.

She'd never even been fully able to imagine the kind of insanity that might entice a person to do it.

But *oh*, she did now.

And it wasn't comfortable. The wall was hard and a little cold. But Caleb was hot and the delicious, beautiful kind of hard at her front.

It was…all-consuming, intense, insane.

But she wanted to tear his clothes from his body so that she could see him, so that she could touch him. So that she could taste him.

She wanted her mouth on him. All over him. But she wanted him in her, maybe even more, and she couldn't seem to breathe or speak around it.

He kissed her, down her neck, down her collarbone, tugging at her shirt. She helped him, ripping it up over her head, struggling as her shoulder blades pinned the thin fabric to the rough wall behind her. She wiggled, managing to jerk it up over her head, and flung it so that it landed over the banister of the adjacent staircase.

He yanked her bra down, exposing her breasts, the band and underwire digging into her ribs. But she didn't care. He licked her breast, sucked her nipple into his mouth, a satisfied groan on his lips.

"Take me," she whispered. "Here. Now."

She didn't know who that woman was, making hot, breathy demands of him.

"No," he refused. She clawed at his back and he grabbed hold of her wrists, gathering them in one hand and pinning them up over her head, his hold bruising, arousing.

And he kissed her, kept on kissing her. Kissed her until she thought she would die. Deep and hot licks against the inside of her mouth that made her shake and shudder. Made her feel hollow and aching, desperate with her need of him.

She rocked forward, trying to bring that hard part of him against the center of her need, but he managed to stay angled just enough that he denied her.

This wasn't *fun*.

It could never be considered *fun*.

Not when it felt like he was denying her basic survival.

Then he bit down on her neck where it was sensitive and raw from how close her blood was flowing to the surface of her skin, from the scrape of his whiskers, and she cried out.

"Please," she begged.

"I want a bed," he growled, nuzzling against her jaw. "I want to spread you out in front of me and eat you all up."

And then he pulled her away from the wall and began to carry her up the stairs. The very same stairs she used to often carry her daughter up to bed, and there was something sharp and real about that. About the invasion of this man in her home, in her life.

It had been one thing to go to Caleb's new house, a house that had no memories, no baggage, and climb on his lap there, to ride them both into oblivion in a place that carried no weight or sense of their lives.

But here…

Even Caleb had climbed the stairs countless times, but never carrying her. Never with her in his arms, restless and needy.

The destination had never been her bedroom.

This was *real*.

This change in what they were. This change in her, what she needed and what she was going to accept.

She wanted to pull away from it, because it was so deep, so intense.

And then they were at the threshold of her bedroom.

The edge of the woods.

And he took that step inside, momentous and huge, and yet so easy for him.

As she didn't want to turn back. Didn't think they could.

This time he stripped her clothes off her. She wasn't in control. Not of how fast it went, not of what she revealed. He took her pants first, and then her underwear, her bra still shoved down beneath her breasts, and it seemed a very strange and male order of operations that she couldn't think about once he had his hand down between her legs, his rough, clever fingers teasing a response from her that rippled from the inside out.

He stood back, pulled his T-shirt over his head, and her throat went dry.

Yes, she had been aware of his body for some time. But looking at it as she did now—as her own personal playground, which she was allowed to climb on—was different. Very different.

She watched as he slowly undid his belt buckle, and she clenched her thighs together, waiting for a sight of him, yet again. It was thrilling to see Caleb naked, and she let herself fully marinate in that.

In the forbidden nature of watching her friend undo his jeans and push them, along with his underwear, down to the floor. Of her friend, intensity lighting up his blue eyes, advancing on her.

Looking more like a predator than he did like the man that she had shared countless dinners with. The man who'd given her the hardest news of her life. The man who'd held her while she'd wept. Who'd held her hand while she'd brought her daughter into the world.

He was nothing like that man at all. And it should scare her, but it didn't.

She liked it.

She wanted to be hunted by him.

She wanted to surrender to it.

And she didn't know what that was, those feelings.

She had known desire, but it wasn't dangerous like this.

Wasn't all-consuming.

This had taken her and transformed her into a creature she didn't even recognize. One who was ready to beg for his body.

She scooted to the edge of the bed, reached out and put her hands on his thighs, angling her head and sliding her tongue along his length, reveling in his flavor—salt and musk and Caleb.

It turned her on so much to put her lips on him there, to put her tongue on him.

He gripped her hair, holding her tight. "I said I wanted to taste you," he said.

"But I want you," she said. "Indulge me in a fantasy?"

That seemed to undo him. He shuddered, some of the tension going out of his body as he relaxed his hold on her, and she angled her head to swallow him whole.

He was a large man, and she couldn't quite take all of him, but she used her fist as best she could at his base to hold him steady as she pleasured them both this way.

She felt the muscles in his thighs begin to shake, and then he moved her away from him, lifted her and laid her back on the bed. He came down on the mattress below her, wrapped his arms around her legs and jerked her forward, leaving her completely open to him, spread out, and before she could protest, he lowered his head and began to feast on her with an intensity that rocked her.

She reached up, grabbing hold of her headboard and holding on tight while Caleb, her Caleb, consumed her.

She looked down just as he looked up, and familiar blue eyes collided with hers while he was doing…that.

She shuddered, digging her heels down into the mattress as the beginnings of her release started cresting. And he finished her off when he pressed one finger inside her as he continued to pleasure her with his mouth.

She arched off the bed, her body drawing tight like a bowstring before releasing. Hard.

But he didn't stop. He pushed her over the edge into some kind of blinding space where she could do nothing but tremble and gasp incoherently. Until she could do nothing but surrender to wave after wave of sensation that she thought might never end. That she thought might destroy her completely.

But it wasn't done. He kissed her hip bone, kissed his way up her body, pressed himself between her legs and moved his hot, heavy flesh between her slick center.

She moaned, arching into him, not sure how in the world she wanted more when he had just given her a release unlike any she'd ever experienced before.

He cursed, lowering his head against hers, breathing hard. "Please tell me you have condoms."

"Yes," she said, wiggling out from underneath him, getting off the bed, her knees buckling. "My legs don't work."

"Good."

She turned around and saw him looking at her, a satisfied smile on his face. Then he got up off the bed. "Point me in the direction of the condoms," he said.

"There's a new box sitting on the bathroom counter. I had just grabbed a couple before coming over to your house."

He went in, and she took a moment to look at the sight of his naked body. That broad, muscular back, his perfect, beautiful ass.

And then he returned, the entire box of condoms in his hand.

And she didn't question the quantity, because if there was a limit to this thing between them, she wasn't sure they could find it.

It was like a sickness. Like a desperate hunger.

And at the moment she felt completely lost in it.

Lost in these dark woods with him and why the hell not?

He took the condom out and took care of the practicalities himself. The sight of his masculine hand holding tightly to his arousal kicked her own up several notches.

She was overcome then by the desire to watch him touch himself.

He said he'd done that while he thought of her.

Just the idea felt unspeakably dirty. Wrong.

She'd never been attracted to that kind of thing. To the forbidden.

If she'd wanted anything, it had been ease. Sweetness. Something nice.

He made her crave this deep, dark thing that she didn't even have words for.

But maybe, maybe part of that was that where she was out in her life, experiencing all the things she had, with the freedom she had, and the responsibilities, it was just thrilling to know that something could still feel that way. Illicit. Exciting.

And somewhere, in all the intensity, buried in the glittering, broken fragments of their desire for each other, was something bright and sparkly and wonderful. An oasis in the middle of the darkened woods.

He came back to her, positioning himself between her legs again as he sank into her slowly. And when he was fully seated inside her, she locked her ankles around his, clung to his shoulders. And she didn't look away from those burning blue eyes. No, she looked right into them. It was amazing. He was amazing. Every single thing about this was amazing.

Caleb, buried deep inside her, for the second time in such a short space, making her need like it had been years and not hours.

It was as sharp and hard as the last time, but now, when it broke over her, when her release took her and he pulsed inside her, when the walls came down and he shook with his release, she gave herself to it. To him.

And it was like someone had turned the key inside her and opened the door to a piece of herself she had never known existed.

And it was scary, not knowing what was on the other side.

But she was ready to walk in.

And so she clung to his shoulders and followed where he led.

CHAPTER FIFTEEN

SHE WAS ASLEEP. Her blond hair a tangle over her face.

He couldn't look away.

This was a moment that Caleb had never, *ever* let himself fantasize about.

What it would be like to lie in bed with Ellie when the passion had faded. Because this was something other than sex. But maybe… Maybe this was the friendship still.

He didn't know. This kind of blissful contentedness that made him want to sleep, but also made him want to fight against the loss of consciousness, because he never wanted the moment to end.

It was a strange thing. This deepening, shifting relationship he had with Ellie.

He'd seen her naked years ago, in the hospital when she'd been in labor, but of course he hadn't looked at her body in a sexual sense, not then. He'd seen her strength. He'd seen her as a warrior. And he'd been there to hold her hand when she'd needed it.

It had been another moment that had tightened the thread around them.

Holding her in her grief.

When she gave birth.

When she was sleep deprived and sad because she was being a mother to a newborn, and doing it all alone.

He'd cared for her needs.

And now he'd seen her naked in a whole new way. Seen her as a strong, beautiful woman. Not in sadness or pain, but in pleasure.

This was something else.

Something quiet and…content. And he and Ellie hadn't gotten a lot of content.

She shifted, and her hair tangled tighter across her face. He brushed it away, untangling her. And her blue eyes fluttered open.

"Good morning," she mumbled.

"It's not morning," he responded, looking at the sky outside.

"Oh," she said, her throat scratchy. "I thought it had to be."

"No. We've still got some time."

The corners of her lips turned up. "I don't think it's physically possible to have sex this many times in the space of a few hours."

"That sounds a lot like a challenge, Ellie."

"I mean, maybe it is," she said, her smile turning impish.

He kissed it. That smile.

"See? I'm fun," he said.

The smile turned sad. "You are. Caleb… I don't know what was going on with me. It's not you. It's me."

It felt like someone had reached inside and taken all that desire in his gut and twisted it around. And he realized that a little bit, he wanted it to be him, and not just *her*.

Wanted whatever the hell this was, whatever the hell her reaction was, to be way more about him than it was about her. He wanted her to want him, but somehow, this, even on the heels of the admission that she had wanted him before, made everything feel a little bit hollow.

"Well. Good."

She sat up and kissed his shoulder, the gentle, erotic gesture breaking through some of his thoughts.

He was just a man. And it was difficult to think with all of his blood rushing down south.

"Do you want me to make food for the Christmas tree–harvesting day?"

He blinked. "What?"

"I was just thinking." She lifted her arms up, stretching, her breasts rising with the motion, and for a moment he lost every thought he'd had in his head. And his world was only her.

"We're going to be harvesting the trees so that we can get the lot set up."

"Yeah," he said slowly, dragging his gaze up to her eyes.

"Well, I can make food." She looked impish. Like she knew exactly what he'd been looking at a moment ago.

"Sure," he said slowly. "But you know, I'm bringing in a whole crew to handle the trees that are going out into other parts of the state."

"Well, I didn't figure we would be harvesting thousands of trees. But it can be our own little party for the local lot trees."

"Yeah," he said. "I'd like that."

But *like* seemed an anemic word. He wasn't particularly sure he even *liked* it very much. Because the whole thing sounded domestic, her helping him with the ranch, cooking for him. Ellie had cooked for him a lot in the past. Then he'd cooked for her. But it hadn't been all tangled up in sex. And now it was.

"I should probably get going soon," he said.

She frowned. "You said we were going to have sex again. I was looking forward to you rising to the challenge."

That impish expression was back, her brow raised. She had her palms resting on the mattress, slightly behind her back, her breasts thrust toward him. The blanket was down around her waist.

Ellie never could tell what she was playing with. She seemed to trust him, no matter how dark the mood. But she probably wouldn't trust him if she really knew him. If she knew what he had done to Clint, and what Clint had done in response. If she understood that he was a jealous, petty asshole who would never be able to quit regretting the way that he had acted toward his friend.

Because Caleb had known. That Clint's parents didn't give a damn about him. That if his father ever did pay attention to him he had better duck and cover because he was probably swinging fists at him.

That Hank and Tammy Dalton were all the parental love he'd ever known and *still* Caleb had been so consumed by jealousy he'd tried to sabotage that for his friend.

Truly, the only good thing he had ever done was *not* take Ellie even when he'd wanted her. And the fact of the matter was, that wasn't about his strength, but about what Ellie wanted.

If he could have seduced her then, she would have never forgiven either of them.

He couldn't have done that to her.

Even feeling compelled to force her to admit that she had felt some attraction to him before had been petty. Had been wrong. Had put her in a bad position, and he'd done it anyway. To satisfy his own self, his own ego.

"I'll stay," he said.

Because he already knew what a prick he was and nothing was going to change that, so he might as well go with it.

"Vanessa and Jacob are coming here in the morning with Amelia."

"Does my brother know that we're sleeping together?"

"Well, there was no way to be all that smooth about it. I'm sure that they have guessed by now. I said that I was going over to talk to you… And that I wouldn't be by until morning. So…"

"So there's no point pretending it didn't happen."

"Well," she said. "I'm going to need to not be parading my sex life in front of my daughter." She got quiet. "Amelia loves you, Caleb. And I do, too. And more than anything else, I need to know that on the other side we are going to be okay. I think that's actually part of what scared me. I expected a certain thing when it came to sex. Because of the experiences that I've had. And because of that I thought…we'll be fine. Whatever happens between us, sex is only going to add to it, and we'll come out on the other side just fine. I mean…as friends we've weathered the death of a man we both loved dearly. And I thought if we could get through that…we can get through anything. But… I don't know what to call this thing between us. I didn't expect it to be like this. I've never felt like this. This… I don't know. Maybe it's being older…"

Suddenly, anger welled up inside him and he growled, pushing her back onto the bed, covering her.

"Maybe it's me," he said.

She looked up at him, stunned. And then she nodded slowly. "Maybe. Maybe it's you and me."

She bit her lip. "Caleb...this would have terrified me at eighteen. I could never have handled it."

He ignored the unspoken truth between them. That neither of them was certain they could handle it now.

"I can't lose you," she said, putting her fingertips against his lips. "Amelia can't lose you. We lost so much. And I just don't think..."

He kissed those fingertips, lowered her hand so it was resting on his chest. "You're not going to lose me," he said, the vow coming from inside him. Because maybe he wasn't the best, but he knew how to be there for her. "Sex is sex. And when we're finished..."

The idea of her being with another man made him want to destroy things, but he wasn't going to dwell on that, wasn't going to make an issue out of it. Because there were a couple of troops at play here. The fact she needed him—in the capacity she'd always had him, or as everything, husband, a lover, a father—was undeniable.

And he knew he couldn't do one, so he had to do the other. When she did settle down again, it would be with a man like what she'd had. Because she'd made it abundantly clear that it was a life she missed, that the person she was with Clint was a person she missed.

And this... This for them was the beginning of a separation, whether she knew it or not. Because he was the Band-Aid. As much as he was trying to pretend that he wasn't.

Once she did have another man in her life...he couldn't be around the way that he was now. And she might think that she never wanted that, but she clearly did. Because she didn't like sleeping alone, and she didn't like being alone. But he would tell her exactly what she wanted to hear. That nothing would change, even though it already had, and it was too late for it to be anything but forever shifted.

"I'll be here for you as long as you want me," he said. "I promise."

He had promised Clint.

Oh, not while his friend lay dying, because he'd been gone instantly, which was a blessing in many ways. But at the crash site, with tears streaming down his face and rage and grief burning in his gut like coals, he had promised.

Promised to take care of Clint's wife, whom he hadn't spoken to in two months because everything he felt for her was wrong. And he had told himself that he would put it all away, that he would be everything she needed.

And he had been.

He would continue to be.

And she took that promise as good enough, and kissed his mouth, and he kissed her back.

For the rest of the night they didn't talk.

But he took her up on her challenge. And by morning, neither of them had slept. And neither of them cared.

CHAPTER SIXTEEN

ELLIE WAS CONTINUALLY plotting ways to be alone with Caleb again.

She knew logistically she could sneak him up to her room at night, and Amelia would never know, but the idea of it made her feel uncomfortable.

Though there was something about that illicitness that excited her. Maybe she should chase that.

She craved him. Craved what he made her feel.

And she had been turning over the conversations they'd had on the couch, in her bed, in the days since their time together. And she had continued to do that while she worked on the food for the tree-harvesting day.

She and Vanessa had rallied the boys and were responsible for transporting them from the Dalton ranch, where their foster parents had dropped them that morning, to Caleb's ranch. They had them all loaded up, and Tammy was going to follow behind with food and Amelia. Jamie, Gabe and West were coming, as well, to help with the actual harvesting of the trees.

Jamie had absolutely refused to involve herself in any of the cooking.

She was going to use her God-given muscles and affinity for hard work.

Her words.

And Ellie may have muttered something about hard

work while sweating over a chili pot for hours the night before.

But Jamie was Jamie, and there was little point in getting bent out of shape over anything.

When they had the boys loaded in the cars, Vanessa looked up at Ellie. "Are you okay?"

"I'm great," she responded.

"Okay."

"I *am*," she insisted.

Vanessa nodded—clearly not accepting the answer, but in no real space to argue—and got in her car, and Ellie followed suit. She had Marco riding shotgun, Calvin and Joseph in the back seat.

She had probably the quietest carload, though Marco was chatty, and a bit of a smart-ass. But she didn't really mind him. But when the use of four-letter words got a little out of hand, she threatened to start giving pop quizzes.

That earned her a little bit of silence.

When they arrived at the tree farm, there were tables already set up, stations already prepared to go—which she knew was the handiwork of Caleb and his brothers.

Caleb started handing out assignments. Art supplies for Calvin, who was going to work on the tree lot signs, axes for the older boys who could be trusted, and would be cutting down trees. Under strict instruction that they would lose the axes quickly if they weren't safe.

Then there was a station with twine and netting and everything necessary for bundling the trees up for transport.

They were purposed to attack it like a barn raising, a tree cutting that would be made into lighter work by all the hands present. Marco laughed. "Literally no one would believe that this is how I'm spending my day."

"Oh, yeah?" Ellie asked.

"No way. I've never liked outdoor kind of stuff. I live in the city. I never thought…"

"You never thought what?"

"That I would like it here."

Ellie smiled at him. "People change. We see more things, do more things, go through more things, and it… It changes us."

She looked across the space, over at Caleb, who was talking with his brothers and demonstrating how to hold an ax.

He was beautiful. He really was. And somehow, she felt like she was looking at him for the millionth time and the first time all at once.

The familiarity was part of that beauty, but there was a freshness to it, too. And a deep, resonant ache that was only Caleb's.

It had never belonged to anyone else.

"I've never seen anyone change. Not really. Everybody just kind of lives their life where I'm from. You either get a job, and you work yourself in the ground, or…you hustle. To, I don't know, at least to get to something."

"Like sent to a special school out in the middle of nowhere?"

"Yeah," he said. "In my case."

"When things are hard, your options feel more limited. I know that. And I wanted… I wanted something different than what I had. I knew that. And I was good at school. Naturally. So I thought maybe if I worked really hard at it I could get myself a scholarship and change the way that I lived."

"Did it work?"

She nodded. "Yes. But it still didn't make my life easy. My husband died. Money didn't protect me from that. But money is good, and it helps with security. And that's why my life didn't fall completely apart when I lost him. I don't know. But I've had a few different times in my life where things changed whether I wanted them to or not. And I had to decide what I wanted to do in response to them. We have endless opportunities to be different. To be stronger."

"So I should just…leave my family and friends behind and end up staying here? Become a cowboy?" He laughed.

"Yeah," she said. "If you want to. Why not? Or maybe work hard to get good grades, and I'll help you find scholarships that you qualify for. I know we could find something. You don't have to be stuck. You can change if you want."

Marco looked down. "It seems stupid," he said. "I wasn't going to change because of the stupid school. I told my friends that I'd be back."

"I think sometimes the worst part is not entirely fitting in to your new life but knowing you can't go back to the old one, either. And I'm actually a lot more familiar with that than I would like to be. But you have to keep moving forward. You don't owe them a worse version of yourself, not when you know you could be something different. Not if you want it."

"Maybe. Maybe I'll take you up on that scholarship thing." He frowned. "Nobody goes to college in my family."

"Nobody did it in mine, either. Well, maybe they did. I don't know my dad, so I wouldn't know. But nobody I knew did."

He nodded slowly, then turned away from her. "I don't want to miss the ax instructions," he said.

She nodded. And she felt a strange sense of peace

wash over her. She watched him walk away and she was infused with it. She was definitely stuck. Between a change she hadn't chosen to make, and the next shift of her life. Not quite ready for either.

It was like she'd said to Caleb the other night. She missed the girl that Clint had helped her find. But she knew that pieces of her were still in there.

He had splintered her focus, and it was for the best. Because she had still gotten her degree; she was still a teacher. But she was a mother, too, and she was a woman who understood that she could want more than just a career, and still have stability and success. A woman who could have friends, who could have a lover, and not be afraid that she couldn't balance all of that. That she might slip into those patterns her mother had.

So yes, that was still there.

And she had met Marco because of it. Had started the school because of that transition, because of the need for change. And maybe his life would be different because of it, and who knew what lives he would change as a result.

You might not always choose the changes that came at you, but you could certainly make something from them.

But...

The ache. That Caleb ache.

It terrified and exhilarated her, and she couldn't turn away from it, either.

All she could do was hold on tight.

She smiled as she watched the boys work, as they spread out and began to cut trees, and Jamie directed the wrapping and the tying and the hefting of the trees into the big truck that would take them downtown.

Calvin was painting, barely overseen by Vanessa,

who trusted him at this point to take a job like this seriously and to do exactly what he'd been asked.

Her heart felt swollen. Because this was the result of her doing something decent with her pain. Of her moving forward. And following a passion. Following a different path.

She blinked, squeezing her eyes shut. "Thanks, Clint," she whispered.

Because it was the woman he'd helped make who had accomplished this. Who had made her more generous and broader-thinking.

And it was some of that money he'd left behind that had helped to pay for it, and that money had come from his thoughtfulness when it came to taking care of her.

It was Gabe who opened up his truck, turned the key partway and began blasting Christmas tunes while they all worked.

Jamie looked at him with a grouchy expression on her face, and Gabe twirled her once before going back to cutting trees.

Vanessa and Ellie helped lift a giant pot of cider onto a burner to get it going, and then they began to heat up the chili.

West worked to start a bonfire, and pretty soon the whole thing felt a lot more like a celebration than it did like work.

And Ellie gave thanks yet again. For the gift of the Dalton family, which had also come through Clint.

Amelia was delighted by the proceedings, twirling around in the designated zone that Ellie had placed her in, so that nothing potentially sharp or hot could get anywhere near her. Because as joyful as the situation was, Ellie wasn't without her standard maternal paranoia, which had come with the love and happiness her daughter had brought into her life.

A big Dodge Ram pulled up, gold-plating on the rims and around the license plate. And a hush fell over the proceedings.

And then Hank Dalton got out, holding an ax. "What? I'm here to help cut some trees."

IT HAD NEVER occurred to Caleb that his dad might show up. He had figured that Hank Dalton was sitting somewhere in silent protest of the fact that all of his boys had turned out so differently than he wanted. So in opposition to everything he'd worked for.

Though Caleb had a feeling that he respected Gabe partnering with Ellie to start a school. Yeah, that had some of that cachet that Hank would feel he had earned.

Caleb fixed his mouth into a grim line and stopped, pushing the head of his ax down into the dirt. "You here to work, Dad?"

"I figure I will," he said. "After all, this is your place. And family shows up for each other."

He couldn't even be scathing about that, because his dad, for all his flaws, did exemplify that.

He knew that Hank was changing, that he had changed. Caleb was angry about the way that things had gone down between them, but all that was water under a bridge that was more than a decade gone, and there was no reason to cling to it.

Except, sometimes Caleb damn well wanted to cling to it.

Since it had shaped his entire life, who he was and the most shameful moment in his past. But whatever.

"Thanks," Caleb said. "Start swinging an ax, then."

Hank joined in, his actions wordless, all of them chopping trees.

When the crew came out tomorrow, they would all use chain saws, but Caleb hadn't especially wanted to do that with the boys, and anyway, with a crew the size of theirs, it was easy enough to get the amount of trees they would need for the lot downtown. Gold Valley was small, and a great many of the people preferred to go out into the woods and procure their own trees anyway.

But there would be plenty of people who would come out to the town to wander around and experience the festivities of the Victorian Christmas that they had every year, to enjoy the Christmas parade and wagon rides through the streets, and they might end up going away with a Christmas tree as a souvenir. So, it was a good idea to get everything ready. And to treat the lot in Gold Valley like a viable moneymaker. Because it was.

The Christmas music was still blaring from Gabe's truck, something ridiculously light and cheesy, which seemed extra strange given the bit of tension that had settled over the proceedings.

"So you own the school?" Aiden asked Hank.

"I guess technically," Hank responded.

"How come we never see you?"

"Because I'm rich I mostly get to sit on my ass."

"Goals," Aiden said, nodding and swinging at a new tree.

"I think you just became his favorite person," Jacob said.

"Well, not totally," Aiden said. "You saved me from the side of a cliff, so it still has to be you. But you do work really hard. You probably should have gotten rich instead."

Aiden was joking, but the whole thing was so close

to their family drama that it was more bitterly funny for Jacob and Caleb than it was actually funny.

Though Jacob had always seemed relatively fine with Hank, Caleb supposed. It was Gabe who had had the most difficult relationship with him. Openly.

Caleb and Hank had a lot of their problems down beneath the surface.

But they went on quietly swinging axes together, and there was something strangely therapeutic about it. All the Dalton men out working together, even West, on bringing Caleb's vision to life. On supporting the school, and these boys.

Actually doing something good, instead of something destructive, which were issues that they had all struggled with at different times.

Well, maybe not West.

He didn't seem to struggle with much of anything beyond the anger that he felt at his ex-wife. And from everything that he'd implied to Caleb, Caleb couldn't blame him.

They worked until the pale sun was high in the sky, barely visible behind the sheet of gray cloud that had been rolled out over the blue. And when it was time to grab lunch, they all pulled up sporadic folding chairs and pieces of log, and sat around eating chili.

For his part, Caleb stood by Ellie, lingering as she served people, and waiting to eat until she started.

She looked up at him, a grin tugging at the corner of her lips. He wanted to kiss her. But he wasn't going to. Not in front of everyone. More because of Amelia than anything else. Everyone else could deal with not having their questions answered. And wondering. But not Amelia.

The little girl was sitting on a rock next to Ellie,

eating a bowl of chili that was mostly cheese and soda crackers with a tiny bit of chili underneath.

"I've missed you," she whispered.

"Good." Maybe that wasn't the nicest response, but it was honest. She had seen him every day for the past week, so if she missed him, it wasn't seeing him. It was having him in bed.

"This is great," she said. "Thank you for including the boys. This is the kind of thing that… It makes a difference. It really does."

He felt like her talking about something other than them was a deflection, but given the fact they were surrounded by his family, perhaps a deflection was necessary.

"Well, happy to make a difference in your life." And if that had two meanings, well, it was intentional.

Caleb wanted to hang on to the moment. Because there was something wonderfully simple about it. His family here, Ellie next to him. They'd had days like this countless times since Clint had died. But standing next to Ellie felt different this time. It felt like she was with him. Sex really did change things.

Because it was impossible to forget that he'd been inside her. And he didn't want to.

Unfortunately, it was also impossible for him to forget that it wasn't forever. That time was going to move on and forward and away from this moment. This moment when he was standing next to her eating chili, and everything was good and easy and peaceful. When there wasn't another man at her side. When there was nothing between them at all.

So he looked around and took in the details. The crisp rows of pine trees still rising high over the jagged stumps they'd left behind. The velvet-covered mountains awash in green, rich and dark without the intense golden light of the sun to shift the green into yellows.

The house way off in the distance, the one that was his.

It occurred to him then that right in this moment he had absolutely everything he'd ever wanted.

And Hank was here to see it.

Of course, no one knew he had Ellie in his bed, but that didn't matter. He did.

And to get that life, his friend had to die, and that was the damn worst stain over the whole thing. Like ink had touched the edge of a blank page and spread. Spread and spread, the darkness covering everything that used to be crisp and white. But the darkness was his.

So maybe he should just learn to be okay with it.

With this tarnished kingdom that he'd inherited in many ways.

Ellie looked around, then quickly brushed her fingertips against his, a small smile touching her lips, color infusing her cheeks.

He grabbed on to that and held it tight. Maybe he was selfish. But now there were no points for being anything else.

The boys were goofing around, being idiots, and one of them picked up the ax like he was going to swing it, and instead, the head fell off.

Gabe immediately launched into scolding him about safety, while Jamie sat on a stump next to her husband, looking up from her chili, a bemused expression on her face.

"I'll get another one," Caleb said, setting his own lunch down and shaking his head as he wandered off toward one of the barns.

The gravel crunched under his feet, and he looked up,

taking a deep breath. The air had that crisp edge to it that let him know that winter was well and firmly here.

But he'd never felt warmer in his life.

In spite of himself, a smile tugged at the edge of his mouth.

When he got into the barn, he heard footsteps behind him and he turned, his smile widening, expecting to see Ellie standing there.

It wasn't.

It was Hank.

"What's up, Dad?"

"This is a nice place," Hank said, pressing one weathered hand against the old, gnarled post by the door. "You must be proud."

"Yeah," Caleb said.

You must be proud.

He noticed that that was very explicitly *not* an admission that his father was proud.

"You seem happy," Hank said finally. "You seem happy here, doing this."

"I am. I chose it. I went out of my way to choose it, actually, so that should tell you that it's something I wanted."

"I could never believe it," Hank said.

"What?"

"That you boys really wanted this life. I could never believe you wanted it. I just thought you didn't want to do the kind of hard work that required you to sit your asses in a chair and think. I thought you were rebelling against me."

"Pretty damn big commitment for us to do all of this just to rebel against you."

"Well," Hank said. "Gabe basically did."

"Gabe was pretty pissed at you," Caleb reminded his dad.

Gabe had basically gone into the rodeo to prove to his dad that he couldn't control his life. When Gabe had begun slacking at school, Hank had sold Gabe's horses. And there had been nothing his brother loved more than his horses. And so Gabe had gone straight out and made horses, and falling off them, his career. Because that was who the Daltons were.

They didn't do things by half. They did them in a whole, with their middle fingers held high in the air at the person who had dared challenge them.

"Yeah," Hank said. "He was. I figured you and Jacob probably were, too."

"I don't think Jacob is pissed at anybody. No one but himself."

"Maybe not anymore. Maybe it's the same with you. Maybe this is the thing you need to be happy."

"Maybe," Caleb said. "Which you would have known if you would have listened, even once."

"I just wanted you to try." Hank shook his head.

"Like Clint?"

He shouldn't have said that. But he had. So there it was. He might as well have cut his own chest open and shown his dad everything.

"Clint didn't come from anything. He didn't have any parents pressuring him, nothing. His grades…"

"Yeah," Caleb said, gritting his teeth. Because there was Clint, from the grave and in the middle of his conversation. And that wasn't fair. Because it wasn't Clint's fault, and it never had been. That he was good, that he attracted people to him like a tractor beam. That he was smart, and that he was smart in a way that impressed

Caleb's father more than anything his three sons had ever done.

"I know that Clint's grades were amazing. And I know that mine weren't. And that's why you didn't even offer to pay for me to go to school."

"I figured it would get your ass in gear," Hank said, his tone incredulous. "College tuition ain't shit money to me. I could have paid for you, for him, for some of the neighborhood kids. But I wanted you to want it, and somehow, sometimes competing with him seems to make you do something."

"I'm dyslexic," Caleb said.

He hadn't meant to tell his father that. But really it was a secret there was no longer any point to keeping. Tied up with those secret lessons with Ellie.

Clint was gone. He and Ellie were sleeping together.

Why not throw this on out there?

Hank drew up and back. "What?"

"Do you even know what that is, Dad?"

"I know what it is. You see letters backward and things."

"Yeah," Caleb said. "But for me they moved, too. And it makes my head hurt to look at a page for too long. And to go along with that, I'm dyscalculic, and there's something called a sequencing disorder, too. That means numbers are backward, too, and I have a tough time putting things in order on the page. Do you know what that means? It means school is impossible. It means it's harder for me. And I'm not saying that to get out of anything. Hell, there's nothing for me to get out of. But I didn't know that about myself until I was about twenty-seven years old. Because Ellie saw me try to fill something out, and she recognized it. But there was no teacher that thought maybe… And you sure as hell didn't think maybe I needed help. You thought I was lazy. Even Mom thought I was lazy."

"Caleb, I didn't have a damn clue."

"No," Caleb said, "you didn't. Because you're married to your vision of what you want our lives to be, and you never stopped to ask what we wanted. Or maybe why we wanted it. The idea of going to college was torture for me. But watching you offer something to Clint that you wouldn't give me, when I knew that it was about who you thought was better, that was worse. I would rather have turned you down."

"I didn't want you to turn me down. I wanted you to ask me for help."

"Why?" Caleb said, throwing his hands wide. "Why the hell would I ever ask you for help, Hank Dalton? You didn't want to think I needed it. You wanted to tell me to use elbow grease and knuckle down. And you wanted us to do it in an arena you knew nothing about. You didn't go to college. You didn't even graduate high school."

"Yeah, because I was too busy staying home and making sure my rat bastard sperm donor didn't kill my mother and siblings." Hank shook his head. "You want to share secrets, Caleb. I have secrets. Things I didn't want to burden you boys with but I've been confronted with nothing but my failures over the past year. The ways that I messed you all up, so maybe it's time you knew."

Hank's words sent a shock wave through the empty barn. Sent a shock wave through Caleb.

"Do you think it's an accident you've never even heard me talk about your grandparents? We're not just nothing," Hank said. "We're the bottom of the barrel. My old man was scum. He used his fists, his boots, on my mother. He did it on my brothers and sisters. He damn near killed my mother more times than I can count. I didn't have the opportunity to go anywhere. Not until he got himself stabbed and killed in a bar fight. God bless the man that drove that knife through his rib cage. That's when I got to leave. And I've... I've hurt people. Because I've got... I don't know."

"PTSD?" Caleb asked.

Hank waved his hand. "Hell no, boy. I didn't go to war."

Hank all up. No excuses for bad behavior, just plenty of bad behavior.

"Sounds like you lived in the war zone."

"Whatever. It doesn't matter. I thought that money would keep us safe. Because all that stuff... The way that my father was. He would always blame it on being poor. On the money. Throwing beer bottles at my mother's head because he was stressed about the phone bill. About where the space rent for the trailer was going to come next. We were a damned cliché. And I didn't want that for you. I didn't want that for us."

He could see his parents clearly now. All the fights they'd had, and the way that Hank had always just smiled and let Tammy rail at him. Tammy, for her part, had never hit Hank. But she had lit his clothes on fire, hit his truck with a baseball bat.

And Hank had never done a damn thing. Except cheat. Constantly.

And suddenly, he saw his dad in a strange new light. As somebody who might be as twisted and damaged by his past as Caleb was. If not more so. Hell, it had to be more so. Because his parents might not have been perfect, but they were never in danger.

Hank was right. They had been insulated by the

money they'd had, never worried about being thrown out onto the streets.

But more than that, neither Hank nor Tammy had ever put them in physical danger, and never would.

Their fights might have been over-the-top, but they'd never gotten violent with each other.

And he could see now that his father's overly laid-back attitude was likely covering something inside him he was afraid might be dark. And Caleb was well familiar with being a little bit afraid of your own darkness.

A darkness that had come out when he had framed Clint for stealing those weapons. It wasn't the act itself so much as the spiderweb of implications that touched so many things. He'd known Clint had it hard, and he hadn't been able to muster up the strength to care. He'd been consumed by his own dark feelings.

That seemed to keep coming out with Ellie, with the intensity between them.

"I wanted you to be as far away from what I was as you could possibly be," Hank said. "I knew that I was something in the middle. Something better than what I left, but definitely not the best."

"Is that why you cheated on Mom?"

Hank paused for a long moment. "I've said it before, and it's true. It was always easy for me to go away and forget about home. To block everything off and remember the moment I was in, and nothing past that. To do what felt good, not what was right. That was how I spent my childhood surviving home. When I left that trailer, it wasn't there. And when I was home I was in the thick of it. So it was years of practicing that. But more than that I think… I could never accept the kind of love that your mom tried to give me. I wanted to. I wanted to be the man that she seemed to think I was. But I just…

That meant seeing something other than that boy whose dad hated him, and whose mama wouldn't leave, not even for the sake of her own children, and I had a very hard time doing that for a long time. I finally worked through some of it. We went to counseling, you know. I went to counseling."

"I know," Caleb said. "Marriage counseling."

"Oh, more than that. I went to therapy. Because that was a lot of years… A lot of patterns of behavior that I had to figure out the cause of. But I never did make myself perfect, and I made a hell of a lot of mistakes both in my marriage and with you. And it's hard for me still to admit it. Because I'm just still not perfect, dammit."

Caleb gritted his teeth. "No one needed you to be perfect, Dad. Just a little bit less of an inflexible bastard."

"Here I am at the end of my life…"

"That's dramatic, Hank. I don't think you're at the end of your life."

"In comparison to where you're at, I am. So here I am, standing at the end of everything, and I'm damned lucky to have a wife that stuck with me, to have kids that still speak to me, hell, and surprise kids that come and speak to me. Probably some of that because of the money. But I don't even care. Because I made so many mistakes I should be standing here alone in a big-ass house with money and no one around me. But I'm not. Because of your mother."

Caleb paused and then looked his father square in the eye. "But you're mad at her about hiding West's identity."

"That's complicated, too." He cleared his throat. "I always thought your mother was perfect."

Again, Caleb thought of his mother lighting things on fire and hitting trucks with baseball bats. "Perfect?"

"She had a temper. Still does. But she forgave me every single time. She was my touchstone. Patient with me until I got my stuff together. A great mother to you boys. And finding out that even she wasn't immune to…"

"The same kind of petty behavior that you engaged in?"

"Yes," Hank said.

"Well, that's not really fair. Mom doesn't exist to be your angel, Dad. She's just a woman. And that makes the fact she forgave you all those times even more remarkable."

"I expect that's so," Hank said, letting out a long, slow breath. "I didn't mean to make you boys feel stuck. I meant to give you freedom. But I pushed you toward what felt like freedom to me. And I'm sorry."

Caleb took a breath. And he realized it was a decent time to tell his dad about Clint and the guns. To confess his own darkness, and his own part he played in that, but he couldn't bring himself to. He couldn't bring himself to speak it out loud.

It wasn't like even though it had been such a big deal all those years ago, that Ellie would never forgive him, or that Hank would disown him. But the fact was, it exposed the truth about himself that he didn't necessarily want to reveal.

He was comfortable saying he wasn't Clint, that he couldn't live up to it, and it was true.

But he wasn't comfortable with the details.

"It's a good ranch," Hank said finally. "It's a good life. God knows we had a good one. It would have been better if I could have just…"

"Been perfect?" Caleb asked.

"Yeah," Hank responded.

"Sure. But you weren't."

He didn't say it as an accusation, just with acceptance, and Hank seemed to understand that.

"I better bring the ax back out."

"Sure," Hank said. "Let's go chop down some more of your trees."

And Caleb could only marvel for a moment that just five minutes ago he'd thought his life was in a pretty optimal spot. But suddenly, he understood his dad a little bit better, and his dad seemed to understand him.

In this moment… Well, this moment somehow managed to make things even better.

And he was going to cling to that for as long as he could.

CHAPTER SEVENTEEN

THE FIRST WEEKEND of the Christmas tree lot was set to coincide with the Gold Valley Christmas parade. The parade was a big event, bringing people in from many surrounding areas. Gold Valley made sure their time complemented the parade that would be happening over at Copper Ridge, along with the events, so that tourists could feasibly pass between both, sampling candied nuts, coffee, cheeses and any number of other local delicacies while also enjoying the picturesque main streets of both towns.

Caleb, for his part, couldn't remember the last time he had come into town for the Christmas parade. Though, technically, he supposed he wasn't here for the parade. He was here to sell trees. But still.

From his position at the corner lot, they had an ideal view of the parade, and as much as Marco and Aiden, his first shift workers, were pretending that they didn't care about it, he could tell that they were mildly interested.

It was tough to be a teenage boy. He remembered that well. Because you were still very much a boy, desperate to prove that you might be a man, with a whole lot of the desires that men had swirling around inside you. But sometimes that hollow, deep longing existed inside a boy, to run wildly and not care what anyone thought, to enjoy the parade, to not be cynical about Christmas.

He could see that war playing out over them now.

Just a damn sucky part of growing up, really.

But then…he looked over at Ellie, who was setting up some little chairs at the edge of the lot so that Amelia could get a good view of the parade. Yeah, sometimes being a grown-up wasn't so bad. Because he could act on his feelings. The kind of feelings that a man had.

Most important, he knew what to do with a woman.

Yeah, sometimes his knees hurt after a day of hard labor, and his muscles had been pretty sore after all the tree chopping. But he would take that any day over being a fumbling teenage boy who didn't know how to take off a bra.

He was a man who knew what to do with his hands and knew what to do with Ellie's body. And he was pretty damned glad of that.

Amelia got out of her chair and wandered over to where Marco and Aiden were. She looked up at them, an earnest expression on her face.

Caleb shot Ellie a look, asking nonverbally if he should intervene. Ellie shook her head.

"Are you going to watch the parade?" Amelia asked.

"We're working," Marco said gravely.

Amelia wrinkled her nose. "You should watch some of the parade. There are a lot of horses."

"Horses are cool," Aiden said, nodding, shoving his hands in his pockets.

Caleb bit back a grin. Yeah, it didn't matter how tough you thought you were; if a little girl wanted to talk to you about horses, you had to talk to her about horses. And right then, Caleb felt for sure that Marco and Aiden were going to be all right.

"Yeah," Marco agreed. "Cool."

"I brought my favorite one," Amelia said, lifting a

small plastic horse with disheveled pink hair and waving it in front of them. "She's going to say hi to the big horses."

"Very cool," Aiden said.

"Yeah. Very cool."

Clearly, neither boy had any idea how to talk to a child, but they were sure trying.

Caleb looked back over at Ellie, who was doing her best to bite back a very wide smile.

"Bye," Amelia said. "I'm going to watch the parade."

And then she turned away from Marco and Aiden, clearly done with that discussion. She paused in front of Caleb and reached out, wrapping her hand around three of his fingers. "Are you going to come sit with us, Caleb?"

Something tugged in his heart. "In a minute, squirt. I'll sit for a while. But we're working. We're selling the trees."

"No one is going to buy trees during the parade," Amelia said, clearly not understanding why anybody would ever do something when the parade was going on.

"Well, if you're right, I'll come sit."

She let go of his hand and bounced back to where Ellie was sitting, all energy and cheer with her pale blond hair, striped leggings, boots and bedraggled fairy skirt.

He would say he didn't think about kids much at all, that he didn't even particularly like them. That little girl, though… He'd die for that little girl. He'd kill for her.

He hadn't ever really wanted to be a father. Mostly because his relationship with his own dad was so messed up.

But then, the only time he'd ever really had feelings

for a woman, it had been Ellie. And that had been impossible. So he had stuck to his whole plan of never getting married.

Looking at Amelia and Ellie sitting together, their matching blond hair bright in the gray light filtering through the cloud cover, it was so easy to pretend that they were both his.

He had been there when Amelia was born. He'd watched Ellie labor to bring her into the world, and he'd seen her take her first breath. There wasn't another kid on the face of the earth he was more connected to than her.

But he wasn't her father.

And he had never even let himself wish that he was. But something was happening to him now, something related probably to the change in his relationship with Ellie, and it made his chest feel scraped raw inside.

It made him wish he could sit right alongside them, complete the picture. Make a family.

That was messed up. It was all messed up.

Amelia wasn't his. She was Clint's.

That was how it had to be. That was how it was.

He was backup, and he was pretty damned good at that. But there would be a man who married Ellie someday, and he wouldn't be backup. He would be the real deal. And it would be up to Caleb to make sure that Amelia didn't forget who her father had been.

He told her a lot of stories about Clint, from the time she was too young to remember, when they were driving between the ranch and her home. She liked to hear the stories, and he was never sure if she fully realized that the man they were talking about was her dad, or if he had become something of a favorite storybook character to her. But either way, she had some sense of who he was, and that was important to him.

He knew it mattered to Ellie, too. And it was just another thing that he had taken to making sure he did.

Right. Except all this other stuff. It getting all tangled up. And you wishing that you could step right into that empty space that he left. For what reason? To be standing next to her, but not as good as she had? To be basically half the dad that he would've been?

He gritted his teeth and pushed that thought away and turned his focus to the lot.

The president of the Gold Valley Rotary was giving a speech, but the words were muffled at the distance they were down the street, and he went ahead and ignored it while he and the boys organized cash drawers, little electronic squares to swipe cards—which he had been informed by Jehoshaphat was the best way to make money, since nobody carried the real stuff anymore—and counted up trees, just to make some busywork.

But Amelia was right, and while the parade was running, they didn't really get any business, so Caleb made his way over to where Ellie and Amelia were sitting and plopped down on the edge of the curb. Amelia smiled at him, got out of the chair and joined him down on the ground.

"What are you doing?" he asked.

"Sitting with you," she said like he was the most ridiculous human being on the planet.

"But the ground is hard," he said.

She shrugged. "It's not bad."

She rested her chin in her hands, her fingertips dimpling her cheeks as she turned her attention to the parade route with the kind of intense seriousness only a child could give to anything.

The Girl Scout troop was first, all dressed as cookies, carrying banners and handing out candy. Amelia rushed forward and took a piece from one of the adorable cookies, before rushing back.

"Do you want to be a Girl Scout?" Ellie asked.

Amelia frowned. "No. Because then you have to give candy away. I just want to get candy."

Caleb's head fell back and he laughed. "You're smart," he said.

"I am," Amelia agreed, unwrapping her candy happily.

He couldn't help but grin because the pure honesty in that kid was something else. Something he wished like hell a person could keep through adulthood. Before what you should do became bigger than what you wanted.

Oh, to have that simplicity.

If Ellie could have been the piece of candy he'd wanted.

Sorry you got there first, buddy. But she's mine and I want her.

But Ellie hadn't been candy. And Caleb and Clint hadn't been kids.

Ellie had been Clint's wife. And so Caleb had…done what a decent man needed to do. Not what a kid who wanted something sweet might do.

He pushed that out of his mind and tried to focus on the moment, on the parade.

Amelia got up and danced with the intertribal dance group that went by next, and then kept on dancing through the Scottish Heritage Society and their bagpipes.

Then she sat down, this time settling herself on Caleb's knee, leaning her head back against his shoulder for the rest of the event.

He took a breath, trying to get in air around all the sharp feelings in his lungs. He looked over at Ellie, who was watching them with a sad and wistful expression on her face.

He cleared his throat and looked back at the parade, watching as the fire trucks went by, which seemed to enliven Amelia again.

By the time it was finished, she seemed tired and hungry.

"Want me to take her down to Mustard Seed to get her something to eat?" Caleb asked.

"Your mom is coming to pick her up." Ellie looked down at her phone. "She'll be here soon."

"You don't have to stay," he said.

"Well," she said. "The boys are kind of my responsibility."

They looked over at the boys, who were currently standing like posts at the front of the lot, like they were ready to beat anyone up who came near the cash box.

"They're taking it pretty seriously. I think they'll be fine. Anyway, I'm paying them, so they have incentive."

"Are you trying to get rid of me?"

His heart kicked. "No," he said. "I'm never trying to get rid of you."

"Well, then, let me arrange it how I want."

They were both stubborn. A little bit too stubborn for their own good.

He thought again about what she had said. About Clint, and how he made her a more relaxed person. About how he made her someone lighter. And he wasn't entirely sure they did that for each other.

Because he didn't have that kind of laid-back attitude, where he shrugged things off and chuckled about it.

No, he and Ellie seemed to just go toe-to-toe, neither one of them knowing when to back down, even on things that didn't really matter. He wasn't trying to get rid of her; he was just trying to make sure she knew that she didn't have to stay.

His mom showed up about a minute later, gave him a hug and left the imprint of her pink lips on his cheek and the scent of her perfume lingering on his jacket collar. But it was his mom, so he was going to be a man about it and not complain.

Then she took Amelia by the hand. "I'm going to take her to Sugar Cup. Is it okay if she gets a treat?" Tammy asked.

"Sure," Ellie said, smiling. "Have fun."

"You know," Ellie said. "If it weren't for your mom… she wouldn't have any experience of a grandmother at all. And your dad is even sweet to her. They really are her grandparents, Caleb."

For some reason that made him feel…not so great. Because somehow it reminded him of how all those pieces seemed to fit together and didn't much require him. The way that Clint had been like a son to his parents, the way that Hank had admired him. And he understood why. And it seemed… It seemed so pointless and terrible to be worried about it now. But it was all well and good for Tammy and Hank to be surrogate grandparents, but he could never be a…

You don't even want to be a father. And you wouldn't be a good one anyway.

Not as good as what she should have had.

He shoved that away, and just in time, because the first wave of people began to arrive now that the parade was through. That kept them busy, showing people through the lot, chatting, which was mainly Ellie's domain—and helping carry trees to vehicles.

They went on until darkness started to fall, at around 5:00 p.m., now that winter was settling in.

They plugged in the lights that were strung around the tree lot, and suddenly, the space was transformed.

The whole town was.

He looked around, at the white lights that lined the red brick all down Main Street, the way the pine boughs were illuminated by the glow. Like an Old West fairy tale, all lit up bright. The night overhead was clear, the sky an inky velvet-black, the stars glittering like crystal.

If he was a man who believed in magic, he might think that he was seeing some now.

Especially when he looked at Ellie.

The gold from those lights had caught in her hair, making it glitter like a halo; her cheeks were pink from the cold, and so was the tip of her nose. "It's beautiful," she said, her breath coming out on a cloud.

"Hey, guys," he said. "Can you hold down the fort for about twenty minutes?"

"Sure," Aiden said, looking serious, his dark brows drawn together.

Marco nodded. "Yeah."

Caleb inclined his head. "Thanks. We'll be back."

"Where are we going?" Ellie asked.

The town wasn't the only thing that was lit up. The glow from the lights above had her all brightened, too, and inside...he felt like he might glow just as bright. Because of her. "You just looked like you might want to see the town."

"That was...thoughtful of you."

They wandered out of the tree lot, down Main Street and toward the center of the town. Ellie pulled a beanie out of her purse and tugged it down low over her ears. "'Tis definitely the season," she said, rubbing her arms.

"Yeah," he said. "It is." He put his arm around her, pulled her close and moved his hand slowly up and down from her shoulder to her elbow.

She looked up at him, and then looked around. "No one's paying attention."

"Come on, now," she said. "That's not true. It's a small town. People are always paying attention."

"Well," he said. "Oh, well."

He lowered his arm then, but took hold of her hand, lacing his fingers through hers as they walked down the quieting streets.

The windows were still lit, even though the shops had all just closed.

They paused in front of the antiques store, and she looked inside. "Is that a squirrel?" she asked.

He looked in and saw it, a taxidermic squirrel in an extended pose up on top of the stack of antique tables. "Yes, I believe it is."

"I *don't* want that for Christmas," she said.

He laughed. "What do you want for Christmas, then?"

"Well, not a platypus," she said.

"Because they're a scam?"

She laughed, and then the silence that fell over them seemed a little melancholy.

"What do you want?" he asked softly.

"Time alone with you would be nice," she said.

"We are alone," he said.

"We are *not*."

"Basically," he said, looking around.

"If you took your clothes off people would notice."

He grinned. "Maybe."

She looked up at him and smiled. "How about a puppy?"

"You don't want a puppy. You already have chickens."

"Well, the chickens could protect the puppy. Amelia would really like a puppy," she said.

"Do you really want to hassle with one?"

"I should," she said. "I should also decorate for Christmas. I should give her Christmas at our house."

"You've never done that," he said.

"No. Because I was afraid it would make me sad. Maybe it will. But maybe that's not such a bad thing. It's hard to explain. I'm done…grieving in that sense that people think of. I'm not sad all the time. Sometimes it hits me in a wave, but even then… I'm sorry he's gone. But I can't even picture what our life would have been like together right now. Too much has changed. I've changed too much. You just can't… You can't go back. And that, I think, has been the hardest thing for me to come to terms with. And I'm still coming to terms with it. I think I'll always miss him. But it's just… It's in that way that you miss Christmas before it comes around. An ache that has some sweet things with it, too. I need to not be so scared of being sad when it's time to be sad. Especially when it might be making Amelia miss out on something happy."

They stopped in front of the toy-shop window, which had a display of windup toys, all moving together. "That's creepy as hell," he said.

She laughed. "Yeah. I can skip windup dolls under the Christmas tree."

"So you do need a Christmas tree, though."

"Yeah," she said. "We're definitely going to need a Christmas tree."

"Luckily, you know a guy."

"I do," she said.

They paused at the end of the street, right in front of the town tree, which was a permanent fixture, not a cut tree that was installed every year. But a pine that had been growing there for a couple hundred years and got a new string of lights wrapped around it each Christmas.

"Or you can give me that one," she said, elbowing him.

"Sure. Let me get my chain saw."

"I already got what I wanted for Christmas," she said.

"Really?"

"The list. It was my Christmas list anyway."

He hadn't thought about the list in what felt like years, but that was impossible since they had only been together a handful of times. Since this had all just started playing out maybe two weeks ago.

"Well, I think you should expand the Christmas list," he said. "Because obviously you were thinking too small."

"But this is good," she said. "It's what I needed. I mean, look, I'm ready to get a tree for my house."

"What, you just needed...an orgasm so you could move on?"

She made a scuffing noise. "No. Anyway, *moving on* is the wrong word. You wake up one day to a life with the person you love not in it anymore. The decision to move on makes it sound like...they're there, and you could choose to stay with them, but you're not. You're moving on. I was moved. Into a life that I didn't choose. I think what I'm actually doing is choosing the different pieces of it. Making it richer and bigger. At first, all you can do is survive. Set dressing doesn't really matter."

"Did you just call my penis *set dressing*?"

She guffawed. And he really shouldn't be that grati-fied that he'd made her laugh, not in the middle of such a serious discussion. But he knew that mattered to her. And he wanted to do things that mattered. "I would never call your penis *set dressing*. It is structurally integral to my current happiness."

"Great. Glad to know that."

"I don't know," she said. "Maybe I'm not describing it very well. But it's like… You go through the storm, whether you choose to or not. And when everything settles, you have to look at what you're left with. Rebuild what you can, start over with what you can't. You start with what you need to keep breathing. And eventually you get a big-screen TV."

"Okay. In this scenario is my penis a big-screen TV?"

"This is ridiculous," she said.

"Life is a little bit ridiculous," he said.

Because here he was, standing with the woman he had loved once, and they were free to be together physically, because of circumstances he would never in a million years have chosen. Looking at a Christmas tree with her, wishing for more.

But he could see, clearly, in the words that she'd said, this was all part of her rebuilding. A stage.

She was adding things. Luxuries. Pleasure.

And he was glad.

But she would move on from it, too. That much was clear.

But… But if he did it right, then he would be a good memory. A good stop on the road to healing.

And that, that really was something he owed Clint, because while he might have been a decent friend sometimes, he'd been really terrible a couple of times, too. He'd caused him trouble. He'd caused him grief.

He wouldn't do the same to Ellie.

Suddenly, this didn't feel like it was all about him.

He'd come into it in anger, unable to see what the hell she was doing, but suddenly, it was as bright and clear as those lights on the tree.

As was his part in it.

"Come on," he said. "We better get back. They might have burned all the trees down."

Ellie chuckled. "Yeah, maybe. But they probably didn't. Because they're pretty good boys in the end."

"Yeah," Caleb said. "I guess they are."

Good boys who had done some bad things.

And that made him think of his own self.

And his concept of *good*.

But he shut that away and just focused on the way that Ellie's hand felt in his. Because it was a much more pleasant thought.

CHAPTER EIGHTEEN

CALEB DALTON NEVER did anything halfway. At least, that was how it was beginning to seem to Ellie. She couldn't say that she had ever fully been aware of just how much of himself he put into everything.

But she was seeing it now.

With the way he ran the Christmas tree farm.

With the way he was in bed.

And most definitely with the way he had decided to commandeer Christmas at her house.

Because he had shown up early on a Sunday morning with not just a tree, but the most spectacular, beautifully formed tree she had ever seen, endless boxes of decorations, pine boughs, cranberries on a string, a Christmas village and...

Well, it looked like an electric cowgirl ornament.

"Some of it came from my mom," he said, coming in with the first box.

Then he went back out, going to his truck to get more.

She just watched him, the way that his broad shoulders flexed as he carried everything. The barely noticeable strain on his forearms and biceps.

He was...

She didn't even really have words for it.

He had made her laugh at the Christmas tree lot yesterday. He had walked her down Main Street like they were dating. And it had made her feel...wonderful.

So wonderful and light it was easy to forget the way that he had come to her house and taken her with so much intensity. The way that he had made her admit that she'd been attracted to him before…

She shifted that thought away. She was already doing this whole Christmas thing. She didn't need to get into her complicated feelings about Caleb.

It wasn't even anything she ever thought about. Not really. Being attracted to somebody wasn't… It wasn't a crime. It was normal. And she really hadn't even let her brain open that door. Just the one time, and before she was married, had she ever even let herself think what it might be like to kiss him.

But she hadn't kissed him. She'd felt curious about it. In a way that made her stomach tight and her hands sweaty. But she hadn't even really been able to picture what it would be like to kiss him.

And now she could kind of see why.

Because kissing Caleb was not like kissing anyone else.

Not that she had a whole lot of people to compare it to. Just the one.

Yeah, she was starting to feel a little bit more comfortable with their interactions outside the bedroom. And while she craved what happened between them in bed… It was… It was very complicated.

Because it tapped into a part of herself she still wasn't terribly comfortable with. There was an intensity there that she didn't particularly like. One that reminded her too much of all of her mother's screaming breakups.

One that reminded her too much of what it was like to feel devastated and lonely, ignored by her mother and desperate to have attention.

That had been one of the things that had relieved her the most about her relationship with Clint.

She had loved him. And it had been easy. Easy conversation, easy kissing. The sex had felt easy. Easy to be aroused by him, easy to have good, naked fun.

He had been an easy husband. One who had taken care of her, one who had let small things roll off his back.

It helped dial back the intensity in her. That gasping, grasping need for affirmation and love that she'd felt all through her growing-up years.

Caleb did not do that. Caleb seemed to be a lit match to a slick of gasoline down inside her soul, and it was incredibly disconcerting. As delicious as it could be in the moment.

"Here," he said, handing her a ceramic angel.

She looked down at it, feeling unaccountably guilty holding the angelic object and thinking about Caleb naked. She set it down quickly on the side table. "This is maybe overkill," she said.

"Daltons don't know from overkill," he said. "We go big, or we don't go."

"Right."

He positioned the stand in the center of her living room and brought in the tree, getting it situated in the base, tightening the screws so that it sat up nice and tall in her living room.

"Where's Amelia?" he asked.

"She's in her room playing. I can get her when you're ready to decorate the tree."

"Yeah, that would be good," he said.

He brought in a few more boxes, and while he prepped the tree, Ellie went through them. She smiled as she took out some of the more Tammy Dalton pieces. A cowgirl

Miss Piggy who was wrapped in Christmas lights, and that Vegas cowgirl that he had mentioned before.

She took them and put them on her mantel.

"Those don't seem very you," he commented.

"I love them," she said. "They're silly. And not something that I would have done before. Because I would have wanted to make everything perfect. You know, like a Martha Stewart magazine. But life's not perfect. So let's have Miss Piggy on the mantel."

"Okay," he responded.

She bustled around, leaving signs of Christmas everywhere, and when she was done, she felt like she'd been punched in the heart.

Because the little farmhouse had never looked like this. And it was like an explosion of what was happening inside her all around.

Changed. Normal. But a little bit crazy. A little bit extra because so much had been kept pushed down for so long.

And by the time she finished with that, Caleb had all the lights done on the tree.

"Beautiful," she said.

"I'll go get Amelia," he said.

He went up the stairs, and she heard their voices, but not the words. And then she heard one set of footsteps return. She looked up, and Amelia was up in Caleb's arms, her hands clasped tight around his neck, her legs locked around his waist.

It made her ache.

Seeing the two of them together was always a lovely thing; it made her feel good anytime she saw Amelia with all the people who loved her. But this was… It was different. The way that he was holding her, the way that she trusted him.

She was suddenly so very aware of what Amelia didn't have.

A father.

She took a breath, trying to tell herself that she had expected all this to be a little bit emotional. And she really didn't want her daughter to see her having a total breakdown. Or Caleb, come to that.

Caleb got her digging through the ornaments right away, and she delightedly began hanging them all in one clump.

"You might want to spread them out," Caleb said.

Amelia looked at him, stubbornness etched into every line of her face. "They're pretty like that."

"I guess so," Caleb said.

Amelia finally looked over at Ellie as if she had just noticed that she was in the room. "Mommy, we have a Christmas tree." Then she looked around the room. "We have Christmas!"

"Yes," she said. "Caleb brought it."

Amelia leaned forward and hugged Caleb and knocked him off balance for a moment. He put his large hand over her back and patted her, and Ellie's stomach twisted. "Thank you for Christmas," she said.

"No problem, squirt," Caleb said, and she didn't think it was her imagination that his voice seemed a little bit rough.

"I'm going to play some Christmas music."

She took her phone and plugged it into one of the speakers in the room, and set up a Christmas station to play. Gentle piano music filled the room, and they each hung ornaments in relative silence, and Ellie knew that she had made the right choice in doing this. Because Amelia had never looked happier.

She bit the inside of her cheek. That was really the

hardest thing. How much joy she knew Clint would have taken in watching their daughter have these milestones. Have these moments.

She ignored the tightening in her throat and tried to focus on the moment. On the joy. Because no matter how much of a bittersweet ache existed inside her, there was joy right along with it.

Because she was here to watch Amelia. Because she had her.

"I think it's pretty good," Caleb said, surveying the tree. Which was beset by a completely lopsided bottom, clearly decorated by a child who thought that *more* was infinitely better than *less*.

"Maybe," Amelia said, appraising the tree. And then she stuck another ornament right into a cluttered spot.

She and Caleb shared a smile.

"We still have to do the star," Caleb said. "But that goes all the way at the very top. So I'm going to have to do that."

"Give it to me," Amelia said, putting up her hands. "Let me."

Caleb picked up the star, and Amelia, holding her forward, and she placed the star right on the top. "Good job," he said, sitting her back down and patting her back. He turned away from Amelia, reaching to plug the tree in, and as soon as it lit up, Amelia's laser focus went right to him.

"Caleb, can you be my dad?"

CHAPTER NINETEEN

THAT TINY LITTLE voice was like a bullet.

It tore through his chest, his lungs. Stole his heart. His breath. For a full second his vision blurred, and he couldn't quite figure out where he was or what the hell he was supposed to do with that sweet, earnest question that carried more weight than any other question he'd been asked in his thirty years.

Slowly, he squatted down, met Amelia's serious gaze. "What?"

"All the girls at preschool have dads. And they're all very tall. And you're very tall. And you brought Christmas. And you let me sit on your lap. And you're handsome."

Each and every descriptor on her list made his chest tighten up just a little bit more, and by the time she was done, he wasn't sure that he would be able to take in another breath. He wasn't sure he'd ever be able to breathe right again.

"I think you should be my dad."

"That..." He cleared his throat. "That's not really how that works."

"I don't understand how it works," she said, clearly frustrated. "A lot of the moms and dads at the preschool don't live together. It's okay if you don't live together."

He looked up at Ellie, who was frozen, her face waxen. And he knew that he couldn't call on her for help. Because he needed to handle this one on his own. If only he knew how.

"You had a dad, honey. You know your dad. You've seen pictures of him. We've talked about them. He…" Caleb cleared his throat. "He died. Before you were born. And he loved you. So much. Even when you were just a little bean inside your mom's tummy." He gave some amount of thanks that he had actually talked with her about Clint before. That he had some rehearsed words to call on, because if he had to come up with it all now on the spot, he would have had nothing.

"I know. But I want a dad that's here," she said. "I don't want one that can't pick me up. You pick me up."

He looked at Ellie again, and she was covering her mouth, a shining tear tracking down her face, partially hidden by her hand.

He looked back at Amelia, and his heart fractured.

"I love you, Amelia," Caleb said. "You know that."

Her green eyes shone with sadness, confusion. Tears. And he hated that he'd put that there. He hated it so much.

"Then why can't you be my dad?"

Damn. *Damn.* Damn the question. Damn the answer he had to give.

Just damn it all to hell.

"Can't I just love you?" he asked, the question cutting his throat on the way out.

"It's not the same," she said. "It's not. It's not fair. Everyone got a dad, and I didn't." Amelia was crying now, inconsolable at the base of the tree, and Caleb wanted to cut out his own heart. Offer it up as some kind of sacrifice. As something. Because what the hell was he supposed to do in this situation? It would be the easiest thing in the world to say "Sure, call me dad, kid." Because why the hell not?

But Clint was her dad.

He deserved to be called her dad.

Caleb was never going to replace him. And Amelia was little enough that she could forget. And that wasn't right. It wasn't fair.

Amelia's little shoulders shook, rising and falling with her breath. "I'm going to ask Santa to make you my dad for Christmas."

And then she walked out of the room, trudging up the stairs.

And Ellie collapsed onto the couch, her hands over her face. "I'm sorry," she said, her voice thick.

"Don't," he said.

"I should have… I guess I didn't talk to her about it the right way. I thought that I did. I thought that…"

"Well, I thought that I did," he said.

Another tear slipped down Ellie's cheek, and she wiped it away. "I should go talk to her."

"Do you want me to?"

"No. Because…you're not her father. I'm sorry. What do you want me to say?"

He didn't know why, but the words lanced him like a sword. "No," he said. "You're right. I'm not. Go ahead."

She got up, wiping her cheeks as she went, and he wondered if he should leave.

But no. He was tangled up in this, and he wanted to be here just in case.

He waited. Braced himself. But Ellie came back only a few moments later.

"She's asleep. I think she must have exhausted herself."

"I'm sorry," he said.

"It's not your fault," she said. "It's not even… It's not even bad. She loves you because you're so great to her. But she doesn't understand. Any of it. And she doesn't know him. She'll never know him." A sob shook her shoulders. "That's the thing that gets me. More than anything else right now. It's that. That relationship. He would have loved her so much."

"He did," Caleb said. "There was never a man more excited to have a baby, Ellie. Trust me."

"You knew how excited he was?"

"Yeah," he said. "I was avoiding you, but he didn't know it. He didn't know about the reading lessons. He didn't know that I… He didn't know. He talked about you and the baby all the time. He never quit talking about it. He was happy. And I don't know if that makes it worse. But you know, some people… Some people live their whole lives and never feel that happy about anything. But he was that happy about you. About her. It really, *really* sucks that he's not here now. Because he should be. But he was happy."

She nodded. "I know he was. But it still…"

"I know. I don't know what to say, and I don't know what to do. Someday, some man might feel like her dad. God knows what your future holds, Ellie, but you're not going to be alone forever."

"No," she said. "Let's just… Let's not talk about it. I don't want to talk about this."

"Ellie…"

"I was afraid that Christmas would remind me too much of him. But it's not even that. It's… She doesn't know. She doesn't remember. She can't. And she won't."

"I don't know the answer," he said. "Because one thing forces his memory aside, and the other forces her to have a hole in her life."

"I know."

"But I'm not her dad either way."

"I know that, too. Well," she said. "Merry Christmas."

"I'm sorry."

He got up, getting ready to leave. "Don't go," she said. "You started all this. The least you can do is… give me something nice."

"Are you sure?"

She had been pretty hard-line about not having sex when Amelia was in the house before. In fact, they'd only been together a couple of times because of that.

"I wanted to protect her," Ellie said. "But I can't protect her. She has to know about the world way too young. And she's asleep right now, and I'm going to let her sleep. And I can't… I can't take away any of the pain that she might feel. I can't fix any of this. So…just make me feel good for a little bit."

"You know it's not fun with me, Ellie."

"I don't want fun. I want to feel something. Something other than this. And I know you can make me. Caleb, nobody makes me feel like you. Nobody ever has."

And that was a double-edged sword, twisting like a knife in his chest. Because it wasn't happy. And it wasn't love. But it was just theirs. And that was something.

She made him crazy, this woman. And she made him sane. He didn't know what the hell to do with himself, didn't know what the hell to do with her. And somehow, he knew exactly what to do all at the same time.

She needed him. This particular brand of passion that they had.

And he couldn't be what Amelia needed. He couldn't

even be what Ellie needed all the time. Because he couldn't be Clint, and he never would be.

It was the story of his entire damn life.

But he could give her this. And no one else could. By her own admission, no one else could. And so he pulled her into his arms, and he kissed her. Kissed her with all the feeling that had been inside him for so long. Everything that he had denied.

Because had he ever stopped loving Ellie Bell? He didn't think he had.

He had told himself that he didn't because it was impossible. And it was impossible still. But hell, he was ready to marinate in that. He was ready to drown in it. To put his head under and consume it. Be consumed by it. She was everything. And if he was nothing in the sight of that, then that was just fine.

Kissing her was like a drug. He wanted more. Only more. Always more. There would never be an end to it. Never be an end to this. She made him want. She made him feel.

And more than anything else, she made him wish that he were different.

She was the only person that he had ever tried to be different for.

Ellie.

His sweet Ellie, who had changed his entire world the first time he'd laid eyes on her, and had changed it every day since.

That was the thing. He couldn't say he didn't believe in love at first sight, because something in him had shifted from the moment she had walked into the room. But even more powerful, things had shifted inside him all the days since.

Love might have hit at first sight, but it had changed

and deepened, taken root over the years, and that was something that left him in awe, and completely enraged and terrified him.

Because what could he do with it?

When he had been young, when he had been a boy, he had thought that maybe…

Maybe that day on the hill, watching the sunset, they could have shared a kiss that might have created a lifetime. But what would he have done with it?

He didn't even know what a lifetime was at that age.

And she had said herself that she didn't think she would have been able to handle this thing between them back then. And he could see why.

It was enough to leave him scorched and reduced to ashes even now. What would it have done to them then?

He had seen what his father had done with the love he wasn't ready for. And Caleb would have rather cut his own heart out than hurt Ellie that way.

He still would.

But he wouldn't think about any of that. Because it didn't matter. The future of the feelings he had didn't matter. All that mattered was now. Because this was his one moment. To let himself feel everything he did for her, to let her feel it.

She wasn't married. Not now.

She was not his friend's wife. And she was more than his friend's widow.

She was the woman that he had fallen in love with when she'd been eighteen years old. And she was the woman that he loved now. And every single woman she'd been in between; they were all one beautiful woman, rich and vibrant. A woman who knew how to laugh, who still laughed, even in spite of all the pain that she had endured. She was brave. His Ellie was so very brave.

And he wanted to honor that.

The other times they had come together... It had felt like he was challenging her. Asking her to take that unbearable desire that existed inside him and shoulder it, because God knew he had for so long. So very long.

But now...

He wanted to worship her. Wanted to give her everything she needed. Everything she deserved.

If it was his one chance to help her understand what she was worth, what she meant to him. Well, he was going to take it.

It didn't matter what the hell it gave him, if it gave him anything at all.

And he didn't know when that had shifted. When it had flipped. But it had. So he kissed her, and he put everything in that kiss.

He wanted to lay her down underneath the Christmas tree, strip her there. But with Amelia in the house, even though she was sleeping, he figured it probably wasn't the best idea. But someday. Someday he would. He made that vow to himself because he felt he shouldn't make it to her. Not now.

He took her hand and brought her up with him, held her hand as he led her up the stairs and into her room. He wanted to give her something different. Different than what she had, and different than what they'd shared. He wanted... He wanted to be enough. He wanted to be more.

He'd never wanted it so much in all his life.

There had been a part of him that had given up on it all those years ago. The part of him that had framed Clint for the guns. He had tried to best his friend by making him seem worse, rather than trying to make his own damn self better.

Well, that was over. It was done.

He was going to be the best for her. Here and now. To the best of his ability. It was what she deserved. Not less, that was for damn sure. And he'd been so worried about one of those men in town getting their hands on her because they weren't good enough to sully Clint's memory.

But he had given it to himself. And he had worried a hell of a lot less about being worthy of touching her.

Because that was the thing.

At some point the specter of Clint had to lift away. And it wasn't about comparing.

It was unavoidable in the beginning, the comparison. But right now it had to be the two of them, and there couldn't be anyone else in this bed with them. Couldn't be anyone else between them.

And this felt momentous. So maybe...

Maybe it was building to something. Something big or something terrible.

But he wasn't going to turn away from it.

He wasn't going to turn away from them.

He had told himself this entire time that it couldn't end with them together. But now he wanted to know why the hell not.

It wouldn't ever be the same as what she'd had before. But like she'd said, what they had between them was different. Not like anything she'd had before. Not like it had been with anyone.

And it was the same for him.

She was Ellie Bell, and she had been singular, perfect, magical, tempting, in ways that no one and nothing ever had been before. From the first moment that she had walked into his life.

"Ellie," he whispered as he laid her down on the bed gently.

He stripped her clothes from her slowly, revealing her body to his gaze. That pale, perfect skin, her lush curves.

"The first moment that I saw you," he said as he unhooked her bra, "I knew something changed. Something in the air. Something in me. I'd never seen a more beautiful woman in my whole life. It was like the world stopped. And the sun shone around you like it was a spotlight, only for you."

She blinked rapidly, her eyes glistening with tears. "Caleb…"

"I need you to know that. I need you to know that even though it hurts sometimes. That even though it was hard later… I can never be angry about that moment. Because it changed something in me. I tried to be angry at it, but I can't. It was like seeing in color for the first time."

She looked away from him and he kissed her neck, kissed a line down over her breasts. Hungry and hot, utterly perfect. For him.

She fit him in every way. And he had known that from the first moment he'd seen her.

And she needed him. She needed him, even if he wasn't the perfect fit.

They both needed him.

He unbuttoned her jeans and slid them down her legs, kissed his way down her stomach and parted her thighs wide. They would never get over this. Tasting her. Pleasuring her. She arched against him, moving her hips in time with his tongue, with his fingers. And he could lose himself. Lose himself forever. With Ellie. In Ellie.

He loved her.

He always had. There hadn't been a moment when he hadn't. It was why the easiest thing in the world had been to take care of her these past years. To never even look at another woman.

Because once she wasn't married…

Well, his body hadn't even been able to muster up a kind of vague biological interest he'd managed to keep while she was completely off-limits.

And waiting for her to be ready had been easy. Caring for her daily life… That had been something he wanted in a way, far above sex. He couldn't explain it.

But that was because the first moment he had seen her he hadn't just wanted her in bed. He wanted her in his life.

Becoming her protector had satisfied something in him.

Had eased something in him that had been feral and hungry for years. And when she had shown interest in being with another man… Well, that was when that beast that had been satisfied gave a big *oh, hell no.*

Because he had waited. And he would have done it forever without ever being able to kiss her. Without ever being able to touch her. But if any man was going to have her, it had to be him.

And he would take whatever she could give him back. Because he wasn't going to be able to live his life without her.

That had always been true.

But now that he had her…

He was an idiot. He thought that he was moving to a tree farm, making a separate life, because he was ready to draw a line underneath what they'd shared? No.

No.

He wanted to do that because he wanted to start making a life that was theirs.

That was what it had been time for.

Not to move away.

But to move into something else. Together.

He pressed two fingers inside her, and she arched up off the bed, crying out her pleasure as she pulsed around him. But he wasn't done yet. He continued. Because he had to do something to show her, and the words wouldn't work. Not right now. Not for the two of them. There was too much…stuff still between them to go there just yet.

But he could show her.

And he felt free.

Because there had been so many years when he couldn't. When he had to hide it.

But right now it wasn't about anything but them. Them, and the beauty of the feelings that he had for her. Not the curse of them, but the wonder of them.

And so he pleasured her until her voice was hoarse, until she was leaving track marks on his back with her fingernails.

And only then did he get a condom and maneuver himself between her thighs; only then did he allow himself a slow, brilliant torture, sliding into her tight, hot body. Sliding home.

He held his breath for a moment. Listened to the sound of his own heartbeat echoing in his head.

He cupped her chin, slid his fingertips down the valley between her breasts. Pressed his hand against her chest and felt her heart. Felt it raging like his own.

She looked at him, but she didn't speak. And he kissed away the questions that might rise up on her lips. Flexed his hips forward and decided to focus on carrying them both to oblivion. Because right now reality was so sharp. And it was cutting him so deep. Because right now it hurt to breathe.

In that brilliant, wonderful way it hurt to breathe on a cold, crystal clear day, when you hiked up the side of a mountain and looked down over the valley. When the air cut your lungs. That was what it was.

But he needed something to help numb the pain, and if anything could, it was the pleasure he found inside her. But each moment of pleasure only served to amplify the pain. Until they twisted and wound together into an unbreakable cord. And that he supposed was about right.

For this. For this all-consuming feeling that burned inside him. Like a beacon on a hill that couldn't be put out. No matter the years, no matter the barriers.

He would burn for Ellie Bell until the day he died.

And it was a clear, joyful, brutal realization to have, buried deep inside her as he was.

She was wonderful. Beautiful perfection.

And whether the world ran on fate or not, he didn't know. But from that first moment, he felt like he had been made for her. Made to be there *for* her.

In every way.

And he would. He pledged that, with his body, with his lips against hers, even though he couldn't do it with words.

He surged inside her, making that vow over and over again. He and Ellie had been together a few times now, and each and every time, it had been an angry race to that ultimate moment of completion.

But now it didn't matter. Not really.

He wanted to stay on this journey forever. Wanted to be with her, just like this.

But it couldn't last. He couldn't last. That soft whimpering sound she made in his ear, the way she held on to his shoulders... It was all too much. And when she raised her head and arched into him, whispering in his ear: *Caleb.*

It broke him. And he splintered like glass as that simple word, that declaration, that it was him she was with and no one else, that it was the two of them here in this bed, it was what undid him completely.

His growl as fractured as the rest of him, he thrust into her one last time, shaking as he found his release. He buried his face in her neck, and inhaled Ellie. Filled his lungs with her as he shook and shuddered, as he squeezed his eyes tightly shut, the stinging behind his lids foreign and intense. He punched his hands in the bedding, and he rode out a release that was like a storm. When he rolled over on his back there was sweat rolling down his face, and maybe other moisture, too, and his heart was threatening to pound a hole through his rib cage.

And then he pulled her up against him and held her there, her hair fanned over his chest.

"Caleb..."

"I'm staying the night," he said.

"But Amelia..."

"Is four and won't think anything of it. I'm here all the time."

He expected her to argue, but she didn't.

She buried her face in his chest and he felt wetness on her cheeks, and he knew it wasn't sweat.

"Are you okay?"

"I don't know. I will be. I will be." She repeated the last part, more to herself, it sounded like to him. "We all will be."

They would be. He would see to it. He was formulating a plan, and he had a feeling that she wasn't going to like it. Hell, he knew he wasn't going to like it. But he was done sitting on the sidelines. He was done letting things in the past have free rein over the present, and the future. Life was short.

And that was one lesson he seemed to have failed to learn in all of this.

He had said it to Jacob, but he hadn't seemed to be able to take it on board himself.

Death was tragic because of love. And they had all loved Clint very much. He wasn't a man who could be easily replaced. He wasn't a man who could be replaced at all. But that wasn't the idea. It was the wrong way to think about it. It wasn't about stepping into his shoes; it wasn't about being a stand-in.

It was about what he could give. And there were things—he knew it. It was about being the one who was here now.

But in order to do that, he had to bring something to the table.

More than just Christmas decorations. More than just sex.

And he knew exactly what that was.

CHAPTER TWENTY

WHEN ELLIE WOKE up the next morning, she smelled coffee.

And that was weird. She did have a coffeepot that she could set the timer on, but she never did it. Not on weekends, because she didn't know when she would get up. And anyway, even on weekdays she usually forgot to set it all up before she went to bed.

But not just coffee. She also smelled…bacon.

She looked around at her decimated bed. And then slowly, memories crept back to her. Caleb.

Caleb had spent the night.

Caleb, who kept changing the damned rules on her.

Last night had been…different.

She had been ready. Ready to hop on and ride that man into that blind intensity that they seemed to be able to find together. But he had done something else. He had been gentle. He had told her all those wonderful things. About what he'd felt when he'd first seen her. Then she had scarcely been able to believe it. It had made her feel… He made her feel.

And that terrified her. In about a thousand places.

In about a thousand ways.

Last night he had been…

They had been…

She rolled onto her side, ignoring the tightness in

her throat. And a tear leaked out and streamed down her cheek anyway.

"Caleb," she whispered.

Then she heard the sound of a small, chattering voice, and she rocketed into a sitting position, swinging her legs over the side of the bed and flinging herself toward the door.

Amelia was up. Up and chatting with Caleb, who had spent the night in her bed.

She pulled on her pajamas and then rushed downstairs.

"Mommy," Amelia said as soon as Ellie entered the kitchen. "Caleb is here. And he made bacon and biscuits."

"Biscuits?" she asked.

He winked. "Tammy Dalton made sure her boys knew how to make biscuits."

He was dressed. Totally dressed. Wearing jeans and a long-sleeved shirt—sleeves pushed up to his elbows and revealing those forearms that made her whole body go tight—and his cowboy hat. It was, of course, the same outfit he had on yesterday, but there was no way that Amelia would realize that, or what it meant.

She was hoping that Amelia wouldn't give Caleb a repeat of last night.

That had torn Ellie's heart out through her throat. And it didn't seem like Caleb had weathered it very well, either.

Except...

She thought of all that beautiful sincerity he'd given Amelia. His answer hadn't been what her daughter had wanted to hear, but he'd taken such care with it.

And then she thought of the sincerity he'd put into their time in bed last night. The way that he'd talked to her. The way that he'd looked at her. The way that he'd held her.

Amelia, for her part, didn't seem to remember what she had said to him last night, but she supposed that was how it was when you were four, and didn't realize that you had effectively stabbed both adults in your life in the heart with your words.

She had never seen Caleb look quite like he had, and the graveness with which he had taken the question had made her feel more than any other response could have.

He had chosen his words so carefully with her. And with so much love. Not just for Amelia, but for Clint. With so much respect for the fact that Clint was a father who would never get to know his daughter.

And with such deep care that Amelia was a child who ached to have a father.

"Thank you for breakfast," Ellie said.

"No problem," he said. "I'm pretty hungry this morning."

The way his eyes burned into hers, she had a feeling it wasn't bacon he was hungry for.

Well, her, too.

No. She was hungry for bacon. But she was also hungry for Caleb. She could be hungry for both.

He turned away from the stove and grabbed a mug of coffee, handing it to her. "Fixed just how you like it."

"You don't just get to make my coffee," she said. "You don't know exactly how I want it."

"I've watched you make coffee about a thousand times," Caleb said. His blue eyes bored directly into hers. "I've watched you make coffee a lot more closely than any man should. And I know exactly how you like it. Because I have paid attention to every little thing about you for more than a decade."

Lord, his eyes. So blue and serious on hers. Eyes she'd looked into countless times, and how had they ever not made her breathless?

Because they couldn't. Because you were with someone else.

But he had always been there.

And this…this feeling in her, it had been there, too.

"And they say men aren't observant," she said breathlessly.

"Well, honey, for the purposes of this conversation, I'm not *men*. I'm *me*. More important, you're not *women*. You're *you*. And that's why I know."

He took a sip of his own coffee, the gesture careless as if he couldn't possibly be aware that he had jumbled things around inside her with his words.

Except the slightly smug expression on his face when he set his cup back down on the counter suggested to her that he just might.

She took a sip of her coffee, and it was perfect.

And she did wonder, if he was that insightful about the coffee, if he could possibly be that insightful about what these things he was saying might mean to her.

"Are you done with your bacon?" she asked Amelia.

"Yes," Amelia said brightly.

"Why don't you find one of your favorite ponies to show Caleb."

"Okay!"

Amelia scrambled from the room, and Ellie knew that she had bought herself a few minutes while her daughter tried to decide which of her plastic ponies was her favorite.

"I need to talk to you," she said.

"About?" he asked, his expression far too innocent

for a man who'd done all those things to her under the cover of darkness, in that soft, cozy space upstairs.

"Last night."

"It was good," he said.

"It was," she said, breathing in deep. "It was different."

"I feel a little different," he said.

"About what you said to me… About the first time you saw me…"

"I have something to tell you," he said slowly.

"Well, I'm trying to tell you something," she said.

"I know. But I feel like if we're going to have that talk, we need to have this one first. And it's going to sound like a small thing. But I need you to understand what it has made me feel about myself. And I know… I know it's not something that you hate me for. Though you won't be that impressed. You'll wonder why I didn't tell you. And it's because it's something I don't even like thinking about."

"What?"

Terror gripped her, and she realized the idea of Caleb *not* being this stalwart man that she had built up in her head actually did terrify her. He said often that he wasn't as good a man as Clint, but they were just different men.

Caleb was intense.

Caleb was the kind of man that you could imagine easily going out on the battlefield back in the days of yore and defending his family with a broadsword. He was that kind of good. She would never have trusted her daughter's safety to him constantly if she didn't believe that.

That he was the kind of man who would die to protect her. He was. It was that simple.

She knew that about him, knew it in her bones.

"You know, Clint was always smart. He did well in school. And he practically lived at my house. He did his homework there. After an hour or so, he would be finished, and I would still be sitting there with a bad attitude and a headache. And my mom would bring him cookies, and tell him what a great job he did. And over the years that stuck in me. I loved Clint—don't get me wrong. But there were things that he could do... There was a way that he was... He attracted people. He lit them up. You know that. He didn't have an ounce of anger in his body, and for a man who came from the kind of house that he did... It was pretty incredible. And I don't know... In hindsight I wonder if he was pulling a Hank Dalton."

"I don't think my husband had a bunch of secret kids," she said.

"That's not what I mean," Caleb responded. "Sometimes I think he was on his best behavior, because of the kind of household he came from... There was a lot of bad behavior. A lot of anger. He probably wanted to get as far away from it as he could when he wasn't there. He probably never wanted to give my parents a reason to not let him be at our house. I never thought of it this way, because I was a kid, and kids are selfish. But I was born into that family, and he stepped in. He was the one with the precarious position, and I imagine he always felt like he had to perform to keep it."

"He loved your family," she said softly. "I don't think he felt like he had to perform."

"I think by the time we were adults it was a habit. But when we were kids... He loved my parents, and they loved him. And now I'm so glad of that. I'm glad that he had good parents. Even if they were mine. But at the time, being forced to compete with him, especially in academics…"

"Of course it was so much harder for you," she said. "And no one knew why."

"My dad thought that I was being lazy. And he couldn't stand lazy. Because you know, in Hank's mind, he pulled himself up by his bootstraps, and if he would've had the opportunities that I did… If he would have been able to go to school, that's what he would've done. My dad is a smart man."

"You keep talking about Clint and your dad and saying that they're smart. You're smart, Caleb. A learning disability doesn't mean you aren't smart. You can't help the way that your brain puts these things together."

"I've tried for a lot of my adult life to take that on board. But it's tough, when you spent your childhood feeling like the class idiot. I hated school because it was out of my control. I hated doing homework with Clint because he was always better than me. I hated it so much. And there was nothing I could do about it. I could get stronger. I could learn to fix an engine. Those things, those physical things, I can control them. And so I threw myself into that. Physical labor, because I knew that I could build up my body, and I couldn't figure out how in the hell to build up my brain."

She shook her head. "You know those things aren't exclusive. Hard work isn't less. Hard work doesn't mean that someone is stupid."

"I know," he said. "I know that because of you. Because you were the one who helped me see it. All those years later. But for a long time I was bogged down in that. And when… You know how Clint's home was. His family was poor, and they lived on the edge of town. And they basically had no interest in him whatsoever.

He loved to come over and spend time in my dad's study. And look at all of the... All of the weird stuff in there."

"It is like a Western museum."

"Yeah, it is. And he had these guns. Old ones. Polished up and hung on the wall. From John Wayne movies. And they're worth a hell of a lot of money. Clint loved them. Because like me, like all of us, he was fascinated with the West. Fascinated with cowboys. He made it clear. He would talk about them every time he would go in there. Talk about how he'd love to have something like that. And then one time he laughed and said he'd just have to sell anything that valuable for money anyway."

She blinked and looked away. Everything about Caleb's expression made her feel a sense of building dread, and she couldn't guess why.

"My dad offered Clint money to go to school. And I was so angry. Because he didn't offer it to me. He offered it to all my brothers, and when it came time for him to give me my talk, my offer, that I was going to refuse the same as they did...he didn't give it. But he told Clint. Free ride anywhere he could get accepted to. And that he was proud of him."

Caleb breathed out, sharp and hard. "That was it. I wanted to break it. I wanted to destroy it. I wanted to... I wanted to ruin that relationship that they had. Because it wasn't fair. Mine was my birthright, and his was... He just stepped in and showed me up every chance he got. How fair was that? So I took the guns. I took the guns, and I put them in Clint's truck. Put them underneath the tarp. And when the guns went missing I made sure they got found there."

"What happened?"

"Clint said he did it. He looked at me, straight in the

eye, and he said he did it. And he apologized. And my
dad forgave him, because if there's any one person who
is imperfect on this earth, it's him. And then I found out
later that Clint didn't take the money to go to school.
Because he didn't think it was fair to me. We never
talked about it. But I think he knew. I think he knew
all that time, and he just took the blame, because that's
how much better than me he was. I couldn't stand it.
I tried to ruin his life, Ellie. And when he showed up
at that barbecue with you, everything in me wanted to
steal you, too. It took everything to sit back and let him
have you. And I almost didn't. Ellie, when we were having those lessons…you were married to him. My best
friend. And no matter how much I was jealous of him,
I loved him. And still… I wanted you. And that's why
I've spent all this time struggling with the idea that
he's the better man. He got you, and he deserved you. I
fractured his relationship with my parents. God knows,
honey, if I had just waited a couple of years to try and
get what he had… It would've been you, and not money
for college that I didn't even want."

The very idea of Caleb pouring all his energy into
stealing her away from Clint made all of her insides
seize up. What would she have done if that intense blue-
eyed boy that had taken her up riding had tried to kiss
her that day? If it hadn't simply been a moment that
existed in her own head?

She didn't know the answer to it, and it scared her. It
made her feel like she didn't know who she was.

And when his face came back into focus, as it was
now, and not as a twenty-year-old kid, riding horses
with her up on the ridge, she could see that he was tortured by it all. Still.

"It's the one thing I wish I could've said to him,"

Caleb said. "I wish I would have shaken his hand and said you always were the better man. And I'm damn sorry that I tried to take you down to my level, instead of trying to get up to yours."

Ellie's throat tightened. "He thought the world of you," she said. "And never once did I ever think there was some reason he thought you were less. He would've said any day of the week that the better man was you. And then in the end, it wouldn't have mattered. Because you're two different men. Not the same. You can be two different kinds of good."

"What I did to him wasn't good."

"I would've done the same thing," she said, her chest tight. "Caleb, I wouldn't have responded to that any better. I grew up fighting for everything I had. I was jealous of everyone and everything. There wasn't a single person at my school that didn't have more than me, and I hated them all. I didn't have any friends. I didn't let myself date. My life was small, jealous and petty. I was empty. I had a void that my mother wouldn't fill. I wanted love I couldn't get. You needed affirmation, and you never got it. You needed someone, anyone, to recognize that you weren't fundamentally lazy. What that does to a child… Can you imagine? Can you imagine if someone told Amelia every day of her life that she wasn't good enough because she wasn't trying, all while she was giving it her best? It's a crime, Caleb. And when you feel those things, when you feel that kind of desperate, your world shrinks down to your own hurt. Your own problems."

Suddenly, she saw herself so clearly, because in so many ways she had been doing it for the past several years since Clint's death.

The way that she had just asked Caleb to have sex

with her, as if it wouldn't bother him in some way. And now that she knew his attraction to her had been a long-running source of guilt for him...

"Sometimes we are so hurt we can't look past that hurt," she said. "And I have a long history of doing just that. I wouldn't have been any better than you. So maybe... Maybe on most days Clint took a higher road than you. That one time. You had other opportunities in your life, to do good or bad, and I'd say you did good."

"Yeah," Caleb said.

"And you know what? I think that we did pretty well. Clint had a haven in your house, but it compromised yours. That's real. You can't overlook that."

"But it was nothing he did wrong."

"No. It wasn't. You were just both young. But you know, on some level he must've realized it. Not taking that college offer from your dad. Choosing to go fight fires with you."

"He wouldn't have wanted a desk job anyway," Caleb said.

"No," she agreed. "He wouldn't have. He would've been miserable. He loved what he did. And more than that, he loved doing it with you and Jacob. He liked making a difference. And you were his brothers. You were."

"It's not your job to make me feel better about this. That's not why I told you. I just wanted you to understand."

"I understand why you feel the way you do. But you need to understand that...what you've shown me of yourself matters a whole lot more. You're my protector," she said. "When grief threatened to drown me, you were there. And if I hadn't had your arms to hold me up out of the waves, Caleb, I don't know what I would have done. You were there when Amelia was born. You were… You're a man who does. And all those actions, all that hard work, it matters. In the end, it's everything. Because if somebody says a whole lot of pretty words, but can't be there when it matters…then it doesn't matter."

"Ellie…"

"And you wouldn't have."

"I wouldn't have what?" he asked.

"You wouldn't have stolen me away from him. Because it's not who you were. It's not who you are."

He shifted uncomfortably. "I don't know if I could have lived with this feeling for the rest of my life and not done anything."

The words stabbed at her. Because it made her wonder, too. For a moment. But they wouldn't have. She knew. Clear as anything. Because whatever pull they felt toward each other, they'd both loved Clint. Because they both cared about things like vows, and other people's hearts.

Because she would never have touched Caleb, and if she'd never touched him she would have never known the real power of the electrical current that arched between them sometimes.

They would never have opened the door.

"You wouldn't have," she said. "Because…whatever you think, Caleb, you protect people. You would never have hurt him, not that way. Petty stuff you did when you were a boy…it's not the same."

"Purple and yellow," Amelia announced, holding two ponies high over her head as she entered the kitchen. "These are my favorite."

"Very nice," Caleb said. His eyes were still on Ellie.

"Caleb," she said. "Play ponies with me."

"For ten minutes, okay. Then I have somewhere to be."

"Tree lot?" Ellie asked.

"Yeah," he said. "I've at least got to help the boys get set up. I'm not comfortable leaving them to their own devices yet."

"Understandable."

"Let's play under your Christmas tree," Amelia said.

"My Christmas tree?"

"Yes," she said, frowning, a deep groove appearing between her pale brows. "Aren't all the Christmas trees yours?"

"No," he said. "I brought this one to you. And now it's yours."

Amelia beamed happily and took Caleb by the hand into the living room.

And something in Ellie's heart cracked. And she stood there in the kitchen, trying to breathe around it. Hoping that somehow she could soothe that back together by rubbing her fingertips over her breastbone.

But it didn't work.

And just when she was feeling like she had some things together, she was wondering if she was going to break again.

And the very idea terrified her.

CHAPTER TWENTY-ONE

HE SPENT EVERY night at her house. For three weeks. He went to bed with her, woke up with her. And if Amelia noticed that there was anything different about it, she didn't say anything, and since she was a four-year-old child, he had a feeling that if she had noticed there was something different, she would have said, and loudly.

For his part, he couldn't really read Ellie. Couldn't really understand what was going on with her. She clung to him at night, her breath on his neck as they slept. And in the morning she often had trouble meeting his eyes.

Even after that talk they'd had, where he had sort of bared his soul and all of that.

But the past three weeks had only strengthened his resolve. It was Christmas Eve Eve, and all of the last-minute trees were gone from the lot. And he had a pocket full of cash, and was on his way to the one jewelry store in town.

It was a nice store, not filled with fine jewelry so much, but handmade, one-of-a-kind pieces, which he knew would appeal to Ellie even more.

He needed to find just the right thing. She had delicate hands, so nothing too chunky. And she sparkled.

But he didn't want to get her a diamond solitaire, because she'd had one of those before.

Because he knew exactly what her wedding rings

looked like, the ones that were in her jewelry box in her room.

She had taken them off when she was eight months pregnant with Amelia, because they hadn't fit her hands, and she had never put them back on.

But he knew them. He knew them without having to look at them, and he wanted something different.

Because what he knew, what he was resolved in, what he was going to say to her, was that they were different.

He walked into the jewelry store, looked at everything under the counter, pausing when he found a white gold band with fragments of sunstone wound through delicate strands of metal. It was perfect.

That kind of sunstone could only be found in Oregon, completely unique to the terrain out in the high desert, and he felt like that matched the way that he felt.

A feeling that could only be found between the two of them. And no one else.

It wasn't a traditional engagement ring. But she didn't... Theirs wasn't a traditional relationship. It wouldn't be a marriage in the same way her first one had been, not for her.

He was okay with that. He was.

He got the ring wrapped up and then he started to head over to the toy store.

If he was going to give Ellie a ring, he was going to have to give Amelia something.

But on his way down there, he paused.

There was a red truck with wood slats nailed to the side, and a sign hanging over the top.

Puppies.

Puppies for an eye-watering price.

But he imagined last-minute Christmas puppies were something of a premium?

"What kind of puppies are these?" he asked. "Solid gold?"

The old man sitting in the lawn chair in front of the truck looked up at him. "Bernedoodles. Bernese mountain dog and a poodle. They don't shed."

"Well, that seems like a bonus."

"We had a bigger litter than we anticipated, and seeing as it's Christmas, we thought that since they were ready to go home now, we might take the ones that weren't placed and see about making them a perfect Christmas surprise."

Caleb walked over and looked in the back of the truck and saw two adorable, ridiculously fluffy puppies. Black with brown and white, like little cotton mops.

"Do they get big?"

"Pretty big."

That worked for him. What he could not have was a small mop dog. And any dog that he got Amelia and Ellie... Well, he hoped it would be his, too.

And... Ellie had mentioned wanting a puppy. And while he was pretty sure she was kidding, he might as well come with jewelry and a puppy.

He was doing his part to bring as much to the table as possible.

"We've got a girl and a boy," he said, pointing to the two in the back of the truck.

The one that the old man had indicated was a boy came up to the end and jumped up, putting his paws on the tailgate and giving Caleb a pleading look.

"Better be the boy," Caleb said.

Not because he was a soft touch, but because otherwise he was going to be completely outnumbered by women.

The very idea made his heart lift.

In the end he spent more on the dog than he did on the ring. And when he drove back toward the house, he had the dog sitting in a seat next to him, and the ring in his pocket.

When he pulled up to the house he realized that he couldn't exactly produce the puppy without Ellie seeing it first.

What the hell was he going to do with a dog if Ellie didn't actually want it? And there was no way he could show it to Amelia and then take it.

"Good thinking, Dalton." He pulled his phone out of his pocket and called Ellie.

"Hello?"

"Hi."

"Are you calling me from outside the house?"

"I am," he said.

"Why?"

"I did something. But I realize that I needed to make sure that you knew first."

"That's scary." The front door opened and Ellie appeared. She waved then hung up her phone, putting it in her pocket. And then she walked over to where he was, her eyes widening when she saw into the truck.

He rolled his window down. "Merry Christmas."

The puppy ran over to the unrolled passenger window and stuck his head out.

"Caleb!"

"Do you think Amelia will be happy with a puppy?"

"She's going to freak out. But...why a puppy?"

"You said you wanted one."

"I was *kidding*." But she was looking at the puppy like he was made of pure delight.

"I was afraid of that."

"I can't *not* take him now. He's so fluffy."

"I know," he said.

"Someone was giving these away in town?"

He chuckled. "Not giving them away."

"What kind of dog is it?"

He explained the mix as best he could.

"You bought me a designer dog?"

"I guess I did."

"Well, I'll take it."

Suddenly, Ellie looked excited. "Should we save him for Christmas? Keep him at your parents' house until then. Christmas morning... She's going to absolutely flip out."

"Yeah, she is."

"Caleb... This is the kind of thing that I would have absolutely... If my mom ever would have..." She blinked. "Thank you."

"What?"

"You brought...this magic back to us. And we needed it. Because I know what it's like to grow up without it. And it's not about money, or gifts... Not really. It's about being able to believe in magic. In something. The kind of insane magic that puts a puppy under your tree on Christmas morning. I don't want Amelia to grow up afraid of the world. Angry at it."

"She won't," he said.

"I didn't have a lot of chances because my mom was so bitter. It was easy to absorb it. I don't want to do that to her."

"You've never been bitter. Of all the things... I find

that the most amazing. Because after everything you've been through…"

"But sometimes I did forget that her childhood shouldn't just be sad. I'm so conscious of what she doesn't have, and I know that she's becoming conscious of it, too. But it is different."

"I know," he said.

"Sometimes I feel like I'm trying too hard to make us both conscious of what we're missing. And we should focus more on what we do have."

"Can you get in the truck for a second?"

She looked around and opened the door, gently holding the puppy at bay while she got inside and sat on the seat.

The puppy, who was going to need a name, tramped across her lap back and forth, and she laughed. "Did you want to talk? Because it's not going to work like this."

"Okay, maybe we should get out, and the puppy should stay inside."

"Is it a boy or girl?" she asked.

"It's a boy."

"Okay, well, I will think of a suitably jaunty name."

"I'm scared now."

The two of them got out of the truck and rounded toward the back, meeting in the middle.

"I've been thinking a lot. About what Amelia feels like she's missing. About us. And about what we're doing here. I've been thinking about it constantly for the past three weeks. Don't think that I just fell into your bed and stayed there without realizing what was happening. From the first moment I met you I wanted you. Not just to sleep with you, but to take care of you. To be with you all the time. To talk to you, laugh with you. And I've had pieces of it over the years. And I'm damn grateful for that. For you. I couldn't have everything then, and it was a good thing I didn't. A good thing we didn't. And I would never suggest that I could replace what you lost. But I've been here for you. I've been here for Amelia. I was there when she was born. And..."

He swallowed hard, his heart thundering. "I want to keep being there for you. I want to keep doing this. And I don't want another man to step in and do it for me. I know that I'll never be the same. You'll never be the same. But we can be... We can be us. I want you to marry me."

Ellie looked like she'd been slapped with a fish. "What?"

"I want you to marry me. Marry *me*, Ellie. Let me be your husband. Let me be Amelia's father. I'll...I'll tell her about Clint. I'll make sure she knows, that she understands what a great man he was, and how much he loved her. But I want her to have someone that she can call dad. And I will... I will not be able to survive if it's someone other than me. Because someday it will have to be. Because if it's not me now...then you're gonna find someone else. And Clint... It could be him. I could let that happen. I did let it happen. But I can't... Not again. If there's going to be someone other than him, it needs to be me."

"Caleb..."

He reached into his pocket and he pulled out his ring box. "I got you a ring, El. It's not a traditional engagement ring." He opened the box. "But I know you've done this before. And I know that what we have is going to be...our own. And that's what this is. That's what that shows you. And I don't need you to walk toward me in a white dress. I know that you gave that to someone else. But I want *you* to be mine. And more than that, I want to be yours. I want to be Amelia's."

For a moment he thought she was going to turn and run away. For a moment he thought that she was going to push him, deny him.

Her lips were pale, her eyes glittering with a sheen of tears.

"Yes," she said. "I'll marry you. I'll marry you. Because...you're right. You're right." She swallowed hard. "She needs this and we...we work. We work like this. As a family."

"Can I put the ring on you?"

"Let's save it," she said quickly. "Let's save it like we're saving the puppy. For Christmas. Let's just... Let's just wait. And then we'll tell everyone. And then it'll be real. And we can... You're right. We can just have a wedding at the courthouse. It..."

He forced a smile. "Good."

"Good."

She wrapped her arms around his neck then, kissed him quickly. And he wondered why the hell this didn't feel happy. Not at all.

He put his ring back in his pocket. "I guess I better run the puppy over to my place. If I don't he's going to pee in my truck."

"Yeah. That sounds like a good idea."

"I'll make sure he's there Christmas morning. We can keep him in our room on Christmas Eve."

"Where are we going to...? Are we going to move to your house after this?"

"Let's talk about it after Christmas," he said. Because for some reason, he couldn't bring himself to talk about it now. Maybe for the same reason there was nothing but sadness in Ellie's eyes.

"Okay. We'll do logistics and things then."

"Ellie…"

It was on the tip of his tongue. To say that he loved her.

But it seemed wrong right now, and he didn't know why.

"I'll see you."

"Yeah," she said, nodding.

"I should probably stay at my place with the puppy tonight. But you know my parents are having a big get-together tomorrow. So I'll see you there probably."

"Okay," she agreed.

"And then we'll bring the puppy over here, and he'll be ready for Christmas morning."

"Good."

"Okay. Good."

And he got in his truck and started the engine. A man who was engaged to Ellie Bell.

A man who finally had everything he ever wanted.

And he'd been prepared for their engagement to be different. For it to be something other than what it had been for Ellie and Clint.

But he hadn't been prepared for it to hurt.

CHAPTER TWENTY-TWO

ELLIE FELT TERRIBLE, but Amelia's excited chatter was giving her a headache. They were on their way to the Dalton family Christmas Eve celebration, and she really should have a lot more patience for her daughter. Well, she was having patience externally. Internally, she felt like she was being stretched on a rack.

She had felt that way ever since Caleb's proposal.

She had said yes. She was marrying him. She had agreed to it.

And she felt like…like crying. Crying until she was hollowed out, and there was nothing left inside her.

She had no idea what the hell was happening.

Of course, she hadn't expected him to propose. And she really hadn't expected herself to agree.

But everything he'd said… It made sense.

Down to the ring that was nothing like the one she had taken from Clint.

The one thing he was wrong about was that there was no other man she would marry.

If she didn't marry him, she wouldn't marry anyone. That much she knew was true.

He seemed convinced that he had to get in there before she was swept off her feet by someone else.

Before she offered up some other replacement father to her daughter.

Which…she couldn't do. She would never do.

Amelia loved Caleb. More than anything. She knew that. In her heart, Caleb was already her father, whatever she had been calling him.

So much so that she had forthrightly and innocently asked if he could simply be her father.

She knew that this was the right thing to do. That it would give Amelia everything she wanted. That it would give her stability, that it would give her happiness.

She hadn't thought anything could overshadow the puppy, but this would do it.

So why was she…panicking?

She did not the hell know. It made sense.

They made sense.

And she repeated that mantra to herself over and over again.

It made sense.

Sensible was not what she would call what happened between them at night. Not at all.

For the past three weeks he had spent every night at her house, except for last night. And nothing they had done was sensible. They couldn't keep their hands off each other.

In the middle of the night, he would reach for her, even in sleep, and she had lost track of how many times they'd come together. Expressing things with their bodies that she didn't have coherent thoughts for.

Let alone the words.

Something about that didn't line up with sensible.

She was a mess.

She was engaged, and she should be happy.

Even though it wouldn't ever be the same as the first time.

The first time.

Oh, she remembered that engagement well.

He had taken her out to dinner. She had suspected that it was coming. They had looked at rings together a few different times while out shopping. He knew exactly what she wanted. So while neither the ring nor the proposal itself had been a blinding surprise, she had been happy. Brilliantly so.

He had gotten down on one knee, and he had made a joke. He had made her laugh, and they had hugged, with that glittering ring on her finger. She had put it on without hesitation.

She hadn't ached when it was done. She hadn't felt hollowed out and empty. Hadn't felt desperate somehow.

Caleb hadn't gotten down on one knee.

She blinked and shook her head.

She had to get a grip on herself before she went inside. Then right when she pulled up to the house, she managed to get some of her jitters under control.

Caleb was on the front porch when she pulled in.

"Hi," he said.

"Hi, yourself."

Her heart twisted. Not exactly a joyful leap.

But she felt herself drawn to him, like a magnet. She wondered if it would ever fade. The intensity, and the depth of what she felt.

It was so strange, so unlike anything she had ever known existed.

She walked up cautiously, Amelia trailing behind her, still chattering. "Hey," he said.

"Hey."

How could a friendship like theirs be uncomfortable? She had wept in his arms like she would never be happy again. She had come apart in those same arms, her cries of pleasure instead of grief when they were in bed. They had licked every inch of each other, seen each other naked.

And still, there was something wrong right now that she felt deeply afraid of.

Something that made her feel naked in a way she hadn't yet been with him.

And that was silly. Because she had been more naked with this man than she ever had been before.

The kind of sex they had was uninhibited and wild. Exposed pieces of herself she hadn't known existed.

She'd enjoyed sex before.

But it hadn't broken her open.

She felt like he was destroying her, in a thousand ways, and she couldn't figure out how to turn away from it. Couldn't figure out if she wanted to.

Or if she even could.

"Ready for the party?"

"Very ready," she said.

Amelia flung her arms around Caleb's legs. "I missed you," she said.

"I missed you, too, squirt," he said, wrapping his arm around her and patting her on the back.

She was making the right choice. She was.

For Amelia.

And all those other things that were cutting her up, they didn't matter.

She was just feeling shell-shocked because of the change. Because change was never fun, and she particularly had had some very bad experiences with it.

They walked in, and the house was already an explosion of warmth and noise. West was there, and so was Gabe and Jamie, Jacob and Vanessa. Also, McKenna, the other Dalton half sibling, and her husband, Grant.

Ellie didn't know Grant Dodge well, but she knew that they had gone through similar things.

He had lost his wife nearly ten years ago to cancer. And while her death had been expected in many ways, she knew that it had destroyed him.

Seeing him now, looking so happy…

Maybe she could will herself into that place. When they watched the two of them together, one word came to her mind.

Brave. Grant Dodge was brave.

Because the smile he had now was reckless, because the hold that he had on McKenna was possessive and tight and sure.

She looked over at Caleb. He held her like that, with that certainty. But she was Grant in this scenario. Not him.

Except, somehow, it felt different.

She wasn't afraid to marry Caleb.

Her stomach twisted. And she called herself a liar.

She took in a deep breath and moved in deeper, giving out hugs to everyone she knew, laughing and trying to look appropriately at ease.

Caleb, for his part, never behaved in any way other than a platonic friend, but he did keep close to her.

Not that that was incredibly strange.

Because he always kept to her. He always had. Even before the engagement.

Looking at him made her heart feel too big. Made her skin feel too tight.

Suddenly, she was overcome with the urge to throw her arms around him and never let go. To hold on to him forever.

She wanted to put him in a glass box. Something that might keep him safe. Keep them both safe.

And that didn't really surprise her, not given the state of things.

Loss had a way of making you keenly aware of the fact that it could happen to anyone, at any time. That, and the anxiety of it, was something that she had wrestled with a lot in those first couple of years. But this was different. Not the same even a little, even at all. She didn't know what this was.

It was like that feeling she had when they were in bed together, like that feeling she had when they made love, so foreign and entirely unlike anything in her experience.

Well, no. It was like one thing.

One thing that she'd always been afraid of.

Mom, why can't we just have Christmas together?

It's not Christmas without Dave.

Why can't it just be Christmas with me?

Because it's not enough, Elizabeth. Leave me the hell alone.

She swallowed hard and looked away from him.

She meandered over to the table, eating meat and cheese in silence until she felt far too self-conscious to remain in the room.

She went into the kitchen, where she found Tammy, who was baking away.

"Hi," she said. "How are you?"

"Good," she said, smiling.

"Really?"

"I will be," Tammy said. "We will be. Things are… resolving. Hank talked to Caleb, and I guess Caleb said some good things to him."

"Really? He didn't tell me that."

"I thought he told you everything," Tammy said.

She thought back on all the years that he'd spent very much not telling her everything.

"He's starting to," she said.

"Good. We all need someone like that. Someone we can share our hearts with."

That made her think of literally reaching into her chest, pulling out her heart and sharing it with Caleb. Literally giving him the source of her life and trusting him with it.

Because that was what sharing her heart with Caleb felt like.

That was what this...this feeling in her felt like.

She didn't like it. Not at all.

"Yeah," she said instead of saying any of that.

"Hank and I have made our share of mistakes. As parents. As spouses. I imagine we'll keep on doing it. It's a journey."

Now that, that made Ellie feel slightly better. It was a journey. And whatever journey she and Caleb were on, they could keep going on it.

"You look thoughtful."

"I am," she said. She needed to tell Tammy. She did. "Caleb and I... He asked me to marry him."

Tammy stopped mixing biscuit dough. She pulled floury hands out of the bowl and wrapped her arms around Ellie. "Oh, sweetie. I'm so happy."

"You are?"

"Yes. I'm so happy that you have him. I'm so happy he has you."

She hadn't known what Tammy's reaction would be. But Caleb was her son, and even though she had loved Clint, of course she loved Caleb, too.

"I love you both," Tammy said as if she read her mind. "I love you all. I want you to be happy."

"Don't tell anyone. We were going to tell Amelia on Christmas. And…after that we'll share it with everyone else. But she needs to know first."

"Of course. Of course."

"Can I help with anything?"

"Why don't you preheat the oven for me. My hands are greasy."

She did so, finding comfort in the simple motion. In Tammy's presence.

"Are you going to have a big wedding?"

The question was innocent, but it made her mind jump back to her wedding. The wedding she'd already had.

She could picture herself so clearly, a bride walking toward her groom. Except…

All she could see was the best man.

Standing there, looking at her. The intensity and those shocking blue eyes pinning her to the spot.

And she tried, she tried to picture Clint, and she couldn't. It froze her. Immobilized her.

She couldn't picture him.

She should be able to. He was the love of her life. Her first love. Her only love. And he had been the groom. Caleb had just been the best man. And there was no…

Clint was Amelia's father. And he was gone. It wasn't fair.

It was Caleb she saw. Caleb who made her ache in all these horrible, uncomfortable ways.

It would never be enough. That was why it ached.

She would never be enough, not for this.

It was bigger than she was, and she'd never wanted that. Not ever. She'd wanted safe, and sweet and kind. And it had been enough.

Why wasn't it enough now?

Why was Caleb all she could see?

"I…I don't know," she said.

"Are you okay?"

"Excuse me for a second."

She rushed out of the kitchen and out the front door without saying a word. She took a gasping breath of the air outside and put her hand to her chest, trying to calm her rioting heartbeat.

A moment later she heard the door open. But it wasn't Tammy who had come out after her.

"Are you okay?"

It was Caleb.

She looked at him and felt…

Everything.

Her heart was bruised, each thump against her breastbone physical pain. "I…I don't know."

"What's the matter?" he pressed, those blue eyes electrifying her. Pinning her in place.

She'd looked into them once a long time ago and seen the possibility of a different future. And after that she'd made it a point to look into them and see only a friend.

But here they were.

Here they were, and it was too much. It was just too much.

"I…I don't think I can marry you," she said.

His face immediately turned to granite. "What?"

Terror was clawing at her; even as she was drawn to him, she wanted to run away. It had been like this from the moment she had said to him: *It should be you.*

She had been so sure that her words had flipped the switch. Sure that he was the one that changed, and suddenly he looked at her with burning intensity. But she could see now that he always had. It wasn't him the switch had flipped in—it was her. Because suddenly she could see. See what had always been there. What had terrified her then, and why it should terrify her now.

It was too much. It was all too much.

It brought her back to the sad, lost little girl she'd been who had wanted too much from a mother who was never going to give it to her.

Who could never, ever be enough.

It wasn't what she'd wanted. She'd gotten what she'd wanted. Companionship, care. She'd had it and it should be enough. Why could she never get enough?

And now here she was, with this man who should have been enough just as he'd been. But she'd let him in, and now she needed more and she didn't even know what more was.

And already he eclipsed Clint and…

"I can't. I can't do this. It's not right. It's not fair. You were his best friend."

"Ellie, that hasn't been an issue this whole time."

"But it is *now*. You were our best man. You are my friend. And you… You don't even really want me," she said, reaching, looking for an excuse. Something, anything, to avoid the intense, crashing terror that was caving in all around her.

Making her feel small and fragile, making her *feel*.

She didn't want to analyze these feelings that were rolling through her.

She didn't want these changes.

And the only way that she could think to keep from having to look at them, to keep from having to examine them, admit to them, was to make him go away.

"I'm just something else that he had."

"That's bullshit."

"You said it yourself. If you hadn't blamed him for

the guns… If you hadn't done it then, you would have done it with me. You told me that."

"But it doesn't mean that I didn't have feelings for you."

"How can you ever know that?" She couldn't. She'd never be sure. How could she? Her own mother hadn't thought she was enough and she was supposed to believe Caleb just wanted her? And that it had nothing to do with his complicated history with Clint?

"Is that what worries you? That I won't feel enough for you?" He shook his head. "Fuck, Ellie."

He breathed out, the gust of air a harsh sound in the silence, visible in the cold. He looked down and then up at her, his eyes burning with intensity. "I love you. I have loved you from the moment I met you. I didn't even see him standing there when you walked in. Woman, you made the world fall away. And I know that you're never going to love me the way that you loved him, but I don't care. That's how much I love you. I will love you enough for the both of us. And I will love Amelia like my own. I already do. I don't need you to give me any damn thing, woman. Just let me take care of you. Let me have you. Because if you don't, then my life is never going to be anything. Christmas tree farms, cattle farms, what the hell ever. None of it matters. It's all just me trying to fill a hole. And I thought that I could do that. I thought that I could draw a line under you, under this, and call it done. But it's never going to be done. Not for me. He might have been the one for you, but you're the one for me. And that won't go away. He's not here. I am. Let one of us have it."

His words cut her like a knife. And she realized, with that knife, he'd given her an escape. And she felt…

like the world's biggest coward using it. But she was going to.

"I can't do that," she said. "You should be with a woman who can love you right. Who can love you first. It's not going to be me, Caleb. It never could be. I know what love is. I had it."

Her throat began to tighten, those words strangling her. "It's fun. And it made me laugh. And it's not... whatever *this is*. We're friends. And we have wonderful sex. But that isn't love. Whatever this is... I can't live with it. I can't."

"You are my whole life," he said, grabbing her and pulling her up against him. And she knew that anyone from the house could look out and see them now, and she knew he was past the point of caring. "You are my whole heart. I have not taken a breath that wasn't for you in more than ten years, Ellie Bell. Don't you tell me what love is."

That thing he was talking about, that feeling he was proclaiming, it sounded like hell to her. It sounded like horror. Because this felt bottomless and painful already.

"I can't," she said. "I won't. Please. Please don't ask me to do this."

"I can't ask for anything else. I want to marry you. I want to be with you forever. Let me give you this."

"No," she said. "Please. Please, Caleb. Don't make me... Don't make me be cruel. This was just supposed to be fun. It was supposed to be my Christmas wish list. It wasn't about forever. It was never about forever."

"You said yes," he ground out.

"And I couldn't put your ring on. Because I can't. I can't put another man's ring on. I'm not ready, and I might never be. I loved him. I don't love you."

He looked like a man being submitted to torture.

Whatever he'd said about not needing her to love him, she knew that wasn't true. Right then. The look of stark pain on his face was enough to make her crack, break into a thousand pieces.

But what was she supposed to do? What kind of mother would she be if she surrendered everything to him? Not any better than her own.

What kind of woman could she be?

"I'm sorry," she said.

"Don't you dare fucking apologize to me," he said.

"I didn't want to hurt you…"

"You're hurting yourself. You're hurting yourself. Don't bullshit me, Ellie. Don't do it. I have known you and loved you for more than ten years. And I can see that you're scared. That you're scared of loss…"

"You don't know what the hell I'm scared of, Caleb. And you know what? You're not going to. Because my life is going to be my life. And your life is going to be yours. And we should draw a line under it and call it done."

"This is yours," he said, digging into his pocket and pulling out the ring box.

"I don't want it."

"It's yours," he repeated, pressing the box into her palm. "Merry Christmas. I'll make sure that Amelia has her puppy on Christmas morning. Someone will bring it."

"You don't have to…"

"She deserves magic," he said. And then he stopped, a muscle in his jaw jumping, a slight tremor to his lips that shocked her. But he composed himself. "I'm still here to give her that. I'd give it to you, too. If you'd let me. But don't take it from her."

"I would never keep you from her."

"Well, I don't know what you would do. Not at this point."

And then he walked away from the house, headed out toward his truck.

"Where are you going?"

"Oddly, I'm not really in a Christmas mood now. Enjoy the party."

So she stood there and watched him go. And damned if it didn't feel like her heart had gone with him.

She looked down at the ring box in her hand, and she wondered if it was too late for her to salvage anything at all.

She felt like her life had fallen apart, for the second time. Except this time…

This time she had broken it herself.

And she didn't know if it could ever be fixed.

CHAPTER TWENTY-THREE

CALEB DROVE. HE DROVE for hours. To where, he didn't know. Until he found himself turning on a winding mountain road that led up to a place that was somewhat familiar. It had been the base camp of the wildfire they'd been fighting when Clint died.

And the crash site… It was close.

And he didn't know why the hell he had come here, because he knew that wherever Clint was, it wasn't here. His afterlife was sure as hell not going to be spent near the site of the smoldering wreckage that had taken him out of this world.

No, he knew his friend better than that.

He almost laughed at the absurdity, but he didn't think he could laugh again.

Because he didn't know what the hell was going on with Ellie, but it wasn't just about the fact that she couldn't love him, though her saying that had torn chunks off him.

He had accepted it, but hearing her say it…

"I tried," he said, resting his forearms on the steering wheel of his truck. "I tried to be a good man. I tried to take care of her. But I'm just hurting her."

And that, even in the moment, was one of the things that hurt him most of all. That he was hurting her still. He was supposed to protect her, but this wasn't protecting her.

"Dammit, Clint," he said. "Why did you have to die? You could've gone on living, and that would have been just fine. You could've watched your little girl grow up. You made us happy. You did. And I know that things were tricky between us. But… I didn't ever want you gone. I love Ellie. I love her. And you being gone means we both have to try this thing, because God knows… God knows we feel stuff. I know she does for me, too." He took a deep breath, his chest a ball of pain. "If you were just here, it would be simple. I could go on pretending I didn't love her. She could go on ignoring that she was ever attracted to me. We wouldn't have to sort any of this shit out. But you're not here. Because life's not fair."

He cleared his throat. Feeling like an idiot for talking to the wind. But he felt wrong, and he'd never damn well feel right again. So he might as well talk to the wind. Talk to a ghost.

"You were a good man. You didn't deserve my jealousy. And you didn't deserve to lose this beautiful life that you had. And I shouldn't love her. I shouldn't have been…made to love her. I love her. I love her, and everything is twisted up. I know it. No one will ever love her more than I do, though. I can promise you that. I love her now. Hell, if her marrying you didn't fix it, her saying something to me isn't going to, either."

He didn't know why he was here. Because there was no closure to be had.

He got out of his truck and looked around. And he felt nothing. Saw nothing.

Because Clint was gone. Except…

Except Caleb was different. For having known him. Just like Ellie was different for it.

And those pieces, those changed pieces, would never be gone.

But they would keep on changing. And they had. Hadn't Ellie said that very thing? That she wanted to get back to that girl that she'd been, but she couldn't.

Yeah. They were changing, because they were still here.

And they would keep on changing.

And one thing he knew for sure was that Ellie did want to marry him.

Maybe she didn't love him.

But she wanted to be with him.

She at least wanted him for Amelia.

So whatever he needed to do, whatever he needed to say...

He would wait. Because he was good at waiting. He had become so good at it over all these years, and he could wait more.

He could.

He told himself that, over and over again. Told himself that until he thought it might be true.

And he pictured Ellie, as a bride, walking toward him... Except, he knew that she hadn't chosen it. Hadn't chosen him.

And he looked into the emptiness all around him, and he had to accept the hardest truth he ever had.

Even with the best man gone, Caleb still wasn't the man she would choose.

And as much as he didn't want to accept the defeat for himself, there was a point at which he had to accept it for her.

If he really wanted to protect her, then he had to protect her. And if that meant walking away...then he would have to walk away.

But there was one thing he knew. Whether she felt the same or not, he would love Ellie Bell until the day that he died.

And sometimes, life just wasn't fair. Here at the place where Clint had died, that was the most apparent truth.

Life wasn't fair, and you couldn't make it so. Two people who loved each other had to be separated sometimes. And that didn't always mean there would be more happiness. Sometimes it just meant someone else ended up in love alone.

No ONE SAID anything to Ellie about Caleb leaving. And really, she didn't deserve their deference. Not now. Not after what she'd done.

She'd hurt him. Because she'd been terrified. Afraid. Of all the things that were happening inside her. But she just…

She had promised to love Clint. And even if wedding vows only extended until death did them part, she just didn't know…

If Caleb had been a stranger, maybe things would be different.

But he wasn't. He was a man she had known before she got married, and that added a layer of confusion to all of this. Because Caleb didn't feel like a second choice, and that actually frightened her. Down to her soul.

The implications of all of this terrified her. What it meant for them, for the future. For her heart.

What it would require of her.

It wasn't until it was time for dessert that Tammy cornered her in the kitchen.

"What happened?"

"I can't marry him," she said.

"Why not?"

"Tammy… I loved Clint. And I know you did, too. I know you loved him like a son. And he… He was wonderful. He was everything I needed. And… And when I picture my wedding I can't even see him anymore. I see Caleb. And that's not fair."

"Because you love Caleb," Tammy said.

"But this isn't what love is supposed to be. It's not supposed to eclipse everything else. It's not supposed to be all-consuming. That's how my mother was. That's how she ruined her life. Clint gave me this wonderful, measured, sweet love, and I can't even remember it anymore. All I see is Caleb. He's all I…" She swallowed hard. "It's not fair to Clint."

"Honey," Tammy said. "Clint is dead. And you're right. That's not fair. It never will be. But it's true."

"I don't want to forget all these things he gave me." And she didn't want to start over, loving someone else. Clint had made her feel sure-footed. It had all felt easy.

She'd never felt afraid she couldn't get enough from him. Never felt afraid she couldn't give enough.

"You need to quit thinking about yourself so much," Tammy said. "Stop thinking about how he loved you. Honey, do you have any idea what the way you loved him meant to him?"

Ellie couldn't make sense of those words. Because Clint had saved her. He'd changed her. She was just… well, she'd never thought about what she'd given to him. "No."

"He doesn't need you to stand as a vigil to him. He doesn't even need you to love him most forever. Because when he was here…the love that you gave him… It changed him. I had never seen him so happy. His family was such a mess… They hurt him in a thousand ways. And I never thought that he would find somebody to love. I didn't know that he could. But he loved you. And you loved him. And the way that you did it... You keep talking about it like he loved you to teach *you* something. And maybe he did. But you keep forgetting that you loved him right back."

But she'd never thought of her love as mattering. Not really. Her mother hadn't cared. And Clint had loved her but...but she'd never thought of it like this.

"It taught him so much," Tammy continued. "His life was too short, Ellie. And I know he didn't get to be a father. And he would've been a damn good one. But he got to be your husband. And that made him happy till his dying day. And how many people can say they were happy until their dying day? Not enough. But he was. Because of you. Because you gave him that gift. You gave him a gift of a happy life. Caleb gave him that gift. Don't deny yourself happiness because you think you owe him some kind of eternal sadness. Some kind of eternal statue to his memory."

Something felt like it broke inside her. Came loose and a flood of emotion washed forward.

"But I..."

"Honey," Tammy said. "It's not about whether or not he would have wanted you to be happy. It's about the fact that you made him happy. You did your work. You were the wife that he needed. And now he doesn't need you. But what do you need? And if it's not Caleb... then it's not."

Terror curled its way around her heart, along with the rush of relief and clarity.

Need. What did she need?

The idea that she might need someone. That she might need Caleb...

Love is easy.

Love is fun.

Her own words echoed in her head. Those things that she had shouted at Caleb. In desperation. In self-defense.

Love is easy.

Love is fun.

And she thought about Amelia. And the love that she felt for her daughter. How she carried her little girl's pain. The way that her heart had broken when she had asked if Caleb would be her dad.

That wasn't easy. That wasn't fun.

Sure, it was a joy to love her daughter, but there was a weight to it. Something she hadn't appreciated when she had been younger. And…

Something she would have avoided.

She had been able to love Clint at the time because she hadn't realized that love could contain those bright, brilliant things he had brought into her world. But she was older now. And she had endured pain beyond anything she had imagined she might.

And she knew now.

Love had a cost.

Love always cost, because the loss of it would devastate.

Love was heavy. As heavy as it was beautiful. Like a precious stone.

And whenever you had something of value, you worried about losing it.

And then there was…

There was Caleb himself. The depth of what she felt for him. It encompassed her whole body. It encompassed her soul.

This thing that she felt for him…it was different. It

was deep and rich and terrifying, and when that man had looked at her and said that he loved her…she wanted to run from it. Because his love would give, it had for years, but it also took. His love was a demand as much as it was a blessing.

It was why she had turned away from that question in his eyes that day up on the ridge.

And it was why she turned away from him now.

Because love terrified her.

When she had been young she had found an easily digestible kind of love. It had been real. It had given her something beautiful. Stability like she'd always craved. A confidence in herself that hadn't been there before.

It had given her Amelia.

It had been lovely. It had been good.

But Caleb…

Caleb was her heart and soul in a way no one ever had been before.

An enduring love that her heart had recognized from the first day they had met.

And that she'd held at arm's length for safety.

"I've never wanted to need anybody," she said. "I grew up watching my mother need men. And she was only ever hurt by it. I needed my mother, and she didn't give me what I wanted, and I just never… I never wanted that."

"I've been hurt plenty of times. And I hurt Hank. And I would never suggest that anybody should model their marriage off of ours. But you know, sometimes you find that one, and they just stick with you."

"But I chose a different one," she said.

"I know you did. You made the best choice for you at the time. Or you made the only choice you could make."

Those words settled within her, and she took hold

of them. Turned them over and examined them from every angle.

She had made the only choice she could make at the time. She would never have been able to have a relationship with Caleb, not then.

They would've consumed each other.

There would've been no finishing school, that was for sure.

She wouldn't have been able to handle him, and she didn't know if he would've been able to handle what he'd gotten back, as much as he had believed he wanted it.

But now…

She was different. She was stronger.

She had walked through the fire and come out harder. And now she needed what he was.

That man who had always stood there, waiting for her.

He was the only man that would do for the woman she was now.

But she had to become brave enough.

She had to find a way.

Fear was like a wall, standing high before her, and she had no way to see what was on the other side of it. But she knew what was on this side. Grief. Loneliness. And maybe she could stay in her little house with Amelia, and she could be a kind of happy.

But maybe, maybe she could find a future and a hope on the other side of her fear that would make all of this seem pale in comparison.

If there was one thing she did know about love, it was that it had only added to her life.

Yes, losing Clint had hurt. But he had given her things. Things that she hadn't lost, even when she lost him.

He had made her a happier person. He had given her Amelia.

Love was never a mistake.

And Caleb...

He made her whole. And if she had felt broken, for even a moment, when she was standing in her kitchen, watching that man move around her life as if he belonged, it was because those jagged edges were rearranging themselves so that they could fit together.

Because he was hers. Her shelter. Her strength. Her intensity.

He was the man who had brought her through that fire. Through those woods.

She and Clint had had a beautiful marriage, and they'd had daily struggles, but they'd never had to go through something shattering.

But she and Caleb... They had been shattered together.

And here they were. Together. Or they could be, if she could just find it in her to say yes.

"Can you...? Can you watch Amelia?"

"Yes. Whatever you need, honey."

"Thank you. I might... I might have her spend the night... But I didn't bring..."

"I have some extra pajamas here. Don't worry about it. She'll have tons of fun. And I'll make sure she knows that Santa will be here for her."

"Thank you. I have to fix this. But first I...I need to be alone."

She said her goodbyes, and somehow managed not to cry, in front of her daughter, in front of her family. And then she found herself driving back to the farmhouse. The one that she had bought for a life that had ended up not existing.

She walked toward the chicken coop and stood there, watching the little brown birds scurry around beneath the heat lamp.

It seemed like a lifetime ago she had stood in here and reflected on the fact that sometimes she could fantasize about having a whole other life when she was in here.

Well, she'd gone and found a whole other life, and what had she done with it?

She had thrown it away out of fear. Out of guilt.

Her whole insides were a mess.

She turned away from the chickens and then walked to the porch, sat down on the steps and leaned her head against the support.

She could remember looking at this house with Clint, planning a future together that they never got to have.

"I loved you," she whispered.

And something in her got lighter. She would always love him, as her first love. As the man who had made her brave enough to love. The man who had given her her beautiful daughter.

And at first she had imagined she would always love him as a husband. That he would always *be* her husband.

But he wasn't.

She had said that to Caleb weeks ago, but she hadn't really meant it. She had said that she was Clint's widow.

But that wasn't all of her. It wasn't even most of her.

She sat on the porch and closed her eyes. "Goodbye," she whispered.

Not just Clint. But to that dream. That dream that was tied up in this house. In that future.

And behind her eyes, that were swimming with tears, she saw Caleb.

Caleb.

She loved him so much it hurt.

Had she always loved him? She might have.

Beautiful Caleb, whom she hadn't been ready for, and wasn't really ready for now.

But she couldn't face a life without him, either.

Her future was with him. Her future was at his Christmas tree farm—and dammit, she was going to make him keep those Christmas trees—it was in his arms. In his bed.

He wasn't second.

He would never be second.

He was the first of this kind of love. He was the only man that the woman she was now could ever be with.

And she wouldn't have been strong enough before. Wouldn't have been steady enough.

She would've run away from the bigness of the feeling; she would never have been able to run toward it.

And just like she had felt the door open when the two of them had been together that night, a door into a part of herself that she had never before encountered, this time she felt one close, as well. Tightly behind her. And she knew. That it was time. Time to walk forward.

She loved Caleb so much it was terrifying. She didn't know that it would ever be anything but terrifying.

But it was also beautiful.

He was the love of her life. It would have destroyed her to admit that before. But life was complicated, and so was love. With beauty and tragedy at the bottom of each valley, and the top of each hill.

You couldn't stop tragedy. But if you were brave, you could grab on to the beauty and hold it tight.

She could have lived her other life. She would have. And she would have been happy.

She was learning there was a lot of space between

happy and this. This soul-deep connection you could share with another person.

Caleb was the only person who had that part of her.

The beauty in the tragedy was they'd found this. And they would have never, ever known what could be without it.

She and Caleb had a complicated, terrible, wonderful history. But it was theirs.

And she was his.

And she loved him.

No matter the cost.

If Caleb was what she would find on the other side of fear, then fear had no place in her.

And so she stood up, wiped off the back of her jeans and walked forward.

CHAPTER TWENTY-FOUR

THERE WAS NOWHERE else to go. He couldn't sleep. And so at midnight, he found himself out at the barn, getting his horse out of the stall, ignoring the fact that snowflakes had started to fall, swirling to the ground, promising a white Christmas that Caleb thought was a mockery of everything he felt.

White Christmas. Black soul.

Perfect.

He started to lead the horse out of the barn, and was stopped by a figure standing there in the middle of the gravel lot.

"West told me that I might find you here."

"Jacob?"

"Yeah. I went to your house. You weren't there. West said that he ran into you out here once."

"Yeah. I'm going for a ride."

"What happened?"

"What makes you think something happened?"

Jacob snorted. "Well, you left. Also, I know that you were sleeping with Ellie. And I'm not an idiot. That's math that even I can do."

"I'm the one that has trouble with math," Caleb said, hauling himself up onto the horse.

"What are you doing?"

"I told you. I'm going for a ride. I need to clear my head."

"Great. Wait for me."

"Come on—really? Do we need to do this? There's nothing to talk about."

"You love her. You love her, and you need to be with her. So yeah, we need to talk about it."

"I proposed to her, idiot."

He couldn't see Jacob's face in the dim light, but he did see his whole frame shift. "What?"

"She rejected me. She doesn't love me. She loves Clint. She's always loved Clint. And it makes me want to hate him. He's dead, and it makes me want to hate him. What kind of man does that make me?"

"A man that's in love, I would think. Why would you ever be okay with your woman's heart belonging to someone else?"

"He's Amelia's father. He was my friend. I respect that. But he's not here to be her husband. It's not…"

"It's not selfish to want her to love you. It was never selfish to want her to love you. Why shouldn't it be you?"

"Well, she doesn't. So now what? What? You were here to lecture me."

"Yeah, I was here to lecture you about being a hypocrite. Because you yelled at me when I screwed things up with Vanessa. And you told me that if I had a woman that loved me I needed to take the opportunity."

Caleb snorted. "And I would. I'm not a hypocrite. I love her. And yeah, I told myself for a long time that it could never work out. I told myself that we were just having sex, and it wasn't going to end with her being my wife. But you know what? I don't want a life that doesn't end with her being my wife."

It hurt to even say it. His whole chest felt like someone had shoved a broken bottle right through it and twisted. "But she doesn't want to be my wife," he said, the words scraping his throat raw. "So what am I supposed to do about that? I fell in love with the wrong woman, Jacob. I fell in love with her more than ten years ago and I can't undo it. I want… I want her to be mine. I want her little girl to be my little girl. I want a family that I can't have. So fix that. Go tack up your horse and let's go riding. Fix my broken life, bro."

Jacob went into the barn, and Caleb sat there on the back of his horse, flakes coming down heavy and hard now. And he waited. Getting lost in the staleness of the cold, and the stillness of his spirit.

Jacob came out a minute later and mounted up. "All right. Let's go."

The moon was bright, the clouds not covering it, illuminating the ground around them and the falling snowflakes. It was a beautiful night, the perfect Christmas Eve, or early Christmas morning, as the case may be.

Except that everything was broken. Utterly and completely destroyed inside him.

He had hope, he realized. And he had never considered himself an optimist. But he was, it turned out.

And having that last little bit of hope snuffed out was devastating.

He didn't know his own insides anymore. They had been moved and shifted, upended and broken.

He didn't know what he was if he didn't love Ellie Bell. If he couldn't take care of her. And now that he held her in his arms at night, he didn't know how he was ever going to sleep without her there.

They rode up the hill, keeping silent as they did.

"So this is a mess," Jacob said finally.

"Yes," Caleb said. "It's a mess. Welcome to my world.

It's been a mess for so long I don't know what it's like to live different." He shook his head. "So damned long."

"Why won't she marry you?"

"I already told you. She doesn't love me."

"Well, that's not true. She loves you a hell of a lot."

"Does she? Or am I just convenient."

"Why wouldn't I have been as convenient as you? She never cared for me the way she did for you."

"I was there."

"It's more than that. You think she slept with you because you were there?"

"Well, she was ready to go sleep with *anyone*."

"I don't think that's true. And anyway, so what? Is this about you not feeling special enough?"

"No," he said. "I was ready to take whatever she would give. I was ready to take less. I was ready to take nothing. To just be able to be there for her."

"Well, maybe that's the problem."

"Why is that a problem?"

"Who wants that?" Jacob asked. "That's not an offer of love. That's not an offer of a new life, of moving on. You're offering to let her love her dead husband more than she loves you? Offering to let her continue to live in the past? Don't do that. Offer her the world. A new world. Fresh and shining and everything that she deserves. Offer her a diamond. Offer her a white wedding. Offer her everything he did and then some. It'll be different either way because it's you. It's from you. Why would she want a consolation? And if she doesn't want a consolation, then don't be one. Be the first. Be everything. If that's what you want, that's what you have to be willing to be."

The words hit him like a slap to the face. "I… But if she can't…"

"You don't know if she can. You're not Clint, Caleb. You're never going to be. You know that. But you're not his shadow, either. You're your own man. And hell, you know that, too, so why are you acting like it might be different with her?"

"Because it is. Because with her everything is different. It always will be. I can't help that…"

"Why? Because she chose him first?"

"No…that sounds…"

"She met him first. And yeah, she chose him first. But when I was that age I chose a lot of things I wouldn't choose now. Not that he was wrong. It's just that you change. And what you need changes. Who you are is different now than who you were. And the same goes for her. Why shouldn't you take all the good things with the different, instead of just the bad? Your lives already changed. Clint is already gone. You don't get a chance to go back and make any of those things different. But you can make today different. You can make tomorrow different."

"So what do you want me to do?" he asked. "Because she already said no. She already said she didn't love me. I told her I loved her from the moment I'd met her. I might not have offered her the prettiest proposal, but I gave her everything I had inside me."

"Yeah. I believe you. I really do."

"So why the lecture? I mean, what the hell am I supposed to do now?"

His brother was silent for a long moment. "What's your life without her?"

Caleb huffed out a laugh, his breath a cloud in the crystal night sky.

"I'm serious," Jacob said. "What's your life without her? Because I had to ask myself the same question.

Did I want to protect myself, or did I want to go all in? The fact of the matter is, protecting myself… It doesn't mean anything if I don't have Vanessa. Because my life doesn't mean anything. That woman is everything to me. And Ellie is everything to you. She has been for years. So why stop now? Why protect yourself now? Why, when you know what you want. You want her a whole lot more than you want to be safe, don't you?"

"I want her more than anything," he said, his voice gruff. "But if she doesn't want me…"

"But you didn't ask for her. Gave her all of you, and you asked her for what you thought she could give easily. But I don't think that's why she likes you, Caleb. You two… Look, I don't need to know details, but I can see chemistry like yours from miles away. Hell, I bet they can see it from space. What you guys have… Look, I was around when she was with Clint. This is different."

"Yeah," Caleb said. "He made her laugh."

"And you held her when she cried. Caleb, I don't envy what you did. I don't envy the fact that you were the one that held her when her life fell apart, that you were the one that had to tell her. I felt like a monumental coward letting you do it, but…you were the one. You were there for her. You're the one who put her back together. Be that man for her now. That man's not going to go in and offer her half. That man's not going to say let's settle for the smallest we can have. There are no points in this life for people who play it safe. And while you still have breath in your body, you have the choice of taking a risk. Choose it. Choose it because you're here, and you can."

They were here. Both of them. And it seemed a real

tragedy to not be together. But she'd said what she had said, and what was he supposed to do with that?

"So, I just…ambush her with another proposal?"

"I don't know about that. I think she loves you. I think she's afraid of it. Maybe… Maybe she'll come to you."

"So I should buy a ring and wait for her to come tell me she was wrong? Then be prepared to offer her the whole world, and ask for nothing less in return?"

"Why not?"

"Because she might not."

"Well, then you're in the exact same spot you're in now. Maybe a thousand dollars poorer, though, 'cause of the ring."

He forced out a laugh. "Minus my pride if I'm carrying a ring around for a woman who doesn't want it."

"What the hell is your pride doing for you?"

They stopped their horses up on the hill. It was quiet, the blanket of fallen snow covering the ground in crisp, cozy velvet. He would have said it was peaceful, if anything in him had been capable of feeling peace.

"I guess I'm not really using my pride at the moment."

"What does pride matter?" Jacob asked. "It can't hold you at night. It can't love you."

"Ellie might not be able to love me, either."

"Have you asked her to love you?"

"No. It's the thing I didn't ask for."

"It's a risk. But we are men who take risks. We fight wildfires. I think that means we ought to be brave enough to take hold of love when we get the chance."

"Easy for you to say. She said she loved you before you told her."

"True," he said. "You're going to have to be so much braver than I was. Because hell, this is pretty twisted up."

"No kidding."

"But let me tell you… Let me tell you, it's worth it. And let me tell you, as someone lucky enough to have a person who was willing to be that brave for me… some of us need it."

Caleb took a breath, and for the first time he felt something a little bit like hope break through the rock in his chest.

"So what do I do in the meantime?"

"You love her," Jacob said. "And you told her that. She's scared. But what do you think she's really scared of?"

Ellie. *Oh, Ellie.*

It was easy to think she was afraid of loss. Loss because of Clint. But she'd told him about her mother. About her fear of loving too much, of wanting a love she couldn't get back.

Their intensity scared her.

She was a strong woman, and he knew it better than most. He'd seen her grieve. He'd seen her give birth. He'd watched her overcome so many obstacles in life.

But this was the one thing she'd always avoided.

She'd loved the fun in Clint, and she'd been angry at him when he wasn't the kind of fun she'd wanted.

She was afraid of being in love like he was.

In the kind of deep, on-fire love that left you scarred and wounded. That felt like a void when you weren't getting what you gave back.

He was willing to jump headlong into it because he already knew he had no other choice. But Ellie was still trying to backtrack. Trying to hide.

But what would she do if he was just there? Waiting,

like always. If he wasn't like her mother. If he didn't tell her to go away, but if he stayed.

The idea made him want to die a little bit. To have to keep on seeing this woman, to see her Christmas morning and not hold her.

To buy a ring and carry it even if he might never need it.

But he'd offered his whole heart. He'd offered that crazy, intense forever love. And he had to keep on showing it to her.

Because he didn't really think Ellie was scared of forgetting Clint.

Ellie was afraid of what she'd always been afraid of.

Loving too much. Loving alone.

Basically the life he'd lived for more than a decade, and damn, the woman was right to fear it.

He was everything that frightened her. Their passion was everything that frightened her.

She thought it would be volatile and temporary. Thought it would leave her in pain.

But he would show her. Yes, the love was sharp, it was big and it could cut like a knife.

But when you had something that dangerous, that lethal…

You treated it with even more reverence, because you knew it could be fatal.

So he would show that. He would be there.

Even if it killed him.

This was a valley in the middle of a dark wood. But like every other path they'd been on, the only way was through.

ELLIE SPENT THE night in a fitful sleep. She had decided that she would go to Caleb in the morning. Because she wanted to sit with her revelation for a little while. Wanted to process her feelings. Mostly, she wanted to be able to tell him, in all the right words, why she loved him. And what it meant.

She was ready to go and do that in the predawn gray of a Christmas morning that felt more like the dawning of the day of a funeral, when she opened her front door, her heart pounding. It was freezing outside.

The air hit her cheeks, a stinging cold penetrating her skin like needles. It was the fortification she needed.

She was ready to go and make it right today. She'd sat in complicated and painful truths all night, and it had felt like an essential thing to do. And today...today she was ready to be with him.

Go to the tree farm.

She didn't know why, but that seemed to be right. She couldn't imagine he would be at his parents' place yet. He would still be at his. She was sure of that, even if she didn't know why.

It was a white Christmas, and the roads were covered in a film, so she took it slowly, making her way up to his place, her heart pounding in her throat.

What if he didn't want to see her? What if he never wanted to speak to her again? After what she had said. She didn't deserve for him to forgive her. She didn't deserve much of anything.

She wound her way slowly up the drive and to his property. And when she pulled up to the trees, her heart stopped. There were lights strung over all of them, a magical Christmas morning wonderland, with that halo glow and the snow falling everywhere, dusting the trees.

And there was Caleb, standing there on the edge of the trees, his hands shoved in his pockets. He breathed out, his breath a cloud in the cold air.

She parked her car and got out, looking around.

"What are you doing out here?" she asked.

He looked up, shocked. "I…I should ask you the same thing."

"I came to find you," she said. "I was thinking I'd have to drag you out of bed."

"I didn't ever sleep," he said.

She saw the circles under his eyes, the lines next to the corners. He hadn't slept. Because of her. Because of her cowardice.

"Caleb…" She started to walk toward him, her heart thundering. "I'm so sorry. I am so… I am so so sorry."

She had hurt this man. And if she'd ever doubted the power of this love, the power of her love—badly withheld because of her own fear—she couldn't now.

Fear would have kept them apart, and the realization of that now made her ache. She would have kept herself from that love. She would have kept herself wanting, forever.

She'd wondered…wondered about that intense fire between a man and a woman, and she'd seen it in Caleb's eyes when he'd come into that bar and pulled her off the dance floor.

She'd wanted to test it. Taste it.

She hadn't wanted to immerse herself in it because anything that all-consuming was her own personal nightmare.

But there was no flirting with this.

This was all, or it had to be nothing.

So she was ready to give all, because Caleb… Without Caleb her life felt a whole lot like nothing.

Emotion knotted up her throat, made it hard for her to speak the words she was so desperate to say. Her heart was pounding hard, her hands shaking.

But here she was, on the other side of fear.

And Caleb was right there with her.

"I do love you," she said, the words breaking. "Caleb, I was so afraid of this kind of love. All of my life I feared it because the need of it broke me. So I decided not to need it. I decided what I could want and still be… safe. I was happy there. I was happy being safe."

He didn't speak; he only looked at her, his expression carved from that beautiful granite face, and she knew she owed him everything first.

Knew she had to be the one to say it all first because he already had.

Hadn't he already stood there radiating emotion and told her he'd loved her all his life?

He had. And she'd turned away. Wounded him to protect herself.

"I was so afraid," she whispered. "To let go. To move on. Because there is safety in fear, Caleb. There's safety in staying in grief. In holding on to the past. I started to change and what I wanted started to change, too. And when I found myself letting go of it without meaning to, I…I was afraid. Because when I closed my eyes and I pictured my wedding, you were the only man I could see."

A muscle in his jaw pulsed, a blue fire in his eyes, but he stood motionless. "I wanted to get back to that girl I was, and I thought that my Christmas list was going to be the way to do it. But instead… Instead, all of the loss, all of the pain, all of our time together, those years alone, the time with you… I became the woman I needed to be now. And that woman loves you. Only you."

She swallowed hard. It was difficult work, sharing

your soul when you'd hidden it away your whole life. Kept a barrier between yourself and everyone.

But with Caleb she shouldn't do that. Part of her had always known it.

Part of her had always feared it.

But the broken road they were both walking was one they could have only walked together. It was him. And somehow, right now, she felt it always had been. "I've changed. I've survived. And I'm brave. This love, this love terrified me far too much to take hold of it, Caleb. But I can't live in fear anymore. I'm brave enough now to face whatever might come our way. I'm brave enough to be a woman that can love you. Because I know I'm strong enough for it. What we have is…" A smile curved her lips. She imagined kissing him. Holding him. Tangled up in bed with him.

And suddenly it seemed like he saw it, too, because he moved for her, caught her up in his arms and kissed her with a ferocity that made her heart feel like it might burst.

He still wanted to kiss her.

That was a very good sign.

"Forgive me," she whispered against his lips as he continued to take small tastes of her between words and breaths.

"There's nothing to forgive," he murmured. "Nothing. Whatever we have, whatever we are, we had to go through it. To get here."

"I had to break myself first," she said, a tear rolling down her cheek. "To understand why I was so afraid. I chased love as a child, and I didn't get it back. My own mother thought I was too much and I believed her. So I decided to be less. And I found a way to be comfortable there. You demanded I be more, and that was the most uncomfortable thing of all. But now that I know what I can feel, now that I know what love can be... I can never take less again. You ruined me."

"Thank God," he growled, kissing her until she was dizzy. "Thank God."

"You are my heart, Caleb Dalton." She rested her hand on his chest. "And I want to belong to you. You carried me through those dark times."

"You keep saying that. Hell, even I say that. But, honey, you held me in your arms right back. But you got me through, too."

"We can do anything, as long as we're together."

She felt like something was expanding inside her, big and bright and true. Something that would change everything.

In the very best way.

"I was out here for a reason," he said, his voice rough. "Putting up these lights because I wanted... I wanted to go find you today. I wanted to show you that I still love you. No matter what. And I wanted to bring you out here and tell you...tell you I'd wait. Because this isn't the kind of love that passes, El. This is forever. If it would pass from me it would have done it a long time ago. I'm in. For the rest of my life, and I always knew it on some level. My whole body took a vow the moment I saw you."

"Oh, Caleb..." His name was a sob.

She loved him so much. It hurt to love this much.

But he was right. It was like seeing in color for the very first time.

Bright. Brilliant. A little too much.

But you could never go back. You never could.

He took her hand, and he led her down one of the

rows of trees, until the pines enveloped them, the lights overhead shining down on them.

"I wanted to tell you I'd wait. And I wanted to tell you…it does matter if you love me. I don't want a piece of you," he said. "I want all of you. I don't want to have a small wedding. I want to see you walk toward me in a white dress."

She put her hand over her mouth, her heart fluttering. And she could picture it. Could picture herself with him in a suit. A wedding. A real wedding.

"I don't want a small marriage," he continued. "To be someone standing there just taking care of you in the place of another man. I love you. Wildly. Deeply. More than I've ever loved anything in my entire life. Ellie Bell, you are my heart. I want you to be my wife. Be my wife because I love you, and because you love me. Not for Amelia, but for us. Because you don't want to live without me, because I damn sure don't want to live without you."

Ellie thought her heart would burst, and she wanted to speak, but she didn't want him to ever quit talking. This was it. These were the words. This was the deep love, the one she'd craved all her life. The one she'd been so sure couldn't exist, not for her.

"Be my wife," he said, "for no other reason than that this is *love*, and it's *real*. That we light up the night in bed because there's never been another love like this. I'm selfish. Ellie, I want it all. I want your heart, your whole heart. And I don't mean… I'll always love Clint. Whether he's here or not. I'll respect until my dying day that you loved him. That he's Amelia's father. But I want to be your husband. Me, and only me. I want to be the man who holds you at night from now to the end of our days."

He reached out and put his hand on her cheek, stroking her gently. "Be mine because you want me. Not because you're lonely. Be mine because you love me. And love me because… Love me because you can't help yourself. Even knowing how cruel the world can be. Because I love you. And I may never be able to read without stumbling over my words. I may never be the gentlest, most caring man around, but I love you with all that I am. Always have, always will."

Oh, this proposal… This was so different from the one behind the truck. Because she was still closed then. Trying to have what she wanted without letting herself be open. Without letting herself feel.

But she couldn't. Not halfway. Not with him.

It would never be fine.

It would be all, and it would be big. And you couldn't hold *all* with folded arms and a closed heart.

"I was afraid that loving like this, loving with all of me, would always mean wanting. Because growing up, it was. I told you about my mother and the Christmas tree. I told you she said…she said I wasn't enough. That I was needy and I just never wanted to be that again. I wanted safe and contained. I wanted secure, and I found it." She breathed in deep. "But I was still guarded. I was still protecting the deepest part of myself, and, Caleb, you get right down to it. It terrified me. You stripped me bare in every way and I didn't know if I could… I didn't know if I could stand it."

"Sweetheart, why? Why did I scare you so much?"

"I could never do easy with you, Caleb. And I think something in me always knew it. I had to be willing to give you me, all of me. And that scared me, too. I grew up not having my mother's love, not really. And I hoped and I wished I could. I tried to make myself someone she could be proud of until the day she told me I'd never be enough. That's when I realized I had to be enough for myself. So I stuck to that. All those years. I knew, on some level, that if I let myself want you… Caleb, I was so afraid of wanting and not having again. It hurts too much…"

"You have all of me," he said. "Every last piece."

"I love you," she whispered through her tears.

"I love you, too, Ellie. I always have."

"Caleb, I've always loved you, too. My heart changed forever when I went through what I did. And that love that I held for you shifted shape right along with it. But it was always there. I have loved you with an everlasting love. My friend, my lover. My safety. My help, my hope. I have loved you as everything. I loved you with a shattered heart, and you've healed it, and you… You fill in all those cracks. Everything that I am. Everything that I ever will be."

"Ellie," he said, her name broken on his lips.

And then he did something totally unexpected.

He got down on one knee in the snow in front of her and pulled a box out of his pocket.

"You gave me a ring," she said.

"I want you to keep it," he said. "Because it's a special ring. And it represents some things about us that mean the world to me. But I want you to have this, too." He opened the box and produced the most exquisitely beautiful diamond ring she had ever seen.

"Where did you get this?"

"Honestly? Thank God for big-box stores that expect men to be way behind on Christmas shopping. And thank God for their jewelry counters."

"It's beautiful," she said.

"I wanted you to have a diamond ring. I was… I was so focused on not forcing you to see this as the same kind of marriage you had. On not competing. But this isn't about competing. But it is about deserving everything. And you and I deserve everything."

"Yes," she said. "Yes. I'll marry you. I'll wear your ring. Both your rings. Any ring you want to give me."

"There is one more person that I probably need to ask."

"Who?"

"We need to go to my parents' house. We need to talk to Amelia."

CALEB HAD BEEN nervous to confess his love for Ellie. After all, there had been a big risk involved in that.

But he wasn't really less nervous to talk to the little girl who had stolen his heart from the moment she had taken her first breath.

Thankfully, he was armed with a puppy.

It was still early, the sky just now getting rosy and casting the snow in a pink glow.

He and Ellie walked hand in hand to the front door of his parents' house, the puppy—who was still nameless—dangling from his arms.

He knocked, and it took a few moments for the door to open. And there was his mother, all done up already, wearing her traditional Christmas morning red.

She looked at him, looked at Ellie, and at the ring on Ellie's left hand.

"So it all worked out," she said softly.

"I think so," Caleb said.

"We need to talk to Amelia."

"She's up and ready."

They walked into the living room and Amelia was sitting in front of the Christmas tree, a big red bow in her pale blond hair, red plaid jammies still on her little body.

"Merry Christmas, princess," Caleb said.

She turned around and her green eyes went wide as saucers.

"A puppy?"

"Yeah," he said. "A puppy."

"Who's it for?" she asked, wary hope in her eyes.

"It's for you," he said.

The squeal of delight that exited Amelia's mouth was nearly shrill enough that only the dog would've been able to hear it. And oddly, the dog didn't seem off-put. He wiggled in Caleb's arms, and Caleb set him down on the ground. He immediately went to Amelia as if he knew, for sure and certain, that that was his person.

She giggled, the puppy licking her all over.

Caleb crouched down beside them. "I want to ask you something."

"What?" she asked, not even looking up from the puppy.

Damn. This was just as tough as a marriage proposal.

"Do you still want me to be your dad?"

She looked up at him, hope shining in her green eyes that was so pure and radiant and made his chest hurt.

"Because I'd like to be your dad, Amelia. I want to marry your mom. And I want to live with you both. Because I love you. Both of you. And I want to be your family."

Her little face crumpled, and she didn't speak. Instead, she just wrapped her arms around Caleb's neck and cried. And only just barely, through her broken sobs, did he hear her whisper. "I love you, Daddy."

And Caleb would be damned if he didn't cry a little bit, too, because a man would have to be made of rock not to. And he didn't want to protect himself from this. He wanted to feel it. Every bit, all the way down.

Because it was a gift.

The best gift he could've ever asked for in all his life.

Caleb Dalton hadn't made a Christmas list, but he'd gotten everything he wanted all the same.

EPILOGUE

ELLIE BELL COULD sometimes imagine she lived an entirely different life. In fact, for a time she'd thought about that quite a lot. But not for a long while. And certainly not today. Her wedding day. When she was getting ready to walk down the aisle toward the man of her dreams. The man she loved more than anyone or anything on earth.

Her wedding dress was simple but beautiful, long-sleeved, perfect for the winter wonderland they had set up for the big day.

When your fiancé owned a Christmas tree farm, and when you had gotten engaged officially on Christmas Day the previous year… Well, there was no choice but to have the most Christmassy wedding imaginable. At least, that was how they had both seen it. Well, it was how she had seen it. Caleb had been a little bit put out to have to wait nearly a year to marry her. And she kind of liked that. That he was impatient.

But she had wanted a wedding. A *big* wedding, not just a rushed one. One for all their family and friends. One to show the whole world what they were doing. One to make the most real and certain declaration possible.

Because this wasn't second-best. Or even a second chance.

It was *their* chance.

Amelia was the flower girl, eagerly spreading berries and pine boughs down on the ground, preparing a blanket for Ellie to walk over when the time came.

And the dog—who had been named Christmas, of course—was dutifully performing the part of ring bearer for the ceremony.

Ellie took a breath and picked up her bouquet. And took her position around the corner from the aisle, out of sight of the guests and of her groom.

And suddenly, on that pale winter day, the clouds parted and the shaft of light shone down from the sky. A little brightness. A little lightness.

She smiled and looked up.

"Thank you," she whispered.

And then she gathered up the front of her dress and stepped around the corner.

And she saw him there. Dressed in a suit, wearing a black cowboy hat, his blue eyes shining with that beautiful brand of intensity that she had come to know as love.

She took a step toward her new life. A step toward becoming Ellie Dalton.

And when she got there, when they joined hands together, she didn't wait for the minister to tell her to kiss him. She did it right away. Because she had waited a long time to kiss him, and she wasn't waiting anymore.

"I love you," she whispered.

"I love you, too," he said back. "Always."

"Always," she whispered.

And as she spoke her vows, she meant them, with every word, every bit of conviction inside her.

And she gave thanks, for the Christmas miracle she

was witnessing now, and the Christmas miracle she had been a part of a year ago.

One that had all started with a simple list.

And ended with forever.

* * * * *

Emerson Maxfield is the perfect pawn for rancher Holden McCall's purposes. She's engaged to a man solely to win her father's approval, and the sheltered beauty never steps out of line. Until one encounter changes everything. Now this good girl must marry Holden to protect her family—or their desire could spell downfall for them all...

Read on for a sneak peek at
Rancher's Wild Secret
by New York Times *bestselling author Maisey Yates!*

"I'll tell you what," he said. "I'm going to give you a kiss. And if afterward you can walk away, then you should."

She blinked. "I don't want to."

"See how you feel after the kiss."

He dropped the ax, and it hit the frozen ground with a dull thump.

He already knew.

He already knew that he was going to have a hard time getting his hands off her once they'd been on her. The way that she appealed to him hit a primitive part of him he couldn't explain. A part of him that was something other than civilized.

She took a step toward him, those ridiculous high heels somehow skimming over the top of the dirt and rocks. She was soft and elegant, and he was half-dressed and sweaty from chopping wood, his breath a cloud in the cold air.

She reached out and put her hand on his chest. And it took every last ounce of his willpower not to grab her wrist and pin her palm to him. To hold her against him, make her feel the way his heart was beginning to rage out of control.

He couldn't remember the last time he'd wanted a woman like this.

And he didn't know if it was the touch of the forbidden adding to the thrill, or if it was the fact that she wanted his body and nothing else. Because he could do nothing for Emerson Maxfield, not Holden Brown, the man he was pretending to be. The man who had to depend on the good graces of his employer and lived in a cabin on the property. There was nothing he could do for her.

She didn't even want emotions from him.

But this woman standing in front of him truly wanted only this elemental thing, this spark of heat between them to become a blaze.

And who was he to deny her?

Will their first kiss lead to something more than either expected?

Find out in
Rancher's Wild Secret
by New York Times *bestselling author Maisey Yates.*

Available November 2019 wherever
Harlequin® Desire books and ebooks are sold.

Harlequin.com

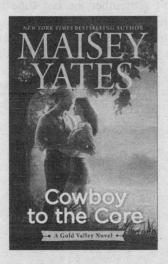

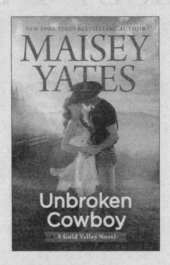